Culture Shock

a novel

by

Janice De Jesus

ALSO BY JANICE DE JESUS

FICTION

Not Just Another Pretty Face

Pretty as a Picture

Soulstice

NONFICTION

Om Struck

Culture Shock

Happy Reading! ♡

Janice
xoxo

Culture Shock

ISBN: 9781724002143

Cover and book design by Ana Galvan

Culture Shock is a work of fiction. Names, characters, places, and incidents are the products of the author's imagination or are used fictitiously. Any resemblance to actual events, locales, or persons, living or dead, is entirely coincidental.

For my parents

Chapter One

Sitting at her desk two rows from the front of the classroom, Lulu felt sick to her stomach. She wished to be invisible.

Mr. Byron twisted his lips, a puzzled expression on his face.

"Please, I'm trying here, okay?"

He sighed and looked down at the sheet of paper on his desk.

"Lawl. Luwal—heyti, ha—hattie. Byetoo…"

This time the entire ninth-grade history class launched into full-blown hysterics. Lulu cringed. *This wasn't funny, at all*, she thought. She hated roll call with a passion. She had yet to meet a teacher who would pronounce her name correctly. Then she sighed and realized that, unless she went only by her nickname, Lulu would have to endure the humiliation of having her full name mispronounced for the rest of her life.

"Settle down!" Mr. Byron admonished, standing up as he narrowed his eyes.

Gradually, the guys and girls in the class quieted down as Mr. Byron waited for complete silence. In the back of the room, two guys snickered for a few seconds until Mr. Byron's glare halted the commotion.

Lulu held her breath as the teacher picked up the paper and took a deep breath before placing his tongue beneath his upper front teeth and pursed his lips.

"Oh, for God's sake, just call me Lulu!"

Twenty-three pairs of eyes turned to the petite, light-brown skinned girl with shiny, long black hair and dark brown almond eyes. Mr. Byron's eyeballs appeared to nearly pop out of their sockets.

Fortunately, most of her classmates knew who she was but unfortunately, they'd witnessed this torture on Lulu every year since seventh grade.

For Lulu, roll call on the first day of school didn't seem to get any easier or any funnier. Only sadder. And always torturous.

Lulu sank down in her seat, flushed, as she surveyed the gazes around her.

"Sorry," she whispered, addressing Mr. Byron. "If you don't mind, I'd rather you call me Lulu."

Mr. Byron inspected his paper once more, his lips forming a straight line.

"Lulu, it is," he said, pushing up his glasses that had slid down his nose. "Hayden Bosworth?"

Hayden, a cute guy with dark brown hair who'd known Lulu since middle school, flashed her a wink of reassurance.

"Here!"

Lulu smiled back gratefully, as a relieved Mr. Bryon moved on. She enjoyed being the center of attention, but not when it came to people bastardizing her name—her God awful-sounding name.

As the teacher continued down the class roster, Lulu began doodling on her notepad with her pen. She began writing her full name—Luwalhati Bituin. Then, smiling to herself, she wrote Luwalhati Abernathy, after Stellan Abernathy, a gorgeous guy in the senior class whom she met in French language club over the summer.

She sat up and furrowed her brows. Then scowling with disgust at what she had just scribbled, she crossed out the previous names she wrote and wrote Lulu Abernathy over and over with nice, broad strokes. *Perfect.*

***

Lulu couldn't bolt out of her history class fast enough. She just had to get out of there. *By the time history class comes around again, all will be well*, she assured herself.

Sara Di Stefano and Kellie Wong, her close friends since seventh grade, rushed to catch up with her.

"Wasn't that just awful?" Kellie said, slightly out of breath as the girls weaved their way through a hallway of kids hanging out by their lockers or rushing to the next class.

Lulu rolled her eyes.

"I'm so over it," she said, fanning herself with her small notebook. The end of August in Walnut Creek was stifling. *But summer isn't over*, her brain argued. "You know, I'm still on vacation mode. What about you guys?"

Sara nodded and pouted as she cast her golden bangs away from her face.

Kellie still seemed preoccupied as she dodged her way through a pack of junior varsity football players playfully wrestling each other.

"What are you going to do about the next class?" Kellie peered at Lulu, who gave her a puzzled expression.

Lulu shrugged. "I don't know what you mean."

Kellie clutched her book bag and swallowed nervously. "I mean about your name."

Lulu stopped in the middle of the hall. She didn't care if she was blocking the way. She knew she had a major crisis on her hands.

"What do you mean *about my name*?"

Sara, who stood behind Lulu, took her index finger and swiped it across her throat as she glared at Kellie.

"Okay, people! You know how I hate my name. It sucks! So, I've decided to change it legally."

Kellie and Sara exchanged looks.

"You're serious?" Sara asked, brushing her bangs away.

Lulu huffed. "Of course. I will eventually. I'll probably have to wait till I'm eighteen or something. I know my parents won't be happy."

The girls continued to walk as the bell's ringing pierced through the hall. Quickening their pace, Kellie and Sara, who both had English class next, veered to the left as Lulu paced herself calmly to the right.

"Have a good math class!" Sara called out.

Lulu didn't respond as she took her time getting to class, even taking out her cell phone to text a message to her Mom about going to the mall after school. She still had a climb to the second floor to Math class but she wasn't worried, even as some stragglers were collecting the last of their belongings before heading to class.

She decided she would miss roll call entirely then saunter in and point to her name on the roster. It was a bold move, but she was willing to do it to avoid humiliation again.

Lulu couldn't wait until Lualhati Bituin was no more.

***

But by the time last period science class came and she was reunited with Sara and Kellie, Lulu realized there was no escaping her name.

This time, someone actually pronounced her name correctly during roll call.

"Luwalhati Bituin!"

The class turned to a small-framed, Asian girl with a flat nose.

Mr. Ostendorf, the science teacher beamed at the new girl, a grateful smile on his face.

"Thank you. And your name is?"

"It is Rowena, sir." The girl pronounced her name with a small vowel sound, instead of "Roweena."

The teacher looked down at the roster. "Ah! You're next on the list. Rowena Bew-hay."

The girl cleared her throat. "No, sir. My surname is pronounced Boo-hi. It means 'life' in Tagalog.

Two girls and a guy snickered.

"Oh god," Lulu muttered, as she sank down in her seat wishing she could disappear.

Who was this girl? And what right did she have to butt in like that? Lulu thought, extremely irritated. *And who the heck refers to someone's last name as a surname?*

Mr. Ostendorf smiled again. "Well, thank you for the language lesson, Rowena. Is it Rowee-na or Rowen-na?"

"Rowena with a small e sound is just fine, sir."

Lulu groaned and buried her face with her arms on her desk. *Was this girl a show off or what?* And what's with all the *sirs*?

She turned to Sara who sat across from her.

"Wake me up when it's all over," she whispered.

After class, Lulu, Kellie and Sara stood in front of the school debating whether they should go to the mall or to the local café to hang out with some juniors and seniors when Rowena passed them and waved.

They stared at her as she strolled over to a nearby bus stop where Rowena sat down on a bench and soon began talking to someone on her cell phone.

"The nerve of her to butt in like that—trying to impress the teacher by showing us all how well she can pronounce *my* name," Lulu huffed.

"Well, did she?" Sara asked. "Pronounce your name correctly, I mean?"

Both of Lulu's friends gaped at her, anxious for her response.

Even though she felt the blood rise to her temples, she remained calm, but firm.

"Well, she did," Lulu admitted, scratching her head. "But that's not the point."

"Did you hear how thick her accent is?" Kellie said, eyeing Rowena as if she were some insect.

Lulu knew that Kellie's own parents, who came to the United States from Hong Kong just a year after Kellie was born there, spoke with accents. She heard Kellie mention how embarrassed she was at times when her parents mispronounced a few English words.

Unlike other American-born or raised Chinese girls who embraced their heritage, Kellie had told her friends she just simply wasn't interested.

"No particular reason," she said once, shrugging. "I'm just not."

But the truth was, like Lulu, Kellie didn't want to stand out. In fact, Lulu knew Kellie understood the whole "real name fiasco." But at least Kellie had a common Chinese last name anyone could easily pronounce.

"Rowena seemed so proud," said Lulu, who couldn't find a better word to describe the new girl. "She reminds me of Virgie, my Mom's friend's daughter. A do-gooder who does all the Filipino clubs and dance troupes and language classes."

"She's just a FOB, Lulu, that's all she is," said Kellie, using the term—"Fresh off the Boat"—to dub newly-arrived Asians. "Who cares if she flaunts her heritage? I wouldn't worry about her."

Suddenly, Sara and Kellie shifted the conversation abruptly as they started talking about a cute pair of wedge shoes they saw at the mall. Lulu watched Rowena as she boarded the bus.

What does Little Miss Philippines have that I don't? Lulu thought to herself.

"I'm not worried," Lulu told her friends. Though she wondered why she didn't sound convincing enough.

***

That night, Lulu dreamed that Stellan, with his dark wavy hair and thick eyelashes held her in his arms when suddenly she felt someone grab her right arm. She turned to face a woman who seemed to be in her thirties with a round face and dark hair looking straight into her eyes. Where had she seen that face before, Lulu wondered? And why did she pull her away from Stellan?

***

Since Wednesday had been the first day of school, Lulu only had to endure Thursday and Friday before it was a weekend again. At least she didn't have to worry about roll call for another year. Still, Lulu had another issue brimming on the horizon—Rowena Buhay. The girl just didn't quite know when to quit.

Lulu cringed at the memory of Rowena coming up to her desk right before one class. Taking a vacant seat across from Lulu, Rowena gave Lulu the grin of a Cheshire cat, only not so charming.

Lulu tried to ignore her by ostensibly scanning the pages of her new science textbook when Rowena started talking to Lulu in what Lulu recognized as Tagalog, though she couldn't understand a word she was saying.

Lulu shook her head.

"So you never learned Tagalog?" Rowena said in English, her voice perky.

Lulu scanned the room. Some students were trickling in but no sign of Sara and Kellie. Where were they? Lulu shook her head and bent down to retrieve her notebook and a few pens. *Why won't she just disappear?*

"So your parents never taught you or you never had time to learn?"

Blowing air out of her pursed lips, Lulu tried to blow off Rowena without actually telling her to get lost.

Rowena leaned over and lowered her voice, eyeing Lulu intently. "I can teach you how to speak Tagalog."

Lulu slammed her science book closed just as Sara and Kellie ambled in.

"I'm not interested," she said to Rowena as she waved to her friends to come over. "That seat's actually taken." Lulu motioned her head over to where Rowena was sitting.

Rowena regarded Sara and Kellie with a wan smile.

"Yeah, I'm actually sitting in the front," Rowena said as she stood up.

Eyeing Rowena as though she were a little bug, Sara feigned sweetness with a forced smile. "Thanks for warming up the seat for me."

The girls watched Rowena make her way to the front of the class as Sara and Kellie claimed the two seats across from Lulu.

"She's got some nerve!" Lulu exclaimed, clicking her pen anxiously.

"What now?" Kellie asked, opening her book bag.

"Little Miss Philippines actually offered to teach me how to speak Tagalog."

"Why would you want to do that?" Kellie asked, scraping the rest of her chipped blue nail polish off her right thumbnail.

Lulu flashed her friend a look of gratitude. "Exactly!"

***

Lulu woke up to the sound of the vacuum cleaner. She groaned, grabbed her pillow, and buried her head under it. When that didn't seem to work, she got up and dragged herself to the bathroom.

She padded downstairs just as her father came charging into the living room with the vacuum cleaner, too absorbed with his task-at-hand to look up or hear her morning greeting.

Scanning the room, Lulu noticed that the camel-colored leather sofa her parents bought a year ago was still covered in plastic for protection—a typical mark of a Filipino household. So too were the tacky, ceramic and plastic knick-knacks, like the Hula girls they collected from Hawaii and Las Vegas which were displayed on the shelves of the faux wooden entertainment center. Saving old knick-knacks, no matter how tacky, was a Filipino trait, Lulu knew after having seen similar ones at other Filipino homes.

Then her eyes focused on more reasons why she was embarrassed to bring friends over—a larger-than-life wooden fork and spoon tacked on to the dining room wall, a huge plaque of Moro tribal swords from the Philippine island of Mindanao and a wooden *tinikling*, a wall hanging showing traditional folk dancers that Lulu had seen in virtually every Filipino home she's been to.

And oh, that framed, creepy black-and-white portrait of someone's great-great-great grandmother, the one with long black hair and beady eyes that seemed to be looking straight at you. At closer inspection, the woman's pug nose, round face with its slight dimple seemed to resemble the face of Lulu's mother. She felt a chill all of a sudden as she realized this was the face of the woman in her weird dream. *Why was that portrait here? And who was she really?* Lulu wondered.

Every cleaning day, in fact, everyday, Lulu hoped those tacky things would disappear and wished her home would resemble more like one of those featured in *Better Homes and Gardens* or *Architectural Digest*, or at least resemble one of her friends' homes—with normal, "American" décor.

Mom and Dad never watch the Home and Garden channel. They're never going to get rid of those things, she thought, sighing as she headed towards the kitchen. On the way there, she stepped on a monkey squeeze toy belonging to Dimar, her two-year-old brother. Lulu shook her head. Chi-Chi, her twelve-year-old sister who still played with dolls, must have placed it there, she figured. They were always playing pranks on each other.

Saturday mornings at the Bituin household meant making your own breakfast if you got up late. Breakfast for Lulu's parents typically consisted of garlic-fried rice and dried fish that surely the neighbors could smell from a mile away, or Cheez Whiz with *pan de sal*, or bread of salt, only they weren't really salty and were more like dinner rolls. *Ugh, major carbs!* Lulu winced.

Since it was getting closer to lunch, Lulu fixed herself a Greek salad—a quick and healthy option. Besides, her busy Mom had forgotten to go grocery shopping—again.

Dimples Bituin, Lulu's Mom, so nicknamed because of the tiny, adorable indentions on each side of her mouth, worked two jobs to support her shopping addiction as well as to help Lulu's Dad, Romar, pay the bills. Dimples, a real estate agent by day, worked as a department store sales associate by night and on weekends mainly for the discount she could get on clothes, housewares and linens to send back to relatives in the Philippines.

As if it wasn't a burden enough to be stuck with a name like Luwalhati, Lulu had to deal with a mother christened with the real name Maria Dimalanta. To this day, Lulu had never found out the meanings of the long, weird names and couldn't care less if she ever would. Even if it turned out that Luwalhati translated into something good in English, Lulu still vowed to one day change her name anyway. As far as she was concerned, Luwalhati Bituin, made no sense and it caused too much stress for most people to pronounce.

Lulu caught sight of a note her Mom stuck on the refrigerator door using a tacky pineapple magnet that read "Hawaii," from one of the family's numerous vacations there. Logistically, vacationing in Hawaii was more relaxing to Lulu than visiting the Philippines. Plus Hawaii was still within the States and not a foreign country. Snatching the note, she sat down to enjoy her salad.

Within a few seconds, she nearly choked on a few olives and feta cheese as she read the note.

"Take a shower, get dressed, going to Auntie Emilia's," the message read.

Lulu dreaded parties at Auntie Emilia's—Auntie Emilia, who wasn't even her real aunt, just a good friend of her parents. Plus, she hated going to Filipino parties in general. Still, *"fiesta" food, like adobo, pancit and lumpia, was probably the only reason to go*, Lulu justified.

But the people there were adults who spoke Tagalog all the time, talking about how their children made the honor roll or scored high on their SATs or got accepted at this or that prestigious university, always trying to one-up the other.

And the kids—they were miniature versions, clones really, of their parents who excelled in private or Catholic schools. Then there were those kids who were Hip Hop wannabes. The FIT-Cs, or Filipinos Into Their Culture, were the worst. They were the ones who danced with Filipino folkdance troupes, formed their own language clubs at school and organized trips to "the homeland."

"Please!" Lulu exclaimed, crumpling the piece of paper.

The vacuum cleaner sound droned off. Lulu heard her Dad's footsteps increase in volume towards the kitchen.

"Lulu! Did you wash those vegetables first? Why don't you eat from a plate, not from the salad bowl? How come you're having salad? You haven't had breakfast yet!"

Romar Bituin's words came tumbling out all in one breath, his accent getting thicker as the volume of his voice got higher.

Lulu sighed. "Dad, it's lunch already."

Romar wiped the sweat from his brow with his shirtsleeve. "Did you get Mom's note?"

"Uh-hmmm," she murmured, drinking carrot juice. Lulu nodded and shrugged, piercing more olives with her fork.

Romar reached into the refrigerator for some coconut juice. Lulu stared at the can containing the clear, liquid and white pulp extracted from a young coconut that she never dared to try.

"You better pay attention to Auntie Emilia's story about her trip," her Dad said, after gulping down his drink.

"Why? It's not like we're going there."

Romar eyed his daughter with a puzzled expression, and then chuckled. "We've got to go some time as a family."

Lulu chewed her olives thoughtfully. "Well, I guess eventually, for vacation sometime in the distant future."

Romar set his can down on the kitchen counter causing a sharp, metallic sound that made Lulu jump.

"Lulu, Dad has good news," he said, excitement dancing in his eyes.

Rolling her eyes, Lulu thought how annoying it was that her parents, like many Philippine-born parents, kept referring to themselves in the third person ever since she could remember. *How annoying and how weird.*

"How about sometime after Christmas?" Romar announced, his eyes dancing.

Lulu's throat suddenly dried up. She couldn't believe what she just heard.

"After Christmas?" That would be in about three months.

Romar nodded like a bobblehead doll. "Yes, soon. Dad got reassigned to the Philippines. My office is opening a branch in Manila and I'll be in charge for a few years until our company trains and hires someone to take over. Which means, we're moving in a few months."

Lulu thought she temporarily lost her sense of hearing and speaking. She stared at her father then at the can of that mysterious juice.

Finally, after what seemed like an eternity, she coughed.

"Who's moving?" she wheezed, out of breath. "Where?"

Romar laughed and turned to throw the can into the bin. "All of us. To the Phillipines."

Lulu sat still for a minute before bursting into a combination of hysterical laughter and whimpering.

"Dad. You guys—Mom, Chi-Chi and Dimar and you—are moving," she said slowly, trying to catch her breath. "I'm *not* going anywhere."

Chapter Two

Lulu sat in the sofa of Auntie Emilia's family room twisting the *pancit* noodles on her plate. A cacophony of voices, mostly high-pitched, and laughter reverberated throughout the house.

Across the way, in the dining room of the house, Lulu's mom, Dimples, gathered with Auntie Emilia and other women around the buffet table as they gossiped about their friends who failed to show up at the parties. As everyone's attention turned to Emilia's friend, Osang Romulo and her diatribe about Peachy Agbayani's husband who was two-timing her, Emilia kept waving her hand as if there were flies over the spread on the table: the roasted pig or *lechon*, cut into small pieces, the *pancit* rice noodles, chicken *adobo*, *lumpia* egg rolls, grilled *bangus* or milkfish, and for dessert, sweet rice cake also known as *bibingka,* corn gelatin or *kalamay* and leche flan. The waving of the hand, Lulu knew after attending many Filipino parties, showed the habit of those raised in the Philippines to swat flies that would typically swarm around during mealtime. For many, the habit stuck even here in America where usually no flies were hovering indoors. It was a habit that often made the one doing it look idiotic, Lulu thought. *Why go on swatting imaginary flies?*

From the living room came the intermittent clacking sound of ivory mahjong tiles over a card table covered in red cloth. Just right before dinner, Lulu saw her dad and

Uncle Jorel, Emilia's husband, among the mahjong players with eyebrows narrowed as they seriously tuned into the game, blocking out any distractions, including other chatter from partygoers, and screaming children running around the house.

Before coming down for dinner, Lulu had just been upstairs where Chi-Chi, her sister's nickname for Christina, played Barbie dolls with girls in the fourth and fifth grade in the "girls only" room, while little Dimar slept in the next room. Lulu made a mental note to start introducing her sister to makeup, clothes and boy talk, now that she was twelve. *Dolls were for little girls.*

Wearing a cotton tank with lace trimmings and blue jeans with rhinestones across the back pockets, Lulu continued to swirl her noodles on her plate as she surveyed the party scene around her and glanced at the widescreen TV in the family room where several people gathered to watch an old Filipino romantic comedy with a weird title—*Sana'y Wala Nang Wakas*, translated as "Hopefully There Will Be No End." Lulu shook her head as she heard but couldn't understand the Tagalog being spoken in the movie. *No end to what? This chaos?* She thought sarcastically as she surveyed the scene before her.

She recalled how earlier, as the guests piled their plates with food at the buffet, Emilia talked about her recent trip to the Philippines.

Emilia explained that even though she grew up in Cavite, a city about an hour from Manila, she hadn't been back since she was twenty-years-old and that was seventeen years ago. She said she had gotten used to living in the United States and found the flies, mosquitoes, the humidity and pollution a nuisance during her recent visit.

"But the shopping malls, *mga mare ko*," Emilia addressed the women as what could be loosely translated to mean "my girlfriends." "The malls are even better there than here, believe it or not. A few of them have five floors. Five floors! Can you believe it?"

Virginia, or Virgie, Emilia's overachieving daughter, stepped in to give her take on the trip.

"Oh, Mom, the malls aren't the highlight of our trip," Virgie said, rolling her eyes, as she reached for heaps full of *pancit*. "I just loved the way food is cooked fresh there. No offense, Mom, but there's so much more of a variety of foods to choose from and not everything's fattening."

Like that would be of concern to you, thought Lulu as she sized up Virgie's slender figure. At 5'6", with her olive skin and long black hair and thick eyelashes, the high school sophomore reminded Lulu of one of the contestants on the Miss Philippines beauty pageant that her parents were prone to watch every year since they subscribed to TFC, The Filipino Channel. Lulu sighed. *The Filipino Channel. What a waste of time and money. They should be watching HGTV like Kellie's and Sara's parents.*

Even though Lulu and Virgie were a year apart and practically knew each other since they were little, they weren't the best of friends. They weren't even good friends. Virgie, one of the FIT-Cs, "Filipinos Into Their Culture," attended St. Bernadette's High School for girls. Lulu knew that aside from being a principal dancer for the Maharlika Filipino Folk Dance Troupe, Virgie also formed her school's first Filipino language club that boasted of Filipino American members who either wanted to learn how to speak Tagalog, those who were already fluent in the language, or those who were non-Filipinos interested in learning the language and culture and finally, those who were natives from the "Mother Country."

The Bituins made no secret they longed for Lulu to be more like Virgie. The "Filipinization" of Lulu had long been a family debate. Lulu's parents couldn't understand why their Lulu never seemed to embrace her heritage.

If they only knew, Lulu sighed, as Virgie continued to talk about her experiences shopping for costumes made of *piña*, natural fibers from the leaves of a pineapple plant for the dance troupe and how she enjoyed her visits with nature to the Banuae rice terraces and the Chocolate Hills of Bohol.

Lulu remembered being a bit curious, a long time ago, to learn about her culture. But somehow, standing out, being viewed as different or weird prevented her from taking that step. She cringed just at the very thought.

Now, as Lulu sat playing with her food, feeling alone despite the crowd around her, she contemplated the family's upcoming move to the Philippines and what excuses she could give her parents for not going.

Offering to live with Auntie Emilia wasn't an option. Lulu knew she couldn't bear to live under the same roof trying to compete with Virgie.

If only I could get a job and have my own apartment, Lulu thought. But that couldn't happen until she was eighteen.

Lulu thought about this girl she knew in middle school who went to live with Buddhist monks from a monastery who took her in after she lost her parents in a car accident. Lulu violently shook her head. *No monastery. Way too rigid.*

Just when she was weighing her options, or lack thereof, Lulu caught sight of a woman who very much resembled the one in the portrait at her home. The woman, who seemed to be about Dimples' age, slowly shook her head as she stared at Lulu.

"Hello, Lulu, are you there?"

Lulu jumped, shaking her head violently then blinked a few times to focus on what she saw. Only this time, the woman wasn't there. Instead, a familiar face from school smiled at her, a hand waving in her face.

"Oh, hello, Rowena."

Rowena sat next to Lulu on the sofa and placed her can of soda on a nearby table.

"Either you're disappointed or not too happy to see me," she said, straightening the pleats on her skirt.

Lulu stared at Rowena's plaid skirt for a moment.

Rowena noticed Lulu's expression. "Do you like it? It's actually part of my old uniform from parochial school in the Philippines. I'm recycling it."

"It's cute," Lulu found herself saying, surprising herself by the compliment she just paid Rowena. Away from the prying eyes of her schoolmates, it was a bit easier for Lulu to let her guard down.

Leaning back on the sofa, Rowena scanned the room. "You seemed to be in a daze earlier."

Lulu shrugged. "I was thinking I'd rather be anywhere but here."

Sitting up suddenly, Rowena grabbed her soda can and stood up. "I knew you didn't want me around."

Raising her eyebrows, Lulu grabbed Rowena's arm. "No, that's not it. I just wasn't expecting you to be here." Lulu gulped realizing how her words must sound as Rowena's eyes widened. "I mean, it's not you. Stay if you like. No one was sitting there anyway."

Glancing around the room with a confused expression on her face, Rowena sat down slowly. "You don't hang out with Virgie?"

Lulu shook her head. "Do you?"

"She's one of my first friends when I moved here from the Philippines during the summer," Rowena said, sipping her soda. "We're on the dance troupe together. She recently came back from her first trip to the Philippines."

"I heard." *And boy did Virgie return with a mouthful about her trip. She just went on and on and on. You practically couldn't get her to shut up*, Lulu thought. *What was so great about the Philippines anyway?*

"I told her all about what to expect in the Philippines and I think it might have helped her with her one-month trip," Rowena said, twisting her ponytail to one side.

Lulu surrendered her plate of noodles to the nearby table. Except for the traditional breakfasts, she liked Filipino food, but this time she was distracted big time. *Please*, she begged silently, *please don't tell me you're going to give me travel tips for the Philippines. I don't think I can take it. I'm still in shock about moving there.*

And then she heard those dreaded words that made it more a reality. "I heard you're moving to the Philippines. Have you ever been there?"

Allowing her eyes to rest on the TV screen that showed a young Filipino couple sharing a passionate kiss, Lulu shook her head. She sighed. *Oh, great, now everyone's going to know. I won't move. I don't want to move.*

"You're going to like it there," Rowena predicted.

"I like it here, my life's perfect *here*," Lulu adamantly declared. *My friends are here and I'm somebody here. After being treated like an outsider in elementary school back in the small town in Louisiana, California's been good to me. There are more people who look like me. Now if I could just do something about my name…*

"Believe me," Rowena continued, taking a quick sip of her soda. "Living there will be an experience you won't regret."

Somehow, Lulu wasn't so sure about that.

***

The Bituins had moved a total of four times since Lulu was born—always because her Dad's banking career took him wherever a new branch opened. While Lulu was proud of her father who worked hard as a bank manager to support the family's lavish vacations, his job had the family packing at every new branch opening opportunity. This time—the Philippines.

Romar said opening a branch in Manila was a bold, but good move on his company's part in an effort to go global. This meant more jobs for Filipinos at home so there wouldn't be a brain drain with most of the country's college graduates moving abroad, he said.

The worst move of all had to be the time Lulu and her family lived in small towns in Georgia and Louisiana for a few years while she was in elementary school before they moved to California.

Lulu never forgot the taunting, the insults, the ridicules the Bituin family endured. She was often made fun of at school for the color of her brown skin. Or her "slanty" eyes. Kids often asked whether she was a "Chink" or a "Jap," terms her classmates often referred to Asians no matter who they were or where they came from.

"I am American, just like you," Lulu recalled telling a skinny, bucktoothed, and blond kid in the fourth-grade when he asked, "What are you?"

"You're *not* American," the skinny kid said, laughing.

Most often, when trying to explain her parents' ethnicity, kids thought she was making the word "Filipino" up, so she was always referred to as Chinese or Japanese or even Vietnamese, her parents being lumped in along with the hordes of refugees who settled in Louisiana since the 1970s.

After bringing a packed lunch of steamed rice and fish her Mom packed one day, Lulu remembered the time she entered a classroom and someone scribbled, "People who eat rice are stupid" on her desk and no one was punished because the teacher had no suspects.

Nor could she ever forget the time her Dad walked her home from school because she was afraid of walking home alone after being taunted by schoolmates nearly every afternoon after school.

"What are you doing here?" one boy asked as he strode alongside her.

"Go back to your country," chimed in another.

"My daddy said that your people killed our fathers, uncles, cousins, and grandfathers in Vietnam and Pearl Harbor," said another boy, pulling Lulu's ponytail. "You don't have a right to be here."

Every day, always the same routine. The boys would taunt her, pull her hair, grab her backpack and throw it on the ground.

Romar suggested he would use his lunch hour from work to walk her home a couple of days each week to show those boys Lulu had someone to protect her but that didn't stop them. Instead of pulling her hair or grabbing her school supplies, the boys would follow behind Romar and Lulu and sing "Chinese, Japanese, dirty knees, look at these," as they pinched then pulled their t-shirts with their thumbs and index fingers to indicate nipples on the chests of Asian women their fathers told them about.

Lulu guessed the gesture had something to do with some Asian women being considered flat chested.

"But who cares?" Romar had wailed.

The Bituins made several complaints to the school board who tried to admonish the culprits. Eventually, notices appeared at school warning kids that showing any type of racist behavior would not be tolerated.

Still, this wasn't enough to heal the deep hurt Lulu felt. *It was only a Band-Aid*, she thought.

"It's a good thing we never taught Lulu and Chi-Chi how to speak Tagalog. They would get teased even more," Lulu heard Dimples say to Romar in the kitchen one day.

Lulu finally got a reprieve when the family moved to sunny, diverse California just in time for middle school to start. This was Lulu's time to start anew. She vowed that she would never be a victim of insults and ridicule again.

It was easy for her to assimilate in her new school in Walnut Creek, as she didn't speak English with an accent so as to call unwanted attention her way. With her exotic looks, flair for fashion, and perky personality that landed her a spot on the pep squad, Lulu fast became a school sensation.

She gravitated towards other girls—"hyphenated Americans," Asian-Americans, Italian-Americans, those who either had no interest in learning about their heritage or whose parents didn't teach them about their culture, friends like Sara and Kellie.

And now Rowena was telling her she would enjoy living in the Philippines. *How could she embrace the very culture that made her an outcast?* In her lily-white middle school, Lulu had seen her classmates make fun of classmates who immigrated from other countries, their manners, and their accents. One couldn't associate oneself with the FOBs, those "Fresh Off the Boat"—if one wanted to be popular.

She once swore she wouldn't make fun of the FOBs. She once vowed never to turn into one of those people who once made life for her a living hell.

Unfortunately, the crowd at high school was about the same as middle school—not as diverse, culturally speaking. Anyone who hadn't assimilated into whitewashed culture stood out. And Lulu knew what it was like to stand out—like she didn't belong.

And so she chose to blend in as best as she could. And the only way she thought was the best way to do that was to not acknowledge her Filipino heritage.

But now, as she thought about how she and her friends were treating Rowena, Lulu shuddered. *I'm becoming one of those people.*

***

Lulu patted herself on the back for coming up with a brilliant plan. She was going to live with Sara while her family was in the Philippines and that was final. This decision came about during lunch at school after Lulu's constant desperate pleas for help. Feeling sorry for Lulu, Sara's parents said it would be okay under one condition: Lulu would have to get her parents' approval.

She felt defiant that morning when she left for school after an argument she had with her Mom.

"You're being unreasonable, Lulu," her Mom said over breakfast. "Why can't you face up to who you are?"

"Who am I? *Who am I*, Mom?" Lulu slammed her fork on the table. "Why don't you tell me? You and Dad want me to be more like Virgie, and yet you never introduced me and Chi-Chi to our culture—never even taught us how to speak the language. If I'm being unreasonable, then it's your fault!"

"Shut up! Don't answer back to me!" Dimples yelled, grabbing a dishtowel and tossing it on the kitchen counter. "Back home in the Philippines, I never answered back to my parents, even when my father, your grandpa was spanking me. We always respected our elders."

Then go back to the Philippines, Lulu thought, as she ran out of the house without saying goodbye and got into a car with Sara and her older brother who was driving them to school.

When she got dropped off later that evening after hanging out at Sara's house, Lulu marched to the front door of the Bituin household, head held up high, ready to make her bold announcement.

A cry pierced her eardrums as she entered into the house.

"Where have you been?" asked Auntie Emilia, who stood in the front hallway entrance.

Lulu moved past her towards the source of the sound. In the living room, Dimples sat crumpled on the floor, her head buried on Romar's lap.

She looked up at Lulu with puffy eyes, tears streaking her face.

"Your Lolo, Mom's father just died," Romar said solemnly. "We just got a call from the Philippines."

Dimples hiccupped and started sobbing again as she heard the words escape from her husband's lips.

She cast watery eyes at her daughter. Even in her grief, Lulu knew Dimples remembered the argument they had earlier—the words Lulu lashed at her Mom she wished she could take back. "We didn't teach you to speak Tagalog because we were only trying to protect you."

Tears welled in Lulu's eyes. Now wasn't the time to bring up their disagreement or moving to the Philippines. Her mother, whom she loved dearly and tried so desperately to understand, was in pain and she needed her.

"I know," Lulu said, simply, feeling awful for the way she acted earlier.

And she knelt down on the floor to give her Mom a huge hug.

Chapter Three

Lulu barely got over the shock of her Lolo dying when she was struck with another calamity—Dimples announced they were moving to the Philippines sooner than they originally planned, and to make matters even worse—they wouldn't be living in Manila. The Bituins would be moving to a small town in the Batangas province where her parents grew up.

Rogelio Villareal Del Rosario, Dimples' father who owned several acres of sugar cane fields in Batangas, a province south of Manila, also owned a hacienda that had been in the Villareal family for generations since the Spanish era and that Dimples, being an only child, had automatically inherited the estate, which included a farm and sugar cane field complete with a cadre of workers.

Lulu didn't know whether to cry or laugh. It seemed that if it wasn't one thing, it was another. Romar told Dimples that he needed to finalize a few work deals stateside first before he left for Manila to open another bank branch there.

So since Dimples needed to help relatives plan her father's funeral as well as settle the estate, Romar encouraged his wife to go ahead and he and the kids would follow later.

But later was still too soon for Lulu.

"I thought we were going to at least wait until summer vacation," Lulu protested.

She was trying to be sensitive to her mother's grief, but Lulu felt she was grieving the loss of her own life as she knew it.

"The bank wants me to go to Manila soon and the earlier the better," Romar said, clicking the mouse of his computer as his eyes fixed on the screen. "But Mom should, of course, take care of family matters and business and while she does, we can get ready to join her later."

"How much later?" Lulu groaned.

The sound of sniffling coming from upstairs silenced father and daughter for a few seconds. Romar shook his head sadly as he rose to head upstairs to comfort his wife.

"I understand it's hard for you to leave your friends," Romar said, stopping midway at the staircase. "But it's not going to be as bad as you think."

Lulu sank even deeper into the beanbag chair in the family room as she tried hard not to cry. She heard sniffling just inches away from her and turned expecting to find Dimples nearby.

But no one was there.

Lulu sighed as she freed herself from the vinyl beanbag chair that seemed to be swallowing her. She had to stop thinking just about herself. *The whole family was moving, thank God, not just me*, Lulu thought.

Chi-Chi skipped past a dazed Lulu, making her jump.

"Do you want a tissue or something?" Lulu asked.

Her sister eyed her quizzically. "What are you talking about?"

"For your nose. I heard you sniffling a few minutes ago."

Chi-Chi raised her eyebrows. "Me? Not me!" She bent over to collect her dolls and their clothes that were strewn all over the family room floor.

"Why are you skipping?" Lulu wondered what Chi-Chi seemed to be so cheery about.

"Well, don't get me wrong," her sister replied, smoothing out her doll's clothes. "I'm sad for Mom that Lolo died and all, but you have to look on the bright side."

For a twelve-year-old, Chi-Chi can sure sound like a grown up sometimes, Lulu thought with a smile.

"Okay then, tell me what's the bright side," Lulu urged, picking up a doll with blond hair and blue eyes and a slender figure. She remembered playing with this same doll years ago before giving it to Chi-Chi who didn't seem to mind inheriting it from her big sister.

Chi-Chi briefly put the dolls' clothes down, eyes boring into Lulu with an air of maturity. "Well, *Ate,* the bright side is that we get to meet all the relatives we're really related to, not just the ones here that we call Auntie and Uncle because they're friends of Mom and Dad." She tossed her black, wavy curls from her rosy, cherub face. "I get to give some of my old clothes and dolls to our cousins since they don't get to go to the mall very often like we do."

"Wait a minute," Lulu said, shaking the doll. "What did you just call me?"

"*Ate,*" said her younger sister, pronouncing the "a" with a sound like "Ah," along with "tay." "Mom says I need to start calling you that. It means big sister."

Sighing, Lulu tossed aside the doll. She wished she were a little bit like Chi-Chi—patient, charitable, amiable. Chi-Chi, who never seemed to complain when Mom and Dad didn't buy her the latest clothing trend or popular doll. Chi-Chi, who seemed to get along with everyone.

***

With Dimples in the Philippines for her father's funeral, Romar stayed behind to search for someone to rent their house for a few years while getting the kids ready for their move.

Not having her mother and Dimar, her two-year-old brother, at home meant only her Dad was in charge and he was always busy working. So Lulu often stayed at home with Chi-Chi packing their clothes for what Lulu considered "a very long, long trip." She couldn't even utter, couldn't even think of the word "move" without wanting to throw up. Lulu needed a diversion.

One afternoon, while watching an animated movie in the family room with her sister, the phone rang.

"Hey, Lulu! What's up?"

It was Stellan, the guy whose last name she planned to take when, in her fantasy, they got married. Lulu could hardly restrain herself as she leapt up from the sofa, cordless phone in her right hand, before sitting back down again.

"Great to hear from you," she said, standing up to move to the much quieter dining area.

"We had an awesome summer, didn't we? With the language club, I mean."

Even though he couldn't see her nodding, she did, enthusiastically, as though she had just won a national spelling bee and could spell a word no one else could—not even the adults who selected the word they obviously had to first look up. It was that kind of awesome.

Together with a bunch of other incoming freshmen, Lulu met with other students to practice French, watched French movies and ate at French restaurants all over the Bay Area over the summer along with an adult tutor. While all the other students were friendly and interesting, Stellan caught Lulu's eye, not only because he was cute, but also because he seemed worldly, well-read and well-traveled. They all had fun as a group but she didn't think he'd single her out.

"I was thinking, maybe you'd like to see a French movie or something?"

Lulu thought her heart had stopped.

"A French movie?"

"Yeah," he laughed. "You're still studying French aren't you?"

She hesitated a few seconds. "Yeah, still." Then sighed. "And probably Tagalog soon."

Wait a minute where did that come from? Lulu wondered.

"Awesome!" Stellan said. "My Mom practically threw a party when I told her I'm finally learning French because she's French and she thought it would be a cool way for me to learn more about my heritage. Well, half of my heritage, at least."

"That's great," Lulu said in what she hoped was her most enthusiastic tone. Talking about one's heritage made her queasy and maybe a bit envious. She had to change the subject.

"So what French movie do you want to see?

"It's called *Etre et Avoir* and it's playing over at Shattuck this Friday night at 8:15," he said. "A bunch of us are going. Do you want to join us?"

So it's not a real date after all, Lulu thought, biting her lip in disappointment. "Sure. Can I bring some friends?"

Friday night, Lulu, Sara and Kellie pranced around from the bathroom to her bedroom upstairs at her house amid a flurry of clothes and body mists wafting in the air as they mixed and matched outfits before facing a large mirror primping themselves.

"I'm sorry about your grandfather and all but I think that it really sucks you're leaving so soon," Kellie offered her own brand of sympathy, as she gripped the handle of the eyelash curler, forcing the clamps to fold a row of lashes, a move guaranteed to make her eyes "pop" or so read the product label.

Lulu huffed in frustration. She always had problems with her stubborn left contact lens. Leaning closer to the mirror, she tried to shove the darn thing in her eye again.

"Hey, maybe you can get Stellan to fall in love with you and the two of you can elope and you wouldn't have to move," Sara said, applying a thick coat of lip-gloss.

The thought of eloping with Stellan made Lulu smile, just as she succeeded in lodging the problematic contact lens on her eyeball. "If only he'd ask me to marry him. I would in a second."

Once they were as presentable as can be, the girls quickly rushed down the stairs and out the front door just as Romar entered the house after a long workday.

"Where do you think you're going?" He grabbed Lulu by the arm.

"To the movies," she answered, eyeing her friends who successfully made it over the threshold.

Romar glanced back at Sara and Kellie. "You girls go on without Lulu."

"What?" Lulu lashed out.

"Your grandfather has just died. You're supposed to be in mourning." Romar's eyes flashed in anger.

"Dad, I feel bad for Mom, really I do. But I didn't know Lolo very well and besides," she looked pleadingly at her friends. "We live *here*, not there."

This angered her father even more. "Don't answer back to me. You're being disrespectful to your Lolo's memory—look at you, dressed like that." His eyes regarded her mini skirt with disdain.

"You are not going anywhere, young lady."

***

She didn't end up going to the movies that Friday night and instead went straight to bed—not having the energy to confront her Dad, not even bothering to change into her pajamas.

She lay in the dark for an indefinite amount of time until the lights went out inside the rest of the house and there was ultimate stillness.

Still upset by the incident earlier that evening, Lulu stayed awake trying to figure out a way she could convince her father she didn't want to move. Suddenly, the sound of music—Tchaikovsky's waltz from *Swan Lake*—cut through the silence.

She froze and groped for the light switch of her beside lamp. Once light flooded the room, Lulu turned to the source of the music—an old jewelry box with a twirling ballerina that had been her mother's given to her by Lulu's grandfather.

She thought it was bizarre that the lid of the jewelry box would pop up like that so she got up to investigate the culprit. It wasn't like the jewelry box was so overstuffed that it opened on its own. She shut the lid before jumping back into bed, switching the light off.

Once she drifted off to sleep after several minutes, her mind weary from plotting ways to get out of moving to the Philippines, she awoke hearing the waltz play again.

"Stupid jewelry box!"

Thinking the latch was broken, Lulu was more annoyed than perplexed as she turned the light back on and slammed the lid of the jewelry box before turning the lights off and plunging back into bed.

Turning to her side, she covered her left ear with a pillow as she pressed her other ear to the mattress. Silence ensued just as Lulu's heavy eyelids surrendered.

Buzzing near her face and ear forced Lulu awake as she waved her hand in the air with her eyes still closed. A sudden, potent prick on her arm jolted her from her bed.

She squinted as her eyes adjusted to the light in her room that she didn't recall turning on again. Or did she? Only, she realized, it wasn't her room and it wasn't her bed she had just risen from. She searched for the mosquito she thought had bitten her, then inspected her affected arm. No mosquito, no bite.

The next thing she knew, Lulu was descending a long, wooden staircase leading to a large sitting room filled with intricately-carved mahogany furniture. She directed her ear toward the sound of a girl laughing in the distance and headed towards the sound, using that light-hearted laugh as her guide.

Lulu seemed to drift through room after room that housed old furniture until she reached a terrace at the front of a house.

The source of the laughter sat on a bicycle—a beautiful, young girl, about six-years-old with almond-shaped eyes, her black hair swept up in a ponytail.

Lulu gasped as she recognized the girl's face—resembling her own face at that age. Only it wasn't exactly her face.

Lulu focused her gaze on a man next to the girl. He was medium-build, with dark, black hair combed to one side and his eyes were twinkling as he smiled at the girl who began to pedal the bike as he held the edge of the seat.

They laughed together as he guided her, slowly at first, as she struggled to steady the handlebars.

Once the girl gained momentum on the bike, the man released his hold and off went the girl as she squealed in fright and delight, whizzing past the house. She made some progress until she lost control, screamed and fell as she tried to turn.

Immediately, the man rushed to comfort the crying girl.

"Hush, sweet Dimples," he soothingly, deeply said. "Papa is here. He won't let you get hurt."

Lulu caught her breath as her eyes darted to the man's face—her Lolo's face.

Suddenly, the man and girl disappeared and all that was left was the sound of crying.

Turning to re-enter the house, Lulu followed the sound of crying which lead her to a closed door. Pressing her ear to the door, she heard muffled sounds, heavy, desperate sounds. Like weeping.

Slowly, she turned the knob, her heart beating wildly as she peeked cautiously, afraid of what her eyes would encounter.

Simple, sweet, small white sampaguitas, a descendant of jasmine flowers, filled the room where at the center stood a woman dressed in black sobbing uncontrollably as she leaned against an open casket.

Lulu's feet padded closer to the woman who raised her head revealing a tear-stained face. But not just any face.

Her mother's face.

Mother and daughter stared at each other for a few minutes until Lulu moved closer to the white casket.

There laid the man who guided the little girl on her first bike ride without training wheels, only this time his face that once highlighted twinkling eyes and a smile now displayed deep creases and gray hair that crowned the now lifeless head resting on the satin pillow.

Lulu drew her breath in sharply. This was the man she never knew, nor would ever know. The man her mother loved dearly, gone forever.

Gasping for air as his hand suddenly clutched at her throat, Lulu found herself jolted back in her own room. She touched her face, surprised that it was damp, her neck throbbing. Outside, the darkness was gradually giving way to the morning light.

Seconds later, the waltz played again, only this time Lulu allowed the music to lull her back to sleep.

Chapter Four

Lulu wished that she hadn't eaten breakfast that morning. As Auntie Emilia's van approached the departure area of the San Francisco airport's international terminal, the food that was still settling in her stomach lurched upward just as her heart sank.

A sign was emblazoned above the sliding doors to the check-in counters as if mocking her—Philippine Airlines.

As she stood there with her rolling luggage, she knew there was no turning back. The eerie occurrence that happened two weeks ago still baffled her. To her relief, the ballerina in her jewelry box didn't make an encore performance.

Since that strange incident in her bedroom, Lulu tried not to analyze what she believed had taken place. She had often heard adults at Filipino parties talk about spirits but shrugged it off as unbelievable and out of this world, and just plain weird.

Still, she couldn't help but think that the incident with the jewelry box had something to do with her grandfather. Could it be that he was trying to communicate with her in the afterlife? Lulu shivered, shaking off that absurdity.

Her thoughts were interrupted by Auntie Emilia's squeal of delight.

"You girls try to have a good time in the Philippines, okay? Try to learn Tagalog while you're there," Auntie

Emilia said, her Filipino accent thickening with every word uttered as she dabbed the tears that were welling in her eyes while still maintaining her smile.

Lulu and Virgie regarded each other for a brief awkward moment before they gave each other a hug. It felt weird hugging like this, Lulu thought. Even though their parents had been friends since they were little, Lulu and Virgie weren't exactly close. Yet, a hug seemed appropriate and Lulu couldn't help but feel that the hug was her last tangible link to her home and so she clung to Virgie just as the latter began to pull away.

Virgie smiled as though she sensed Lulu's trepidation.

"Mom's right," she said to Lulu. "Learning Tagalog can help you make lots of friends. But be careful of those girls who want to be friends with you just because you're a walking dollar bill."

Lulu looked at her, confused. "A walking dollar bill?"

Virgie chuckled. "That's what the girls there call us who are American born."

"Lulu, let's go!"

Romar's voice called out anxiously as more hugs were exchanged. Chi-Chi rushed to follow Romar as Lulu secured her backpack over her shoulder and pulled her rolling luggage. She glanced back once more as Virgie and Auntie Emilia waved.

"Don't worry! Rowena and I will e-mail you!" Virgie called out just as the sliding doors separated Lulu from the world she knew and the unknown she was about to face.

As she followed her father and sister, Lulu felt a pang of regret—she wished she'd gotten to know Virgie and Rowena more as it turned out they, rather than Sara and Kellie, seemed to have been more reassuring and comforting to Lulu the past few weeks as the Bituin family prepared for their move.

It was Virgie and Rowena who took Lulu out to a farewell lunch and advised her not to go shopping for clothes in the States telling her she will go crazy at the malls in the

Philippines as there will be everything she needed there and so much more and for so much less.

It was Virgie and Rowena who loaned Lulu travel guidebooks about the Philippines and helped her shop for *pasalubong,* souvenirs to bring to her cousins.

Surprisingly, Sara and Kellie seemed a bit distant the last few weeks. Lulu thought it was because they were all sad to see her go but she couldn't help but feel disappointed that her own friends hadn't given her a send-off. Maybe they thought she couldn't go out because the family was still in mourning. Still, things had gotten pretty weird since the night Lulu couldn't go out with them to the movies with Stellan.

Oh, Stellan. Lulu sighed. She had just barely gotten to know him. But a glimmer of hope rose within her as she remembered that he had requested she e-mail him to tell him all about her experiences.

She hadn't even left yet and already Lulu felt like she was in a different country.

In front of the Philippine Airlines check-in counters were hordes of people in line pushing carts of cardboard boxes with the word *Balikbayan* on them. Growing up, Lulu recalled her parents filling those boxes with things like cans of SPAM, packs of Bic ballpoint pens, Dove and Irish Spring soap, Hershey's Chocolate, assorted AVON perfumes, a variety of Brach's hard candy, towels and clothes that Lulu and Chi-Chi outgrew to send to relatives.

This time the boxes were piled high—at least two per passenger. Lulu feared there would be way too many boxes for the plane's cargo section to accommodate. This wasn't like simply flying to Hawaii where Filipinos didn't have the dreaded boxes. Paranoia added to the frustration of moving, causing Lulu to harbor silly thoughts. *What if the plane crashed from carrying too much weight?*

Lulu thrust forward as her face dove into the back of the man before her. The old man turned around to give her a gap toothed grin. She turned around to face the source of her unexpected shove but saw no one. Instead, she faced two *Balikbayan* boxes, one stacked on top of the other, being wheeled in a cart, the owner oblivious to Lulu being on the other side.

She turned to her side to face her dad who was talking to Chi-Chi.

"What's *Balikbayan* mean, Daddy?" Chi-Chi's high-pitched voice rose above a cacophony of dialects abounding as the line of people snaked around the counter.

Even though she couldn't speak Tagalog, Lulu had developed an ear for the language she grew up hearing her parents speak to each other—enough to recognize the tones and rhythms. Which was why she was able to notice that Tagalog wasn't the only dialect being spoken there.

Amid a variety of tongue flapping and chirping of words undistinguishable to Lulu, arose the recognizable sound of words from her own native tongue. Only the accent seemed British. Or was it Australian? Lulu couldn't tell.

"Yep, I'm going surfing. I'll be diving, too," Lulu heard a voice say.

She craned her head around the boxes behind her to find the source of the voice. A tall, lanky blonde young man in his twenties who had a tan and wavy hair was talking to two Filipino men who craned their necks up at the man as though they were admiring a skyscraper.

Hours seemed to drag on before the family finally checked in their luggage and Lulu sank into her window seat, Chi-Chi sitting next to her.

With her heart pounding heavily as the plane ascended gradually, Lulu continued to stare at the bay and buildings below—until every image she had known for years disappeared beyond the clouds and she focused her eyes on the magnificent, mighty wing of the Boeing 777 that carried her away from the only life she had ever known.

***

Humid, intense sticky air greeted Lulu's skin as soon as she and her family exited the airport in Manila. It wasn't quite the welcome she wanted and the minute the sweat beads started rolling down the sides of her face and cascaded down her neck and back, she felt a shower was in order.

But the Bituin family still had yet to endure the journey that lay ahead as the drive to Batangas province where her Mom's family lived was still nearly two hours away.

The humidity wasn't the only thing that arrived in the welcome wagon. An onslaught of relatives came charging toward Lulu, her Dad and her sister.

All at once, they started chirping in Tagalog, which Lulu dreaded learning but knew understanding and speaking the language was inevitable.

"*O, kumusta na pare?*" said one male relative wearing khaki shorts and a red, white and blue T-shirt who greeted her Dad with a pat on the back.

"*Oy, ang ganda ganda ng mga taga istates,*" said a woman wearing a cotton, madras dress that Lulu guessed was probably the typical dress of provincial women.

She wished she could understand what they were saying, although after hearing bits and pieces of conversations between her parents through the years, she guessed what the woman said had something to do with beauty.

"*Maganda*, means beautiful," she recalled her Mom saying.

Introductions were finally made and as it turned out, the man was Toting, the husband of Dimples' cousin, Diding, the woman wearing plaid. The two teenage boys were the couple's nephews and the young girl with them was the couple's niece on Toting's side of the family.

Lulu sighed. How in the world was she going to keep track of all these relatives? And she knew there were still many more to meet.

The two teen boys helped load the Bituin family's luggage onto the most bizarre looking vehicle Lulu had ever seen.

"This is a jeepney," said one of the boys who introduced himself as Niel, short for Nathaniel and pronounced *Nee-yel*. Not Neil, he was quick to add.

Niel, who seemed to be about Lulu's age, flashed a grin as he stared at her unabashedly. Wearing faded blue jeans and a white T-shirt emblazoned with the words "Rock and Roll," his black hair wavy and long eyelashes providing an awning for his eyes, Niel seemed cute and incredibly tall, Lulu thought, but definitely not her type.

She sighed. *Like I really know what my type is these days*, she thought.

"What's a jeepney?" Lulu asked, trying to be polite.

"The idea was derived from the GI soldiers' use of jeeps during World War II, but Filipinos built their own versions of passenger jeeps and have used them for public transportation ever since," Niel said, his voice laced with an accent Lulu couldn't help but find endearing. An admission of that realization shocked her. And she was pleased to note he spoke English very well.

Lulu walked around the jeepney, inspecting it closely. From the front, it looked like a regular jeep only it was longer and inside two extended, vinyl-covered seats on either side could hold as many as twenty people—ten on each side if everyone squeezed in tight, Niel explained.

A passenger had to board a jeepney from the back of the vehicle which didn't have a door. As Lulu surveyed the streets near the airport, she noticed that on passenger jeepneys used for public transportation, people were standing on the back ledge and holding on to a bar behind the vehicle, hanging on for dear life as the jeepneys darted and weaved through horrendous traffic.

Niel chuckled as he observed the bewildered expression on Lulu's face.

"No. None of us will be hanging out of this jeepney," he said revealing a flash of perfect, white teeth. "There's more than enough room for all of us. This is actually my uncle's jeepney. He hires a driver to pick up passengers around town. It's good extra business for the family."

Lulu nodded as she marveled at the intricate detailing on the outside of the jeep which was painted in a vibrant mosaic of colors. She eyed a sign hanging above the windshield that read "Lucky Star." Niel explained most jeepney drivers were still stuck in the 1980s as they constantly played songs from groups such as Chicago and Journey.

"Each jeepney is personalized according to the interests of the owner," Niel told her. "Lucky Star was named in honor of Madonna, the singer, who was just starting her career during the time my uncle just graduated from high school and bought this jeepney. And even my sister and the jeepney share the same name."

Despite the excruciating heat and the sweat that drenched her tank top and beige capri pants, and despite being initially annoyed they weren't riding in an air-conditioned vehicle, Lulu couldn't help but smile.

"That's a cute story," she said as she climbed into the jeepney. But what she really thought was, *how corny can you be naming your jeep after a Madonna song?*

Niel stepped up and rushed immediately to help her inside, holding her hand with his one hand and supporting the small of her back with the other. As she sat down, Lulu glared at Niel.

He, in turn, had a look of alarm written all over his face.

"I'm sorry," he murmured as he climbed in.

Flushed, she focused down at her hands and glanced shyly at Niel, regretting the look she gave him earlier.

"Sorry for what?" she asked. "I'm just not used to guys my age being so…"

The word escaped her.

"Gentlemanly," was the only word that came to mind.

Niel's face relaxed at once.

"You'll find that young men here are very chivalrous," said Niel's mom who insisted she be called Auntie Yelling, short for Yellimina.

This time Lulu had to stop herself from displaying another expression of shock, lest she offend anyone. But to herself, she wondered—*Yelling? What kind of a nickname was that?* Filipinos have such odd nicknames that often ended with "ing," she noticed through the years as she recalled some of her parents' friends back home with "ing" nicknames—Angeling, Diding, Rufing, Ning-Ning, Ting-Ting, to name a few.

Then it was Cyril, Niel's younger brother's turn to laugh.

"We don't want you to think that Yelling means that our *Inay* yells a lot," he said of his mother. "Except maybe when we're disobedient."

The family laughed as Niel's uncle, who insisted on being called "Tiyo Tot," drove out of the airport lot.

Lulu carefully noted Cyril's formal use of the word "disobedient," instead of just plain, "bad." She chuckled to herself. Boys in the Philippines were disobedient—but boys back in the States were just downright bad.

Hot air whipped across Lulu's face as she turned to view the mess of cars that weaved through the city streets as drivers blasted their horns.

She wondered, with a sigh, how in the world did everyone know who was following who, which lane to be in and who had the right of way?

This was going to be an interesting two-year living experiment, Lulu thought as the jeepney made its way through traffic and finally into a long stretch of highway towards the Philippine countryside that would be her new home.

***

Dimples, with little Dimar in tow, shrieked and ran to greet Romar, Lulu and Chi-Chi who appeared disheveled as they got off the jeepney.

As Lulu buried her face into her mother's embroidered cotton blouse, she inhaled the fresh, crisp scent of laundry soap and felt a warm surge rush through her body. She didn't realize until then how much she had missed Dimples and her baby brother who clung to Lulu's leg.

After hugs were exchanged and fresh tears sprung from weary eyes, the Bituin family was escorted by tons of still unknown relatives into the garage of a house that had been converted into a makeshift dining area where a smorgasbord of food was laid out on a long rectangular table. While modern homes in provincial Philippines resembled those in the States, the open garages weren't normally used for cars but instead converted as extra dining space for fiestas to accommodate the extended family and guests.

Whether it was jet lag or culture shock, Lulu knew something was amiss. She eyed the nondescript home made of wood and stone blocks. Like the houses back home, this one had a garage, but unlike the houses back home, this one had a terrace which, in fact, was the only feature the house had in common with some of the mansions Lulu had seen in magazines.

While Lulu noticed that it seemed like every relative was staring at Chi-Chi and her as if they were from another planet, she caught her mother thoughtfully eyeing her.

"What? No hacienda? No mansion?" Lulu said, half-joking, half-sarcastic. "I thought you said Lolo owned sugar cane fields?"

Dimples smiled as if struck with a fond memory. "He did. I sold them."

Tightening in Lulu's throat forced her to cough. She knew it was more than just the heat. "You—you sold, what? The hacienda? The sugar cane fields?"

Dimples laughed and hugged her daughter. "I don't have a clue how to run that kind of business and your Dad has no time for that either, especially since he'll be in Manila most of the time. We don't need all that. All we need is this simple house. Your Lolo lived here most of the time anyway since your *Lola* died."

Well, I guess we won't be living a life of luxury, will we? Lulu thought. She turned her attention to the boisterous bunch of people otherwise known as her relatives. They smiled at her looking as if they were unsure of what to say. She responded with a slight lift of the lower facial area which she hoped would be construed as a smile, as her mood prevented her from producing an authentic one. How can anyone feel so out of place and so out of touch, as she was, with the place of her origin? *Well, my parents' origin*, she reminded herself. *I don't belong here. If my grandfather hadn't died, I wouldn't be here. I would've made my parents agree to have me stay back home in the States, maybe live with Kellie or Sara, or heck, even Virgie.*

But, she would wait—at least until she finished high school. She had four more long years before turning eighteen. She would make nice with her parents, attend school, and all the while she would be planning a way to go back home. She wouldn't just ask—she would beg Sara, or Kellie or Virgie, anyone, to have her live with them till she turned eighteen. She had to have something to look forward to while enduring her stay here.

Sweat beads ran down her back as if they were in a race. The relentless, hot sun beat down on her so she sought refuge in the garage where relatives were helping themselves to the food and others were swatting flies with what looked like cheerleader pom-poms clasped to the end of a wooden stick. Without warning, Lulu felt a prick, followed by an uncontrollable itch; she peered down in horror to see swarms of mosquitoes circling her legs.

"You have fresh blood," said one of the elderly women, who handed her a plate. "The mosquitoes aren't used to you yet."

And they never will, Lulu vowed. *I won't give those mosquitoes a chance to know me because I don't plan on staying long.*

Lulu recognized the usual fare but noticed a few unfamiliar dishes of assorted colors and smells.

As she sat down wearily, Lulu realized she was famished even though the airline food was satisfying—rice and chicken *adobo* for dinner, marinated pork *tocino*, eggs over garlic fried rice for breakfast and *pancit* and *lumpia* for lunch and assorted snacks—Lulu longed for a home-cooked meal to eat as she stretched out her tired, achy, stiff limbs.

Several relatives—she couldn't remember all their names—continued to stare at her and Chi-Chi as they ate and fanned themselves but Lulu didn't mind. She simply smiled politely and glanced over at her Mom who was caressing her Dad's back with her hand.

Dimples' shoulder-length hair was tied in a loose bun that rested lightly on the nape of her neck, soft tendrils flowing. Despite the dark circles under her eyes and the simple short-sleeved black outfit she wore, Dimples sported a wan smile. It had been nearly a month since Lulu's grandfather died, but Lulu knew her mother's pain was still fresh.

"You like the *Dinugguan*?"

Niel's voice pierced Lulu's thoughts.

He nodded toward her plate with a smile. Lulu examined her dish. She had finished her *pancit*, chicken *afritada, menudo*, and *lumpia* but was still working on the rice she had covered with some extremely dark sauce—a pork stew, one relative helpfully described.

"It's a bit chewy," Lulu admitted, shoving a spoonful of stew and rice into her mouth.

Niel continued to nod. "Hmm, yes, that it is. Pigs innards usually are."

As if he caught himself saying something he thought he shouldn't, Niel zipped his lips shut.

Suddenly, the stew which tasted vinegary and garlicky didn't seem to rest well in her mouth as she chewed ever so slowly.

"Do you know what you're eating?" Cyril asked, overhearing their conversation.

All of a sudden, Lulu wasn't so sure she wanted to know the answer but knew she was going to hear it whether she liked to or not.

"Pig innards stewed in its own blood," Cyril helpfully supplied with a grin on his face.

Niel shoved his brother away. "Get lost! You did that on purpose to find out how she'll react." He turned to Lulu, apologetically. "I'm sorry, he's a bit of a brat."

With her mouth still full, Lulu nodded waving her hand to excuse herself as she rushed to find a garbage pail.

In a flash, Niel was at her side with a brown paper bag. Lulu hurled a mass of eaten and uneaten food into it. Unable to make eye contact, Lulu turned away, wiping her lips.

"I take it you've never had that dish before," he said.

She shook her head. While Lulu had heard of the pork's blood stew back in the States, she had never tried it.

Niel closed the bag tightly and strode away explaining in Tagalog to relatives that Lulu was still recovering from airsickness and jet lag.

With her relatives looking on, Lulu smiled helplessly as Dimples pursed her lips.

"*Anak*, why don't you go inside and freshen up a bit," her Mom suggested.

Gratefully, Lulu welcomed that idea and sauntered over to the door leading to a kitchen that she was surprised to find immaculately clean. She wondered, *How in the world were they able to prepare a meal and still maintain a spotless kitchen?*

Using this time to explore the house, Lulu noticed that it was made predominantly of concrete though still had parts of the house such as some floors and beams on the ceilings made of bamboo and narra wood.

She chanced upon a building that wasn't quite connected to the house but rather an annex and thus the answer to her clean kitchen mystery. Lulu entered to find plates, utensils, and dozens of small and huge pots strewn about. There was a sink and what seemed to be a stove top sitting on a table. Most intriguing was a space filled with soot and ashes and burned wood with two clay pots that were filled—one with *menudo*, the other with that dark, pork blood stew.

Feeling nauseous, Lulu quickly exited the kitchen annex and re-entered the house. She trudged through a large formal dining area with a long, sturdy table and chairs made of narra.

She proceeded to the sala where she found more narra chairs with red velvet cushions. Since it's customary to leave one's shoes outside, Lulu walked around with her bare feet touching the terracotta mosaic-tiled first floor.

She went up a staircase—the steps and banisters made of Philippine mahogany—leading up to the second floor which to her delight boasted of an all narra-wooden floor. Peering into each of the four rooms, she guessed which one was the master bedroom as it had the largest bed with embroidered cotton sheets.

Upon entering the room, she immediately felt a chill in the air. The room started to spin, or was it Lulu who started to spin—she wasn't quite sure as she clung to a bedpost to steady herself.

Taking a deep breath, she hoped she wasn't contracting a case of food poisoning on her first day in the Philippines.

With slow, even breaths, Lulu gradually made her way to the dresser where her eyes scanned some old photographs, some of them clearly taken decades ago.

That was when she saw *her* face—the face of the woman she saw at Auntie Emilia's party. The face of the woman whose portrait hung on the wall of the Bituin family home only this was a different picture entirely. In this photo, the woman was with a man—but not Lulu's grandfather. By the way they were dressed, it appeared as though this was a wedding picture from over a hundred years ago.

Lulu picked up a sepia photo in its pewter frame to inspect it closely. The woman's face was round, her eyes equally so, but she appeared frail in the elegant dress she was wearing. *Maybe it was the corset all women had to wear back then, it had to be*, Lulu thought.

The man in the photo looked quite dapper wearing a black suit and white shirt and bow tie. He seemed to bear a slight resemblance to her Lolo, Dimples' father—the same wide forehead, dark circles under deep-set eyes, high cheekbones.

From the corner of Lulu's eye, she noticed someone flit past the doorway and she raised her gaze just as the same music box melody she heard continuously that one night in her bedroom back in the States permeated the room. *That couldn't have been the music from the jewelry box*, she thought. She hadn't packed it in her suitcase; she remembered packing it with boxes and furniture that had yet to arrive from the States. Placing the photo back on the dresser, Lulu paced slowly toward the hallway to find out who was there. Seeing no one, she strode to the next room and figured it might have been Chi-Chi searching for a bathroom.

Taking note of the interior, Lulu noticed that each room was a smaller version of the master bedroom. She also noticed there wasn't a bathroom on the second floor. *So if there wasn't a bathroom on this floor, where the heck was it?* She wondered.

Lulu noticed that as she descended the stairs, Dimples was lying on the sofa, her eyes closed. She could hear voices outside but they were not as boisterous as the crowd seemed to have dwindled.

Leaning toward her Mom, Dimples' eyelids opened slowly as if sensing Lulu's presence. She peeked at her daughter with eyelids half-open.

"You should rest, you are tired, *anak*," Dimples said, affectionately calling her the Tagalog term for "child" as she had when Lulu was little, brushing Lulu's hair with her fingers.

Lulu shook her head. "Mom, it's you who should rest."

"Hmmm," Dimples smiled as she closed her eyes again.

Lulu sat on the edge of the sofa as she watched Dimples breathe, her stomach and chest rising up and down in rhythm with her breath.

"Mom," Lulu began, slowly. "I'm really sorry about Lolo."

With that, Dimples' eyes flew open and she sat up slowly. Mother and daughter stared at each other until Dimples gathered Lulu in a tight embrace.

"Oh, I'm just so glad the whole family is here," Dimples said in mid-embrace. "I know it was hard for you to come here, *anak*, but I know you'll come to love it here as much as I always have."

With her chin on her Mom's shoulder, Lulu assessed her surroundings, not knowing exactly how to respond to Dimples' remark.

Just then, a woman started descending slowly down the staircase. Lulu immediately observed the woman wasn't wearing a "duster," the Philippine version of smock-frocks or sundresses like other provincial women wore. This one wore a long-sleeved black dress with a fitted-bodice and black gloves, an unusual choice in humid weather, Lulu thought.

Still tight in Dimples' embrace, Lulu observed the woman's feet as she noticed the stranger wasn't making a sound as she glided down the wooden steps. With the woman's long dress covering her feet, Lulu couldn't make out whether she was wearing shoes or not.

Then it dawned on her—a long gown, a long-sleeved dress and gloves—in this weather? Lulu then focused on the face of the woman whom she guessed was about Dimples' age. She let out a gasp.

The woman from the old photo upstairs!

"What's wrong, *anak*?" Dimples stared at Lulu with a startled expression.

Lulu glanced at her Mom, knowing that since Dimples had her back turned, there was no way she could have seen what Lulu just saw. Or believed it either.

When Lulu's eyes darted toward the staircase again, there was no sign of the woman.

"Are you okay?" Dimples said, worry written all over her face.

Lulu took a deep breath.

"I'm fine, Mom, just tired I think."

Dimples stood up. "Okay, then go upstairs and take a nice long nap. I'll wake you up at dinnertime."

Maybe it was just jet lag, thought Lulu, that made her see things or people that weren't there.

"Mom, if it's okay, can I take a nap here on this sofa?"

Dimples smiled. "Of course, *anak*."

She kissed Lulu lightly on the forehead before joining the group of relatives gathered outside where the air seemed a bit cooler than indoors despite the oscillating electric fans.

Lulu sank her body down on the sofa, afraid to succumb to sleep. Yet she feared what she would see if her eyes remained open.

"Rest, that's all I need is rest."

Minutes later, Lulu's heavy eyelids finally surrendered, just as a soft breeze caressed her cheek.

Chapter Five

A sharp piercing sound jolted her awake. But when Lulu's eyelids sprung open, she didn't know where she was. Then she remembered she wasn't in her own bed back in California and instead she was lying on a sofa in a home—her new home. As she recognized the screeching noise of a rooster crowing as dawn was barely breaking, with the soft moos of the cows from a distance, Lulu realized she'd been asleep several hours and had skipped dinner altogether.

It turned out Lulu continued to sleep off and on for a couple of days and even then she hadn't quite gotten over her jet lag as she would wake up hungry for breakfast at night and yearn for bedtime in the morning.

One thing was for sure—Lulu couldn't stop thinking about the woman she saw, if in fact it was a woman or…a ghost? Even the mere thought of ghosts made her cringe. Who believed in ghosts? *Certainly, not me!* Ghosts were the last thing Lulu wanted to talk about. But she found that moving to the Philippines, to be specific, moving to a provincial part of the Philippines where, her mother told her, people still believed in ghosts, meant exposing yourself to the wonders, and inconveniences, of rural life that never cease. Like believing in ghosts and bathing in outhouses.

Take for instance something as simple as bathing. Lulu found that not only was there no hot water, but she had to grab a plastic pail and pump her own water then carry it to the outhouse/bathhouse adjoining the kitchen and pour water into an even larger pail until it filled to the rim. Then she had to take a plastic bowl with a handle, called a *tabo*, that looked to Lulu like a humongous measuring cup, and then dip it into the pail before splashing cold water all over her body. How about washcloths and loofah scrubs? Forget it! That's what those large, smooth oval stones were for, her mother said.

"Aaaaagh!" Lulu yelped as the cold water violated her body, nearly paralyzing her from the chill. Scrubbing stones over her body was going to take some getting used to. She made a mental note to ask her mother to boil some water to add to her bath next time as she dried herself and slipped into a bathrobe then hurried back to her room upstairs.

But once she got dressed in a white, cotton peasant blouse and khaki skirt, Lulu started to feel beads of sweat streaming down her temples, neck and back.

"Great," she said, sarcastically. "I'm going to need another bath.

She couldn't believe that it was nearly November and it still felt like summer. Not a San Francisco Bay Area, Mediterranean summer but a humid, Louisiana summer.

Not surprisingly, Chi-Chi seemed to adjust really well in her new surroundings. Already she and Niel's sister Madonna, who was Chi-Chi's age, were practically inseparable as they spent a lot of time choosing clothes for their dolls. Two days ago, Lulu found them raiding Dimples' closet of old clothes, which the girls tried on as they giggled. And Chi-Chi seemed to be a hit with the girl cousins as well. Lulu wondered whether she would befriend one of her cousins and if they would have anything in common.

And the guys were just another issue to deal with. Lulu sighed, lamenting over the fact that spending the remainder of her high school days in the Philippines meant she would probably go dateless until she returned back home to the States for college.

"Oh, God! No!" she wailed at this pathetic realization one day.

"What's wrong? Don't you think Filipino guys are cute?" asked Chi-Chi, braiding her doll's blond hair.

Lulu glared at her sister. "I haven't seen a cute guy yet, have you?"

Chi-Chi shrugged, unraveling the blond doll's braids. "We just got here, Lulu." She began tying the doll's hair with a ribbon. "Don't you think Niel's cute?"

"Ha!" Lulu laughed. "His hair's too thick and wavy and he's way too nice."

Putting her doll down, Chi-Chi looked puzzled. "And that's a bad thing?"

Lulu shrugged. "He seems eager to please."

Tossing aside the ribbon, Chi-Chi started combing the doll's blond hair with a pink plastic comb. "I heard that's how Filipino guys are—they're chiver, chiveralous."

"You mean chivalrous," corrected an annoyed Lulu, rifling through her unpacked suitcase. After a few days, she was still unwilling to unpack, still hanging on to the hope she could convince her parents she didn't belong in the Philippines. "Whatever. I don't buy it. I mean what's the deal? Don't they have any pride?"

"Are you saying you'd rather go after the guy?"

"No, I'm saying do they have to be so chivalrous? It's kind of corny, don't you think?"

"I think it's kinda romantic."

Lulu cringed, preferring to think about Stellan and how straightforward and genuine he seemed to be.

"I didn't say they were all nice, Lulu," Chi-Chi grimaced as she combed through her doll's tangled hair. "I just thought Niel seemed like a real nice guy, that's all."

"And that's his problem," Lulu huffed, tossing blouses onto the bed and floor as she was sorting them by color and style. *Why did I bring some of these sweaters over here? I'll never wear them.* "He's too nice and seems corny to me, like he's trying too hard to impress me."

Chi-Chi got up, giving up the battle on the unruly doll's hair. "Can I have him, then?"

"He's too old for you," Lulu said, playfully throwing one of her sweaters at Chi-Chi who threw it right back.

***

Walking downstairs one day, Lulu found the living room was filled with relatives who were there days earlier for the welcome party and still even more relatives in the kitchen and dining room. But where were Mom, Dad, Chi-Chi, and Dimar?

"*Ining*, there you are!" Diding called out as she got up from the floor where a number of women were gathered around the *Balikbayan* boxes filled with goodies from the U.S. now scattered all over the floor and coffee table. Women and children were huddled over the small bottles of perfume, lipsticks, candy, soap and school supplies Romar bought at the stateside drugstore to give to relatives who looked like scavengers after a treasure hunt.

"You need to eat lunch now," Diding said, grabbing Lulu by the arm and leading her to the dining area.

"Where's my family?" Lulu asked acclimating to all the still unfamiliar, smiling faces staring at her as though she were a Hollywood star.

As soon as her question escaped her lips, Lulu knew she had said the wrong thing.

"Your family?" Diding said, looking puzzled as she scooped heaps full of rice onto a plate followed by two extremely round, extremely red sausages. "*Aba*, look around you. We're all here."

A skinny woman with dark, crepe-like skin and a gap-toothed grin playfully slapped Diding on the arm. "She means, where are her parents and siblings?"

Diding smacked her palm on her forehead. "Oh, I see! I see! They are in town buying groceries. They left early while you were asleep."

Lulu pouted briefly at the thought of having been left behind, then made an effort to smile at her relatives who continued to stare at her while she ate. She wasn't accustomed to having this heavy a lunch—garlic fried rice and *longanisa*—but she had to admit, it was rather tasty. She just wished she could enjoy her meal without an audience.

"*Ang kinis-kinis ng kutis niya, parang artista,*" said the skinny woman, Clara, who turned out to be Diding's older sister.

Diding flashed a wide grin as she sat next to Lulu. "My sister said you have a clear complexion—like a movie star's."

Lulu politely smiled at Clara, not really knowing how to respond. She was considered to be rather pretty back at school in the States—but like a movie star?

"You can be a queen at the May festival," said Claudia, another relative.

With raised eyebrows as she chewed her food, Lulu eyed the women, who cooled themselves with *anahaw* fans.

"The Flores de Mayo or Santacruzan," answered Claudia, a woman Lulu guessed was in her forties with jet-black hair tied neatly in a bun at the nape of her neck. "It is a fiesta held in May every year in honor of the Virgin Mary. I help organize the events and choose the pretty maidens who will participate in the parade. You can be either Reina Elena or Reina Imperatriz who are usually the prettiest girls in town."

Placing her fork down, Lulu nearly choked on her food. Were these people for real? First, they said she had movie star looks, and now she was the prettiest girl in town? *I wonder what the other girls my age look like here?* She wondered.

"*Kumusta*, Titas!"

Just then Niel and Cyril appeared and immediately went to the elder ladies in the group and placed the backs of the women's right hands on their foreheads one by one as Lulu curiously watched.

The boys both greeted Lulu with a nod, a quick raise of the eyebrows, apparently a common way of greeting.

"Are you just about done with lunch?" Niel said, flashing Lulu a shy grin she thought was rather cute.

"Actually, this is kind of breakfast but yeah, I'm all done," she said, standing up and gathering her plate and utensils which Clara whisked away from her.

"You go with Niel, Cyril and Madonna. They will show you around town," Diding said. "Maybe you'll see your Mama and Papa there."

Frankly, I'd rather tool around town just Niel and me, Lulu thought but felt grateful for the chance to get to know Niel a bit more. She followed the guys to a much smaller jeep than the "Lucky Star" parked a few yards from the house. After Niel helped Lulu climb into the Jeep Wrangler, she sat down next to Madonna in the back seat. Suddenly, as Lulu watched Niel confidently take the driver's seat, his toned, brown arms gripping the wheel, Lulu shuddered as another thought crossed her mind.

"Niel, are we related?"

Carefully navigated by Niel, the jeep hummed over the dirt road from the compound onto a paved main road leading to town. Once the jeep was safely coasting along, Niel glanced back with a quick smile at Lulu.

"Why do you ask?"

She shrugged and chuckled a bit. "It seems I'm related to just about everybody around here." Little did he know she secretly hoped that wasn't the case with Niel.

As Lulu brushed away her hair that whipped across her face from the wind, she set eyes on a few bamboo homes, called *bahay kubos*, with roofs of shaggy *nipa* shingles and further out lay fields of sugar cane as far as the eye could see.

"Homes made out of bamboo are rare these days," Niel said, as if reading Lulu's thoughts. "You want to know what's beyond those sugar cane fields? The Balayan Bay and miles and miles of beachfront property. We'll have to organize a picnic sometime."

Turning to her left, Lulu cast her gaze across the lush fields, trying to imagine the vision that lay beyond the palm trees and banana trees—the feel of her toes digging into smooth, grainy, white sand caressed by the lull of ocean waves. Closing her eyes, Lulu tilted her head back to let the sunlight wash over her face as the excited chattering between Madonna and Cyril in Tagalog seemed to fade away.

"By the way, the answer is no."

Niel's deep voice reeled her back to the present and when she opened her eyes she found his own eyes meeting hers via the rear view mirror. The jeep suddenly lurched onto another dirt road that lead to another paved one that was lined with palm trees. Lulu guessed this road was leading to town and thought a number of rustic buildings appeared as though they were built more than a century ago.

Turns out she was right. Niel told her these "*bahay na bato*," wood-and-stone houses along the street were built during the Spanish colonization. Structures along the road typically consisted of businesses on the bottom floor and homes on the top floor that showed off picturesque wrap-around capiz windows and a square symmetry of the Geometic style. Some of the homes boasted of metal cutwork awnings and fancy grills within their *ventanillas.*

Twisting the handkerchief she held in her hand, Lulu still couldn't believe she was in the Philippines. The whole experience remained too surreal for her. All around her were shards of evidence showing layer upon layer of cultures—Chinese, Spanish, Filipino and Malay. The buildings ignited a sense of nostalgia that Lulu had never experienced before—a sense of connecting, of belonging to a past she found herself wanting to know more about. Only for a moment did she allow herself a glimpse of her life back in the States where her home, school, and some of the shops were less than fifty years old. At first, Lulu thought, it was best to be a part of a culture where everything was new. Considering her need to escape the prejudices of the past, living in a place that didn't have a past seemed safe. But as she viewed the centuries-old architecture that seemed to whisper her name, drawing her into the past, Lulu couldn't help but return the favor with long, admiring looks of wonder, despite her initial animosity.

"Neat, huh?" Niel said, meeting her eyes in the rear view mirror.

"I've never seen such old buildings in all my life," she said, trying to take it in all at once. "They have a certain charm to them. They're haunting, but in a good way."

Niel drove steadily along the main thoroughfare until a huge basilica came into view up ahead as they were approaching the town square. Lulu thought the Baroque-style edifice was majestic, with its thick brick walls bolstered by quadrangular buttresses and a bell tower hovering over the plaza luminous and mighty protecting the townsfolk like a lighthouse guiding ships on a foggy night.

At the center of the plaza was a bronze statue of Filipino patriot Jose Rizal. The statues of the country's national hero, whose book was known to spark the Philippine revolution against the Spaniards, were found in virtually every town, reminding Filipinos of the bravery they showed in the fight for their independence from Spain.

Knowing this made Lulu's heart swell with pride but also with embarrassment since she didn't know much about Philippine history. Seeing the statue of Rizal, his stance so proud and honorable, made Lulu want to learn more about him. Could it be that the Philippines had already had an effect on her? And so soon?

It's not like I want to settle and live here forever. She assured herself silently that the move to the Philippines was temporary. She shook her head as if trying to ward off the magic spell her immediate surroundings seem to cast on her, just as Niel parked the jeep alongside jeepneys and tricycles in front of the basilica.

"Every town has a huge church," Niel told Lulu and as he helped her get out of the jeep the handkerchief she was holding dropped on the ground. Their foreheads butted as they both stooped down to retrieve it and they laughed as they eyed each other.

"*Gutom na ako!*" whined Madonna, who yawned and scratched her head.

Niel shot his younger sister a warning glance. "We haven't shown Ate Lulu the church yet. We'll eat afterward."

Madonna pouted then turned away as Niel smiled meekly at Lulu. "Little sisters," he said.

Lulu raised her eyebrows. She wasn't used to being referred to as "*Ate*," by someone other than Chi-Chi. When Lulu noticed her mother calling her older female cousins "*Ate*," the day they arrived, Dimples explained that any female who was older was "*Ate*," whether they were related or not. "Yeah. I know all about sisters. But we really don't need to see the church just yet. Let's eat."

"But you just had breakfast. Or was that lunch?"

Shrugging her shoulders, Lulu observed Madonna's hopeful face. "I'll join you guys for a snack then."

Lulu followed Niel, Cyril and Madonna through a whir of buzzing tricycles and honking jeepneys to the public market, or *palengke*, across from the church. While darting and ducking to avoid being toppled over by vendors carrying baskets of fish or vegetables on their heads, Lulu followed behind the siblings in a single file through the narrow alleyways of the public market.

Whistles and catcalls showered the group—or it seemed like it was directed to just Lulu—as they passed the various specialty vendor stalls and shops along the way selling everything from *anahaw* fans and t-shirts and jeans to shampoo and snacks.

The sound of chopping greeted the group farther into the market where Lulu encountered an array of butchery stalls with meat vendors selling fresh cut poultry, pork and beef. Even farther down, in their own little, pungent nook as though the rest of the vendors ostracized them by smell alone, sat the fish vendors with pails of fresh catch.

Trying to avoid appearing rude by pinching her nostrils with her fingers, Lulu held her breath as they strode by the fish vendors, staring men and women whose dark skin weathered by hours in the sun. Lulu caught Madonna curiously eyeing her and just then, the young girl took a handkerchief from her pocket and placed it over her nose and mouth. Lulu took the cue and fished for her own handkerchief and did the same. *The handkerchief did come in handy after all, thank God*, Lulu thought.

Just when she thought they would never get there, Niel beckoned them over to a corner of the market where a bar counter was set up with red vinyl cushioned stools. He motioned Lulu to a seat next to him while Cyril and Madonna took seats on either side of them.

As Lulu looked around curiously, she noticed a couple of other diners sipping, or rather slurping their soups loudly.

"Isn't the weather a little too hot for soup?" Lulu exclaimed, alarmed at herself for voicing her thoughts aloud.

Niel chuckled. "We will have *mami*," he said, pronouncing the word in the same way a child would ask for his mommy.

Another puzzled look from Lulu elicited another chuckle from Niel. "It's basically chicken broth with egg noodles, with a whole egg cooked into it—quite the specialty here. You should try it."

Sure Lulu liked the idea of the soup—a welcome treat especially during cold and rainy winters back home but in tropical, humid weather—she wasn't so sure. Still, she was willing to give it a try. Heck, she thought, when in

Rome…actually, when in the Philippines. *If I endured pig meat stewed in its own blood, I can endure this.*

And endured the soup she did. While hot liquid entered her mouth and seared her tongue and throat, a stream of sweat poured down Lulu's back and neck and she figured she could use another bath. But the experience was worth it. The soup was delicious.

A bath had to wait until they got home. After their soup stop, Niel accompanied Lulu to an Internet café so she could e-mail Kellie, Sara and Stellan while Cyril and Madonna checked out a nearby bookstore. Then the group took Lulu on a quick tour of the basilica, the centerpiece of the town, with its alluring frescoes of the saints. The construction of the church started in 1749 and was completed ten years later. A stone arc depicting angels and doves welcomed guests. Standing a few meters from the church, was the four-layered bell tower. The church was listed as a National Cultural Treasure as its construction was supervised by Filipino seculars during the Spanish Colonial Period, Niel pointed out.

They also went to the Catholic school, which used to be a monastery located just next to the church, where Lulu would attend school in a few days. She tried not to think about her first day of school, concentrating instead on the Spanish-style buildings that reminded her of the California missions back home.

School. The more Lulu thought about going to a new school and in a foreign country no less, the more she felt sick to her stomach with anger at her parents for moving here and fear of the uncertainty that lay ahead.

Chapter Six

The group of four aunts, a rambunctious bunch consisting of Tita Claudia, Diding, Clara and Norie, ranging from ages thirty to seventy and collectively known in the family as "the Titas," gathered one evening in the kitchen to make a dinner of *tinola*, soup with chicken, green papaya and fresh garden vegetables, fried fish called *galungong*, *pinakbet*, a vegetable stew, sliced Indian mango with *bagoong*, fermented krill, and steamed rice.

The Titas kept casting frequent glances at Lulu who was propped on an easy chair in the family room which had a clear view of the kitchen. As they prepared raw rice for cooking by sifting it first using a flat, round bamboo-woven winnowing basket or a *bilao,* the Titas hoped the kitchen activity would draw Lulu, whose face was buried in a teen romance novel, into the kitchen. What they didn't know was she was secretly watching the Titas squatting on the floor while sifting rice, with its swishing sounds in the baskets, ever so delicately, and with seemingly little effort, that made Lulu think there was nothing to it.

As her eyes peered cautiously above the top of her book, Lulu observed the way the Titas held their *bilaos* firmly while gracefully tossing the rice upward and, as if in magical slow motion, saw how the rice stayed suspended in air for a microsecond until a thin stream of rice finally cascaded down into the baskets.

Shoosh, shoosh, shoosh, went the rice sifting in the basket. There had to be a trick to doing that, thought Lulu, as she squirmed in her chair, eager to try the method.

Even though Lulu didn't completely understand what they were talking about and could only make out a few words, the Titas' chatter and laughter were infectious. She even found herself suppressing a chuckle at Tita Claudia's amusing, asthmatic laughter. Lulu thought about joining them to prove she was making an effort to get to know her relatives. But even though the Titas knew English, Lulu feared her inability to converse in Tagalog would make her feel like an outsider.

Shoosh, shoosh, shoosh. It seemed the sound of the rice sifting was calling out to her. Lulu observed as Clara, the eldest of the Titas sat with her back against a loose kitchen cabinet door, which pounded on the doorframe each time Tita Clara sifted her basket with a rowing motion. Tita Diding's brows knitted together as she picked stones from the rice as Tita Norie, the youngest of the group, began telling a story. Lulu wished she could join in on the conversation as she observed how the sun's rays cast soft light through the slats of the blinds atop the Titas' heads as they leaned closer together, apparently riveted by what could be the latest gossip in town.

Lulu enjoyed cooking but her experience at the market, the kitchen utensils and dishes were all so foreign to her; she wondered if she would ever learn to cook Filipino food. Acquiring culinary skills could be a way to fit in her new milieu.

Titas Claudia and Clara stood up to start chopping vegetables and immediately Lulu's eyes went to the two flat baskets that sat temporarily neglected, as the remaining squatting Titas continued sifting. Then, as if her feet and legs had a mind of their own, Lulu found herself getting up and moving over to where Titas Norie and Diding were tending the rice. With smiles on their faces, they eyed her with interest as she sat down with legs crossed. Tita Norie placed a basket in front of her. Lulu shook her head and pushed the basket aside gently. Although she was eager to try sifting, she didn't think she could pull it off so gracefully.

"The point of the sifting is to remove any traces of seeds or tiny stones from the rice mills," said Tita Diding, showing Lulu the proper way to hold the basket with two hands while sifting and tossing the rice.

Even though Lulu carefully shook the basket, some rice still managed to spill onto the floor. She started to give up on her first try, but Tita Diding insisted she try again.

"Don't worry. With practice, you'll be able to sift without spilling," smiled Tita Diding, as she flashed her gap-toothed grin. "See if you can change your sitting position. If you squat, you have better mobility and will be able to handle the basket with more grace."

Lulu shifted her position so that both feet were firmly planted on the floor as she tried not to let her butt touch the floor. The position reminded Lulu of a yoga pose but she couldn't quite remember what it was called. Squatting down on the floor while rocking the flat basket back and forth without losing her balance and falling over proved to be a challenge. Lulu's efforts were sloppy at best as she clumsily shook the rice that showered onto the floor instead of cascading gracefully back down into the *bilao*. But instead of feeling frustrated, she laughed at her blunder as a novice rice sifter.

"That's okay," Tita Norie said, bending down to sweep the spilled rice with her hands.

"Why do you sift so much rice?" Lulu asked, trying to get the hang of the technique without spilling more rice.

"Well, there are so many of us to feed and we love eating rice with every meal," Tita Diding explained in a patient voice as she concentrated on picking seeds from her batch. "Whatever we don't eat tonight we'll save for making garlic fried rice for breakfast."

"Do people always eat rice for breakfast?" Lulu had never heard of such a thing.

The Titas nodded in unison. "You've never had fried rice for breakfast?"

"Mom and Dad sometimes did back home but I didn't care for it—with all those carbs," she said. "I don't understand why rice is that important."

Lulu's response caused the Titas to shake their heads, either from her referring to the States as "home," or reacting to her rice comment. "Tsk, tsk, tsk. That Dimples—didn't teach her girls much about their culture," said Tita Claudia, almost under her breath.

The Titas told her, that aside from rice being such an economic staple in the country, garlic fried rice usually accompanied Philippine sweet sausage, called *longanisa*, or with *bangus*, grilled Philippine milkfish, or *tocino*, sweet cured pork, chicken or beef. Hearing all of this made Lulu's stomach turn, as she wasn't used to eating so much in the morning.

The Titas assigned Lulu to chop a variety of vegetables for the stew that included eggplant, okra, onions, green beans and the frequently used *ampalaya* or bitter melon. Chopping proved to be more fun than sifting. As she chopped, Lulu saw how the kitchen, though sparse and not as equipped or as large as their kitchen back in the States, became the center of familial gatherings as an assortment of cousins and neighbors would stop by to taste a vegetable stew or to drop off some freshly picked fruits and vegetables from the family orchard and gardens.

Later at dinner, Lulu sat with Chi-Chi in the family room with the younger cousins since only a certain number of people could eat at the dining table at one time. Dimples said the cousins were mostly honor students so Lulu assumed they could all speak English, though she had yet to hear them speak to her.

"They're just shy," Dimples told Lulu, as she shoveled a spoonful of rice in Dimar's mouth.

Still, the cousins sat awkwardly as they ate and conversed amongst themselves in Tagalog while occasionally stealing glances at Chi-Chi and Lulu. After dinner, Tita Norie's twin brother, Tito Enrico, a high school English teacher, gathered everyone in the family room for storytelling.

"Why can't we just watch TV?" Lulu asked her mother who was getting ready to put Dimar to bed.

"Because this is what our family usually does after dinner, especially now with the family all together. Storytelling is also a favorite activity when the power goes out during a storm and we all sit together with lighted candles glowing around us."

"But the power isn't even out," Lulu argued. She could think of better things to do with her time—like going to her room to continue reading her novel and be alone. Lulu had always enjoyed reading and now, more than ever before, books had become great companions, a refuge from an emotional storm. None of the cousins wanted to talk to her anyway. But Dimples wouldn't let her retreat upstairs. It would be rude not to participate, her mother said.

"At least, just listen."

So even without a power outage, Lulu sat next to Chi-Chi in the room with the cousins and Titas and uncles as Tito Enrico's baritone voice commanded silence in the room. She was surprised he was telling the stories in English that Lulu presumed wouldn't guarantee her undivided attention. She would act like the obedient daughter, and then tune Uncle Enrico out. Maybe in favor of daydreaming about Stellan waiting for her back home?

Closing her eyes, Lulu mentally calculated how many more days before she would start school and how many months before she would graduate from high school and finally return home. But the oohs and aahs emitting from the relatives around her piqued Lulu's interest that she couldn't resist hearing the rest of the story.

"And the lady in white floated along the lake leaving an eerie glow in her wake." Tito Enrico's words jolted Lulu from her reverie just as a sudden grasp of someone's hand on Lulu's arm made her jump. She turned to see Chi-Chi trying to hide her face on her sister's shoulder.

"I'm scared," Chi-Chi whimpered.

Lulu patted her hand reassuringly. "Don't be. It's just a story. It's not true."

She thought the cousins seemed foolish with frightened expressions on their faces, some smiling awkwardly, some with a hint of fear in their eyes. Even if Lulu didn't believe in ghosts, her cousins' reactions made her curious.

"We never get tired of hearing about the legend of the White Lady," offered Nina, one of the cousins about the same age as Lulu who was pleasantly surprised to be addressed directly by one of the cousins. Maybe ghost stories could be the icebreaker Lulu needed. Or maybe Nina was just showing off that she wasn't fazed at all by ghosts, Lulu thought as she detected what appeared to be a smug look on Nina's face.

But Lulu didn't believe in ghosts. Ghosts, she thought, would have to do something spectacular if she were ever to change her views about them. Instead, she wanted to bolt and take Chi-Chi with her, but something about the expressions on her cousins' faces and the inviting, compelling tone of Tito Enrico's voice kept her glued to her seat. As if sensing he had riveted his audience, Tito Enrico continued his storytelling, this time leaning forward as if preparing to tell a more morbid tale, the candle lights even more prominently casting an eerie glow on his face.

"Do you all remember when I first told you about Lola Josefina? The time I saw her in the middle of the sugar cane fields?" Tito Enrico scanned the room as some nodded and others looked at one another nervously. "I have another Lola Josefina story to share."

Lola Josefina? Lulu looked around to see if anyone seemed as puzzled as she was. *Who was this Lola Josefina?*

Chi-Chi moaned as she gripped the end of Lulu's shirt.

"Do you want me to take you to bed now?"

Surprisingly, Chi-Chi shook her head. Lulu sensed that though Chi-Chi appeared to be frightened, like her, morbid fascination and curiosity seemed to win over fear. The sisters held on to each other firmly for support as they waited for Tito Enrico's story while the crickets outside performed their nightly serenade.

Chapter Seven

"It happened when I was about fourteen or fifteen. I was helping *Tatay* at the sugar cane fields on a hot day. To get a break from the heat, I wandered over to the lake and plunged into the water," Tito Enrico said. Even in the candlelight, his eyes hinted that he had mentally, and maybe emotionally, gone to a place where there was no turning back.

Hesitating a bit to scratch his head, Tito Enrico seemed uneasy as though he was unsure whether he should continue. Then, he sat up straight and, as if wanting to unleash the demon inside of him, he took a deep breath and forged on.

"I had been cooling off in the water for quite some time and thought I heard some rustling near the banana plants. I felt like someone was watching me," he said with slow, unsteady breaths, like he was running a marathon and talking at the same time. "So I turned to look toward the area where I thought I heard a sound and there, standing next to a mango tree, was Lola Josefina."

The whole room collectively gasped as Lulu curiously peered around, annoyed that everyone, including Chi-Chi, seemed captivated by the story.

"What did she do, Tito?" asked Carly, Nina's perky, wide-eyed ten-year-old sister.

Tito Enrico pursed his lips for a second then twitched his nose. "She just stared at me for a long time. Of course, I was younger and bolder then and thought I'd take on a challenge. So I stared right back. Then, all of a sudden, I felt something pull me down in the water, like two hands gripping my ankles and forcing me down. And down I went but by the time I came up for air, the ghost was gone."

A few of the cousins squealed in a mixture of delight and horror as Lulu rolled her eyes.

"Lola Josefina is our ancestor who lived a hundred years ago," Nina whispered to Lulu who nodded politely.

"Who was she?" Lulu asked, eager to get the lowdown on the alleged "ghost."

"Doña Josefina Villareal Del Rosario, your great-great-great grandmother, maintained a simple life raising her eight children during the Spanish era," explained Tito Enrico. "When her husband was declared missing in the fight against the Spaniards in 1896, Lola Josefina placed her eldest daughter in charge of her brood then formed a group of women from the village who bravely scoured the battlefields in search of Lola's husband and wounded soldiers to care for them."

"Is she a scary ghost or a saint, Tito Enrico?" Carly asked.

While Lola Josefina became somewhat of a legend in the barrio, not much was known about her, only that after her death, she appeared from time to time to certain people, he replied.

Tito Enrico scratched his head and smiled. "Well, to me, she's not a scary ghost and she may as well be a saint for all the good she did for our ailing soldiers." He nodded his head and seemed deep in thought as if fond images flooded his memory. "To me, she seemed like a guardian angel for the times I was lost and struggled to find direction in life. She appeared to me when I was almost eighteen when my papa died and I couldn't decide whether I should leave Mama and my family to join the U.S. Navy. Then, a few times when I was homesick, I thought I saw her on the deck of the ship I served on that was headed to Japan. Yes, I think she was there to guide me."

Was that supposed to make me believe in Tito Enrico's story? Lulu thought. Telling ghost stories was fast becoming an annoyance to Lulu, a very unnecessary annoyance. Didn't these people have better things to do with their time? Then she thought back to the time when she first arrived and the woman she saw descending the staircase. *Could that have been Lola Josefina?* Lulu shook her head violently. *No way am I buying into that ghost business.*

When the cousins left later that night, Lulu lay in her bed restless and for once, wishing she were sharing a room with Chi-Chi. It bothered Lulu that her sister believed the story. Could there really be some truth to Tito Enrico's tale?

Sighing, Lulu pulled the light cotton blanket over her head and turned to one side, her back to the window.

"Ghosts don't exist," she said out loud to herself. "They just don't."

Suddenly, a familiar waltz pierced through the darkness of Lulu's bedroom. Without turning to look, Lulu knew it was her newly-unpacked jewelry box again. Only then did she feel more frightened than annoyed. *Was Lola Josefina trying to send her a message? And if so, what was it?*

"Shut up, I say, shut up!" she shouted at the jewelry box as if it or the ghost she refused to believe in could hear her.

She vowed to shut the jewelry box forevermore by securing it with duct tape but before she could get up, the music stopped.

***

On the first day of classes at her new school, on a hot, October morning nearly a month after their arrival, Lulu's stomach was turning from first day jitters and her head aching from lack of sleep from anxiety over Lola Josefina and the jewelry box. So the prospect of staying in bed all day seemed tempting. But she dragged her body up, took the long, arduous but necessary bath and dressed in the school uniform of gray and navy plaid skirt and short-sleeved white shirt.

When she went downstairs, she found a steaming bowl of garlic fried rice complete with hot dog slices and diced scrambled eggs waiting for her. She felt nauseous from the sight and scent of the food along with her fear of facing her new classmates. She couldn't bear to have this huge breakfast, so unusual, so foreign, so unfamiliar from the home she grew up knowing.

"Um, Mom, can I have some oatmeal, instead?" she said, as Chi-Chi shot her a warning look.

Dimples was already steeped in her own sweat, a look of frustration on her face as she was trying to console Dimar who was scratching a rash on his stomach.

"Oatmeal? This isn't the States, Lulu. Make do with what you've got," said her mother who tried feeding some rice to Dimar with difficulty. Then wiping the sweat from her forehead with the back of her hand, she said. "We need a maid."

"Are you serious?" Lulu's eyes bulged with disbelief. "We're not even rich!"

"Mom says you don't have to be rich to have a maid here," Chi-Chi calmly, but helpfully offered, as she ate her rice with seemingly no problem.

Lulu stared helplessly at her bowl of rice, not wanting to sit down for breakfast, a breakfast that could one day be served to her by a maid. Maybe other kids from the States would enjoy the service. But for reasons unknown to her, Lulu couldn't fathom being served to and it frustrated her that she wasn't too keen on the idea. Had this place changed her views already? She was about to express how the concept of having a maid seemed a bit archaic and class-oriented when Dimar let out a howl and Dimples stood up with toddler son in tow and stomped out of the room.

"I tried to warn you Mom's not in a good mood," Chi-Chi said, seemingly absorbed in her rice bowl.

Lulu sank down in her seat. "I feel like throwing up."

Chi-Chi was scraping the remnants of her meal. "Well, don't do it here."

"I don't mean the food as much as being nervous about school," Lulu said, picking up her spoon, having learned that a spoon was the utensil of choice over the fork, which played a supporting role: shoveling food onto the spoon.

"Miss Popular nervous about school?"

"It's different here, Chi." Lulu toyed with her rice. "Aren't you nervous?"

Her sister shrugged. "A little, I guess. But I'm just going to be nice to everyone and hope they'll be nice to me."

Sweet, optimistic Chi-Chi, thought Lulu. *I hope she's right for her sake.*

Since it was their first day, Romar taught the girls how to take the jeepney to school. He showed them where to wait for the jeepney and the location of the jeepney stop they would meet at to take them back home. Lulu at once was thankful for the blasting throwback 1980s music in the jeepney that temporarily distracted her thoughts about school and about ghosts.

And since they were too old to have Daddy hold their hands as they walked to their classrooms, Lulu and Chi-Chi insisted they find their own way around. It was important to make a good first impression, Lulu suggested to her sister. And showing people what a Daddy's girl you are isn't the way to do it. Chi-Chi's sixth-grade class was a building away from the high school girls' building. Elementary school was co-ed but high school wasn't. To Lulu's dismay, the boys' high school was on the far side of the campus. But one exciting thing about their Catholic school was that the college building was merely a courtyard away. Suddenly, Lulu felt a bit grown up because she was technically on the same campus as the college students. Lulu learned from her relatives that most private elementary, high school and college classes in the

Philippines were held on the same campus but housed in different buildings.

When Tito Enrico told her a few days before school started that, at least in their region of the country, there were no middle schools, Lulu practically did a somersault. "While the more Westernized international schools attended by children of diplomats living in Manila have middle school grade levels, the Philippine school system generally doesn't offer them," said her uncle.

That meant, by default, Lulu would jump from being a freshman in high school back home to being a junior at fourteen. That meant, after two more years, she'd be in college. As she thought about the prospect of graduating from high school early, she smiled to herself and practically skipped to her classroom. This was the best news she had in a long time and probably the only good thing about the move so far. *Well, maybe not the only good thing*, thought Lulu, as she wondered whether she would bump into Niel even though he was in college.

But now she had to concentrate on just getting through her first day.

Chapter Eight

Once Lulu entered the classroom, she wasn't sure what to expect and didn't know much about her class except for the room number listed with her name.

Taking a deep breath as though preparing to dive into murky waters, Lulu entered the classroom hoping the girls wouldn't notice her trembling and more importantly, notice she was new. But that was next to impossible as the girls practically all grew up and went to the same school together since they learned to walk and talk. Immediately, about twenty-five pairs of eyes stared at Lulu as she struggled to find an empty desk; nervousness prevented her from meeting anyone's gaze. Even when she did find a desk and sank into it, that didn't ensure she would blend in. Suddenly, laughter erupted. Looking around, she saw unfamiliar faces with mouths open, eyes flashing and for just a few seconds, it was as if her surroundings were on mute, as she couldn't even hear what was coming out of their mouths.

Then, as if someone had pressed the mute-off button, the laughter, this time quite audible, continued. One girl with short black hair and a humongous pimple on her nose pointed downward towards Lulu. To her horror, Lulu discovered the back of her skirt had caught on the back of her chair, exposing her pink, flowered cotton underwear.

She quickly stood up to smooth down the pleats of her skirt before sinking back down in her seat just as the laughter had started to die down.

And all Lulu could think of at that moment was how Rowena felt on her first day of school in the States.

"Girls! Girls! Settle down!"

A haughty voice immediately silenced the room as a rail-thin, gray-haired woman with horn-rimmed glasses wearing a gray button-down short-sleeved shirt and matching skirt marched into the room. As if on cue, all the girls, except Lulu, stood at attention.

"Good morning, Miss Espinosa!" they cried in singsong unison.

The ancient Miss Lucia Espinosa had served as the high school's Tagalog language teacher for nearly thirty-five years. She peered at the students from the top of her eyeglass rims, motioning with an impatient wave of her hand for the girls to take their seats until her eyes grazed on Lulu then on to other girls before resting on Lulu again.

"*May bagong estudiante tayo*," said Miss Espinosa in a croaky voice, peering at Lulu curiously. "*Ano ang pangalan mo, Iha*?"

Lulu felt as though her tongue twisted into a knot. "Excuse me? I don't understand."

A few girls giggled until the teacher glared at them and returned her attention to Lulu. "You don't understand? You don't speak Tagalog?"

"No."

"That's no, *Miss* Espinosa," the teacher corrected a trembling Lulu, who fiddled with the strap of her backpack. "I asked you: what is your name?" said the old woman carefully enunciating each syllable.

Lulu cleared her throat. Here was an opportunity for people to hear her name pronounced correctly but she realized they probably already knew how to say it. "Lualhati Bituin, Miss Espinosa."

"Stand up!" the teacher admonished. "Here in this school, whenever you address the teacher, you must stand up. That's the way we do things around here."

Feeling perplexed and embarrassed, Lulu slowly stood up, wishing she were anywhere but here in this classroom.

"Did you move here recently?" said Miss Espinosa, both hands on her hips.

"Yes, Miss Espinosa. About a month ago."

"Well, then. You will have to learn Tagalog if you are to remain here. You can speak English anywhere else, I don't care. But in *my* class, only Tagalog is spoken."

Thankfully, Miss Espinosa managed to ignore Lulu for the remainder of the class just as Lulu decided she just won't say anything in this class for the rest of the school year if possible. She sat through class as though she wasn't there. Missing her old school and her old friends, Lulu just let the unfamiliar words glaze over her.

Finally, class was over and Miss Espinosa left the room. The students resumed their chatting again as they waited for the next teacher to arrive for second period Philippine history class.

With her initial nervousness behind her, Lulu realized she was in the same class with her cousin Nina, whom she didn't recognize earlier. She waved to her cousin who stared at her blankly then turned away. *Didn't she see me?* Lulu wondered. Was this the same Nina, who only last night spoke briefly to her but today maybe pretended not to know her? Was she really being helpful and friendly that night or just testing her nerves?

Feeling deflated that she would never have an ally in the class, Lulu cautiously observed the girls in her classroom as they waited for the teacher to show up. She tried to figure out which ones were the popular girls. There were some attractive girls, some—if given the chance to find out—maybe with nice personalities, and some who may articulate very well in English. Her mother constantly drove home the point that girls and boys here adored

American culture, though they may not always practice some of the Western customs in provincial Philippines, such as dating rituals. Guys still had to court girls at the girls' homes—in front of the family, sometimes—a traditional practice Lulu thought she would never experience during her stay in the country.

Jolie Reyes, a pretty girl with cat-like eyes, sitting two seats diagonally away from Lulu, eyed her the way a scientist would examine a new specimen, as Nina chatted away with two friends in her corner, still not acknowledging Lulu's presence.

The girls suddenly stood at attention again and this time, Lulu was grateful she had the good enough sense to stay alert and stand along with them—a practice that seemed terribly odd to her.

"Good morning, Sister Ruth!" they welcomed a rotund nun dressed in her traditional habit.

Sister Ruth, who was an assistant principal, informed the class that Mr. Dimasyado, the second period teacher was running late and if the class would kindly wait a few minutes.

As soon as Sister Ruth left, Jolie Reyes was at Lulu's side, along with a thin, olive-skinned girl Jolie introduced as her friend, Aprilyn Ocampo. Clearly, these girls weren't afraid to approach Lulu who smiled at them in appreciation.

"We wanted you to know if you have any questions, you can ask us," Jolie said in heavily-accented English, as she and Aprilyn squatted closer to Lulu.

The girls in her class would be her same classmates throughout the whole school year, Jolie told her.

"In American movies, we see students walk to their different classes," said Aprilyn, twisting a strand of her light brown hair. "It's different here. It's the teachers who come to us."

This was going to be a huge adjustment for Lulu. Gone were the lingering and loitering in the halls between classes or hanging out by the lockers.

"Oh, we should also tell you about the way each class is set up," Jolie added, with an authoritative tone that made Lulu think Jolie could write a book about "How to Survive in a Philippine High School."

The word "caste" came to Lulu's mind when it was explained to Lulu that: "High school girls are classified according to beauty, brains, and old money designated in each grade level. Section A class has all of the above. Section B has the nouveau riche girls who are "somewhat brainy" but not filthy rich or pretty enough," Jolie helpfully supplied.

While sadly, Section C was everything Section A wasn't. Once again, Lulu thought about the archaic "caste system." *What kind of backward system were they running here?* Lulu thought to herself.

***

At the school cafeteria, Lulu stood carrying her tray of ham sandwich and Coke as she scanned the seating area. Nina lifted her eyes to meet her gaze but quickly turned away to continue chatting with friends. As the blood rose to her temples in uncertainty, Lulu nearly turned around to leave the cafeteria hoping to find an empty classroom to lunch in when she felt a nudge on her forearm.

Lulu thought it wouldn't do her any harm to hang out with people from her class even if they weren't popular. Since Jolie and Aprilyn went out of their way to talk to her, the least Lulu could do was let her guard down, just a little during lunch. She knew she had to make the effort to cultivate friendships—with anyone at this point. She needed allies. She didn't need to be seen—the new American girl—having lunch alone.

Jolie was an above average student whose accountant father was working as a janitor for a school district in California while he went back to school to acquire new accreditation for a CPA license. The job also helped him save money to eventually petition his whole family to move abroad. While Jolie's dad's janitorial job was a humbling experience for the family, the fact that her father was making decent American dollars put Jolie and her siblings in the "nouveau riche" category at school but the janitor part kept Jolie from actually making it in Section A.

"I don't get it," Lulu said finally between delicate bites of her sandwich. She was ravenous since she hardly ate breakfast and now with Section A girls looking on, apparently judging Lulu's every move, she was slowly losing her appetite. In fact, in the co-ed cafeteria, she felt the entire high school department scrutinizing her, including the boys. She gulped slowly and tried to will her thoughts away from the stares. "What's the big deal what section you're in? This whole thing seems so backward, so discriminating."

The minute the words flew out of her mouth, Lulu feared she offended Aprilyn and Jolie. But they didn't seem to take issue with her comment.

"You're not upset you didn't get placed in Section A? You should be," Aprilyn wryly commented as she sunk her teeth into a santol fruit. "You're pretty enough and I bet you were popular at your school back in the States."

With that remark and despite her earlier opposition with the high school class system, Lulu shamelessly admitted that Aprilyn was right. She deserved to be with the popular group; it had been that way back home. But it wasn't that way now. She had to start over. She had to prove herself.

"It's a test," Jolie shrugged nonchalantly as she peeled the banana leaf that wrapped her sweet, sticky rice snack, called *suman*. "The Sisters and the girls from Section A and their parents want to know what kind of girl Lulu really is. And when she passes the test, they'll transfer her," Jolie predicted, solemnly.

"That could be sooner than you think," Aprilyn said, whisking away breadcrumbs that had fallen on her skirt.

"Why aren't *you* in Section A?" Lulu directed the question at the girls.

"I'm not fair skinned enough," said Jolie, crushing the banana leaf peel into a ball.

Lulu regarded the fair-skinned Aprilyn who chimed in, "And I'm not pretty enough or rich enough or smart enough to their standards."

"What does the color of a person's skin have to do with anything?" Immediately, the blood rose to Lulu's brain, which felt like exploding from rage. She thought about the time she and her family endured being ostracized in rural Louisiana for simply being who they were.

"Didn't you notice they favor *mestisas* here?" Jolie said, gathering her lunch bag and soda can. "The fairer your skin, the better chances you have at getting noticed."

Lulu looked at Aprilyn who nodded her confirmation. "That's right. There are some ugly girls who have no talent but who get good parts in dance routines, school plays, things like that, but they're mega rich and their parents are half-Spanish."

Lulu shook her head in disbelief. She didn't just leave one discriminating place—rural Louisiana— behind for another one, did she? What were the odds? "That's ridiculous."

"It's true," Aprilyn and Jolie said in unison.

Unsettling thoughts about discrimination—even discriminating against people of your own ethnicity—started to burden Lulu's conscience. Even after she was learning all this from Aprilyn and Jolie, who were being nice to her, Lulu couldn't help but think they thought she was "too good" to be one of them. While Lulu had always enjoyed being popular back home, the fact she still longed for acceptance with the popular girls at her new school was unnerving her. What kind of a person did that make her? Was it so wrong to want to be popular, no matter what the circumstances?

"How long have things been like this?" Lulu pushed aside her sandwich unable to nourish herself for the moment.

"I think ever since the Spanish times, then continuing during the American occupation." Jolie got up and grabbed her backpack. "It's been this way ever since my mother and my grandmother attended this school."

After learning a bit about the history of cultural discrimination in the Philippines, Lulu's guilt-trip staggered but didn't exactly come to an absolute halt. It wasn't her fault that there were people here who had been discriminating against each other based on status and skin color since the turn of the 20th century, maybe even earlier. That was a disorder that existed long before she and all the girls sat in that cafeteria. It was ingrained in the culture, but that still didn't make it right, she thought.

Would Lulu be chastised if the school decided to transfer her to Section A? How would that affect her stay in the school? This would surely be a dilemma, one that Lulu thought she would deal with when the time came. And she was sure it would.

***

Not only did Lulu manage to survive the first day, but also the first week of school. Despite the earlier mishaps with her skirt and not standing when speaking to a teacher, Lulu had to congratulate herself for lasting through the week. Chi-Chi seemed to have better luck as two of her sister's classmates came home with her one day to do homework and play with her dolls.

Being in high school back home wasn't easy, but transferring during the middle of a high school year was a tremendous challenge. Lulu had to get used to a whole new way of doing things besides standing up when a teacher called on you.

People at her new school seemed to engage in numerous religious activities—attending mass, praying the rosary, as well as fundraising events—beauty contests masquerading as fundraisers to see which class could raise the most money for the school.

This year's money contest "Miss Queen of All Saints" was loosely patterned after the Miss Philippines beauty pageant but each contestant was a representative from each high school section.

"It doesn't matter who we pick to represent us. It's nothing but a money contest and the winner is chosen based on which class raises the most money," said the ever-cynical Jolie.

Because of the buzz throughout the school about Lulu being the new girl from the United States, she was unanimously chosen to represent Section B.

"So what do I have to do?" Lulu asked, unsure about her participation in the contest. The concept seemed all too weird.

Jolie shrugged. "Nothing. Just show up."

"I think Lulu means what does she have to do to prepare," said Aprilyn, mindlessly picking at her *Halo-Halo* dessert at a *panciteria* one day after school.

"Well, doesn't the contest have some sort of talent competition?" Lulu asked, putting aside her *Halo-Halo* that wasn't exactly palatable when the shaved ice melted into ingredients like *macapuno*, preserved shredded young coconut, *nata de coco*, a chewy, translucent, coconut gel, red mung beans, sweetened *langka*, or jackfruit, gelatin, flan and *ube* ice cream. The point was to mix the contents immediately and consume it before the ice melts, the girls told her. Lulu was frustrated at herself for not being quick enough.

The looks people in other booths at the stuffy, crowded *panciteria* gave her also frustrated her. It didn't matter whether they were students, kids or the elderly. They eyed her as if she were an unusual specimen. She could have been an exotic insect from another planet by the way they were gawking at her. How could they, out of hordes of people, single her out as someone who wasn't originally from there?

"There is a talent competition and a Q and A portion," said Jolie, smacking her lips after shoveling a huge heap of *ube* ice cream into her mouth and noticing the annoyed expression on Lulu's face. "What's wrong?"

Lulu threw down her paper napkin on the table and folded her arms across her chest. "Don't these people know it's not polite to stare?"

"Staring is what people do around here whenever there's someone or something new or interesting to look at," Aprilyn calmly explained, shooing a fly away from her dish. "It's totally acceptable. And harmless."

"Harmless? You're not the one being stared at!"

"Lulu, you're new here and people think you're pretty. Besides, they're curious because they want to know how someone from the States looks and acts," Aprilyn said, smoothing the pleats on her skirt.

Lulu eyed her friends quizzically. "Uh, I look like they do. I'm Filipino, too, remember?"

Aprilyn sighed. "It doesn't matter. People here are fascinated with those who live abroad. I remember one time my Auntie Gremlyn went to Canada to work for a few years as a live-in maid for some elderly couple. When she came back, everyone in town stared at her as if she was some kind of celebrity. They were more curious to know if her skin had whitened."

Lulu nearly choked on the water she sipped. "Whitened? Did she have her skin bleached?"

"No. Call it ignorance on the part of people from a small town but for some reason, people seem to think when you live abroad your skin lightens," Aprilyn explained.

"That's the most ridiculous thing I've ever heard," Lulu said. "I know some Filipinos from back home in the States and their skin is toasted golden brown and they've never even been to the Philippines."

Aprilyn shrugged and shook her head. "People here tend to fantasize about other people in other places—other places including Manila."

"They just need to get out more." Surveying her surroundings uncomfortably, Lulu motioned her head towards the door. "Can we go now?"

The second Jolie suggested Lulu prepare a speech about what it's like growing up in the United States for the talent competition, Lulu threatened to drop out of the contest.

"Why can't I just sing or dance?"

"Because everyone will sing and dance," Jolie argued. "You have to think of some unusual talent—something to get the judges' attention, something that speaks of your ability to be congenial. This is the Miss Queen of All Saints pageant, you know."

"How about if I just simply walk up to the judges and have a nice conversation with them?" Lulu sarcastically suggested.

Since cooking had been one of Lulu's strengths, she suggested highlighting her culinary skills with a demonstration.

"What will you cook?" Aprilyn asked. "It should be something exotic."

"Will spinach quiche and brownies be exotic enough?" They were Lulu's specialties and not hard to make at all.

"Logistically, it would be difficult to cart an oven on stage at school from the local bakery," Aprilyn said.

"How about the school café's oven?"

"There isn't one," Jolie said. "We generally don't use ovens here because it gets really hot and the weather's already hot as it is."

With this predicament certainly weighing on Lulu's mind, she promised to mull it over and come back with a decision soon.

The more Lulu thought about the contest, the more she thought the idea was ludicrous. But since it was a major school event, she willed herself to make it work in her favor. Initially, she thought about being a total rebel and get herself kicked out of school and cause her parents grief so that they'd send her back to the States. But after her grandfather's passing, she knew she couldn't put her mother through that. Besides, Lulu thought, trying on a new school environment could be a fun and interesting challenge—no matter how weird they do things over here.

***

Lulu learned she couldn't just audition for the school plays as parts were designated only to girls in Section A.

"They've cast the parts for the play already," Aprilyn huffed angrily, furiously leafing through her textbook.

Lulu raised her head, eyebrows furrowing. "I didn't hear or see any audition announcements."

Aprilyn sighed impatiently. "Of course you wouldn't. There weren't any. They just continue to pick the same girls every year."

Aprilyn's passivity began to weigh on Lulu. "I don't see why you have to have attitude about all this," Lulu said. "Why can't you speak up and start changing things around here?"

Slamming shut the cover of the English literature textbook she had open, Aprilyn glared at Lulu, sizing her up and down. "You have no idea what it's like to be discriminated against—you with your fair skin, high cheekbones, shiny black hair, tall height and American accent. You don't know what it feels like."

Turning away, Lulu walked back to her seat and opened her book. *How dare she say that? She doesn't know me at all. No one does.*

After school, as Lulu headed toward the elementary school building to meet Chi-Chi, Jolie caught up to her.

"Don't mind Aprilyn. She's just sore because she's talented and no one gives her a chance to prove herself because of the way things are."

Lulu shook her head slowly. "Why can't anyone change the system? I never heard of people discriminating against their own."

Jolie shrugged. "Because it's always been this way. It's worse here in the *provincia* than in Manila, I heard. But I think that this is typical in countries that were colonized."

"It's sad."

Since Chi-Chi's teacher had yet to dismiss the class, Lulu considered telling Jolie about her own brush with discrimination. She never really talked about it with anyone—reluctant to go back to that dark time in her life. But somehow, she felt compelled to share her story with Jolie.

When she did, Jolie responded with wide-eyed disbelief.

"This was years ago when I was in elementary school and it happened in a small town," Lulu confided.

"It still doesn't justify what they did," Jolie said, shaking her head. "You should share this story with Aprilyn."

"No!"

"It will help her understand that discrimination comes in all forms and that it can happen anywhere. And she'll ease up on you a bit. She thinks you've had it so easy. That's why she gave you a bit of an attitude. But that doesn't make her right."

Even though confiding in Jolie relieved Lulu of the burden she carried since childhood, she still wasn't sure telling people she barely knew was a good move.

"I don't know why I even told you."

Jolie patted Lulu on the arm reassuringly. "That's quite a load you've been carrying. I think you needed to tell someone."

Just then, Lulu caught Chi-Chi surrounded by a group of boisterous, friendly and chatty girls. It seemed her younger sister was adjusting to her new school life. That was so like dear, sweet, easygoing, carefree Chi-Chi whose transition was taking place in elementary rather than the nerve-wracking high school years. Being the new girl in school sure didn't get any easier as you got older, Lulu thought. Especially at a private, Catholic, all-girls high school in a new country.

After Lulu tore her sister away from her new friends, she and Chi-Chi hurried toward the Internet café as Jolie tagged along. Since it was the only Internet café in town, it was crowded at this time after school so Lulu, Chi-Chi and Jolie patiently waited their turn to use a computer by occupying themselves with entertainment magazines. Lulu tried to read some of the words on the page and was able to grasp the gist of a few of the short articles on various celebrities, though she still longed to be able to understand them more.

She practically leapt toward the computer when it was her turn, but slumped in her seat when, to her disappointment, Sara, Kellie and Stellan still hadn't responded to her e-mails.

There was, however, an e-mail from Rowena who was apparently the only one who responded to Lulu's mass e-mail invitation to keep in touch.

"Just wanted to tell you hello and to find out how you're doing over there," Rowena's e-mail said. "I hope you've made some new friends and are trying to learn Tagalog even though most of the people there speak English. I think Tagalog will help you in most social situations. Don't hesitate to ask me for advice about anything. Good luck with school. I'm sure that now your name is finally being pronounced correctly. Rowena."

Lulu read the e-mail three times as, even though it was from Rowena, a girl she hardly knew, it was Lulu's link to life back in the States and, surprisingly, she took comfort from Rowena's words. Before she knew it, Lulu found herself hitting "Reply," and the words just flowed onto the screen as she pounded away on the keyboard.

"Hey there, Rowena. Thanks for the e-mail. How are things going over there?" Lulu typed. She bit her lip, resisting the temptation to ask about Sara and Kellie as doing so would no doubt make it obvious her friends hadn't e-mailed her. "Things are so different here. I met two girls in my class who seem nice. What's weird for me: the way baths are taken here, the sectioning of classes and taking a jeepney to school every day." Lulu was careful not to mention in what section she was placed, nor was she willing to reveal the horrors of her first day as she wasn't sure what her popular friends back in the States might think if they found out. "But I think Filipino food tastes even better here and most of my relatives seem pretty nice." She didn't dare mention Nina's snub. Lulu checked the box at the corner of the computer screen that indicated how much time she had then noticed a line of students waiting to use computers. "I have to go now because we have limited time to use the computers at this café I'm at and I need to save money for my jeepney ride home." Lulu paused a few seconds to fan herself with her notebook as the air conditioning didn't seem to be working at the café. "By the way, Rowena—do you believe in ghosts?"

While resting her palm on the computer's mouse, Lulu stared at the last line she typed and watched as the cursor moved toward "Send," then clicked before she had a chance to change her mind. Then she gathered her things and stomped out of the café with Chi-Chi and Jolie.

On the jeepney ride home, Lulu turned her face away from the people piled into the jeepney, preferring to focus her eyes on the vast sugar cane fields and palm trees they passed along the way. She wondered what possessed her to ask Rowena about ghosts, as she allowed her hair made unruly by the hot wind to whip across her face.

***

As soon as the sisters descended the jeepney, Chi-Chi rushed over to one of the relatives' homes to play with their cousin, Carly, as Lulu continued ambling along the dirt path, past a few vegetable gardens, past a chicken coop and a pig pen toward the Bituin home.

From the corner of her eye, she could sense she was being watched and figured it might have been one of the aunts. She turned to her right with a smile—after all, the Titas had been awfully nice to her. But the sight that greeted her wasn't one of the aunts—at least not one she knew. When she was a few yards away from her, Lulu realized the woman standing near the water pump wasn't one of the Titas washing clothes but the woman whom Lulu saw descend the staircase at the house when they first arrived. Could it be Lola Josefina?

This time, Lulu wasn't so much shocked as she was puzzled and a bit annoyed. If this was the famous spirit of Lola Josefina, why was she "visiting" her? Lulu took a deep breath.

"I don't believe in ghosts," she addressed the apparition who continued to stare at her. "I don't believe in *you*."

It appeared that Lola Josefina wanted to say something to Lulu as the spirit's mouth opened slightly. But Lulu didn't want to be bothered and instead ran all the way toward the house.

On her way to her bedroom, Lulu peered in the doorway of her parent's room to find her mother sitting on the floor going through things in a dust-covered mahogany chest.

"How's school coming along?" Dimples asked removing a large box filled with photos.

"Okay, I guess." Lulu sat next to the chest, scanning its contents—some photo albums and boxes, some ribbons, yearbooks, framed diplomas. "It's the Tagalog class I'm really worried about." Lulu rummaged through some of the old photos, pleased with seeing her mother as a teen wearing the same high school uniform.

"You should have Nina tutor you," Dimples suggested, arranging some of the photos on the floor.

"Not a chance, Mom. Nina's so fake. She's nice to me around the relatives but totally ignores me at school."

"I'll talk to her," offered Dimples, gathering more photos.

Panic struck Lulu. She didn't want a confrontation. She had to firmly establish a good reputation at school. "No! Mom! Please, don't. I'll—I'll manage somehow."

"Still that doesn't seem right. If she starts to give you trouble, you'll be sure to let me know?"

"I promise." Lulu eyed her mother's high school graduation photos. Then Lulu's eyes rested on a familiar face in one of the photos—that of the ghost. But, it couldn't be. Lola Josefina lived a century ago.

Dimples smiled as she noticed the photo her daughter was examining, the one of three young women posing in front of the school.

"That was my cousin Lorelai, who was also my best friend until she died in a bus accident two months after our high school graduation." Dimples examined the photo pensively.

"Doesn't she look like someone you know?" Lulu asked, thinking about the photo in the hallway of their old home and of the face of the spirit appearing to Lulu.

Dimples nodded nonchalantly. "Yes, she resembled Lola Josefina, the one whose portrait hung in our former home, remember?"

"I don't remember you ever telling me about Lola Josefina," Lulu began anxiously. "How did you get the portrait?"

"Growing up, I always saw it prominently displayed in my grandmother's house so when I married your Dad and we moved to the States, the portrait went with us. It was a wedding gift. My grandmother knew I was always fond of the portrait. Lola Josefina's face was always such a comfort to me, especially when I was getting used to living in the States as a new wife and mother."

Lulu remained quiet for a few minutes as she watched her mother arrange the photos by year and then by occasion.

"I've always wanted to organize these," Dimples said, concentrating on the order of the photos.

Lulu took a deep breath. "Mom—has…has Lola Josefina's spirit ever appeared to you?"

Dimples sat up straight, eyes directed at her daughter. "I'm not really sure. But I think there were times I thought I saw her. She was more like a spiritual entity—like I could feel her presence. It's funny. She lived so long ago, but it's like I knew her. It's hard to explain. Why do you ask?"

Lulu shrugged. "I think she may be visiting me." Even as the words tumbled out of her mouth, it sounded weird. "I think she might be trying to tell me something but I don't know what. Or maybe I'm just imagining things. Mom, tell me I'm not going crazy."

Dimples laughed and hugged Lulu, the photos on her lap sliding on the floor. "You're not crazy, Lulu. I heard that Lola Josefina, who became a widow during the revolution, arrived in the U.S. along with several Filipinos after the revolution and the Philippine-American war. She had the chance to work as a caregiver for a rich, elderly woman. The story goes that Lola Josefina planned to save money so her children, whom she left behind in the care of her sisters, could join her as she was so lonely and homesick. But she never saw her family again. She died in 1906 when a train from San Francisco she was riding in with her employer had derailed on its way to Sacramento to visit her employer's family. She was only 39. It's been said that her spirit has roamed restlessly ever since."

Lulu felt a shiver up her spine as she listened to her mother's tale. Now knowing Lola Josefina was a real person who died a tragic death—and in the States no less—made Lulu more curious about her and for the first time, she realized Lola Josefina's spirit was real and not just a legend. *So why was she haunting people?* Lulu ached to know. *And why me?*

Chapter Nine

Lulu spent the evening and most of the next day preoccupied with thoughts of Lola Josefina. She found her mother's nonchalant way of describing Lola Josefina—as if she were a living, breathing person—disturbing.

"But she *was* a real person," Lulu thought aloud as she combed her hair in front of her dresser one morning before getting ready for school.

And a ghost, Lulu added silently, as though she was afraid Lola Josefina might hear her, or worse, read her thoughts. *This was ridiculous, Lulu thought. I don't even believe in ghosts but here I am afraid of one.*

While Lulu tried to reconcile her feelings about the existence of ghosts, she couldn't help but be on her guard—in case Lola Josefina were to suddenly appear. But being overly cautious took its toll. Lulu didn't hear her literature teacher call on her to discuss the merits of *Moby Dick* in popular culture. She couldn't concentrate on her trigonometry pop quiz and was sure she didn't get any of the answers right. She was listless during lunch as Jolie and Aprilyn chatted about the upcoming pageant.

"So have you mastered making your chocolate mousse yet?" Jolie asked, wiping peanut butter from her lips.

"Umm-hmm," replied Lulu, twisting spaghetti noodles in a "ketchup-y" sauce with hot dog slices on her plate. "Why are there hot dogs in this spaghetti?"

Aprilyn snapped her tin lunch box shut. "Because that's the way we do things here." She flicked her bangs away from her face with one impatient toss. "Really, Lulu, you don't seem as excited about the pageant as we are. Maybe your cousin, Nina, is right. Maybe you're not the best candidate to represent our class."

Jolie flashed Aprilyn a scolding glare.

"I resent that," Lulu said, as she pushed her plate aside.

"Sorry." Aprilyn took out a compact from her purse to inspect a small red bump on her chin. "It's just that you seem distracted and the pageant is in a few weeks."

Lulu sighed. She wondered if she should tell Jolie and Aprilyn about Lola Josefina. What would they say? She had never attended an all-girls school before and from what she'd seen so far, she concluded that girls can be relentless yet sensitive, also competitive and catty about the pettiest of things. If she told the girls about Lola Josefina, where else might that information go? Never mind that it may be common to believe in ghosts. It could just be a common belief for adults. Never mind that Nina and the rest of her cousins believed in ghosts. Lulu figured Nina would never admit that in public.

So Lulu chose to remain mum on the topic, opening her schoolbag instead and rifling through her folders erratically like a squirrel gathering as many acorns as she can.

"I'm just worried about my classes—especially trigonometry—and Tagalog," said Lulu, turning the pages of her Tagalog notebook.

Aprilyn and Jolie seemed to buy Lulu's excuse as they stopped pestering her just in time for them to head back to class.

That afternoon, Lulu's paranoia about Lola Josefina continued to distract her as she found herself avoiding empty hallways on campus and feared what might happen should she catch herself alone in the girls' bathroom.

During history class, Lulu couldn't hold it anymore. She rushed to the bathroom hoping there would be another girl using it as well. Her heart beating rapidly, Lulu cautiously opened the bathroom door and to her dismay, not a soul was stirring. Unless that soul was Lola Josefina, Lulu thought, wishing she had gone during lunch. At least the bathroom would surely have been crowded.

Cursing to herself, Lulu hurriedly entered a stall. Just as she was about to finish, she heard a slight rustling noise. Afraid to open the door of her stall, Lulu waited to figure out the source of the sound. Water was slowly dripping from a faucet. The branches and leaves of a tree outside the window were bristling in the wind. Lulu gazed up at the ceiling of the bathroom. It was an old building, she reasoned. It could be the pipes. Quickly, she flushed the toilet.

Taking a deep breath, Lulu slowly opened the stall door and peered from left to right and back to left again. With the coast clear, she stepped out to wash and wipe her hands. Remembering her disheveled hair from the windy walk back to class after lunch, Lulu checked her appearance in the mirror. Her peripheral view suddenly went on high alert. There was another face in the mirror to her right. Lola Josefina. With a smile on her face.

Lulu turned to find no one standing beside her. Trembling, she looked back at the mirror only to discover Lola Josefina's face had vanished.

Had she imagined what she saw in her fright? With a rapidly thumping heart, she pondered her latest ghostly encounter as she hurried her pace back to the classroom.

After school, Lulu wandered around the market, searching for fabric for her pageant dress and ingredients for her chocolate mousse.

Amid the jostling of merchants and customers in the claustrophobic dry goods store at the market, Lulu—sweat beads running down the sides of her face, chest and back—scanned the shelves for ingredients to make chocolate mousse for the talent competition. Not only was it her first time shopping at the market by herself; she had to choose a recipe that didn't require use of an oven. Getting egg yolks and sugar wasn't a problem. It was finding alternative ingredients for semisweet chocolate chips and whipping cream. As her eyes canvassed the store's limited selection in shelves and its refrigerated section, she found there were none. And she'd been to at least three other stores.

Another problem seemed to be the language issue. Although, she knew some of the merchants were perfectly capable of speaking English, Lulu didn't want to draw attention to herself by speaking with an American accent. She ruled out speaking English with a Filipino accent as surely merchants would wonder why she just couldn't speak to them in Tagalog, when the fact was, she couldn't. It dawned on Lulu that she couldn't be stubborn about refusing to learn Tagalog. Since she took it as a challenge to see how well she'd fit in at school, learning Tagalog was no longer an option. It was mandatory. Sure the students and faculty all spoke English. But when it came time to converse amongst themselves in a social situation, Tagalog was the language of choice and Lulu didn't want to be left out of the loop.

"Can I help you there, Miss?"

The voice of a young man startled Lulu but she was pleased and a bit surprised someone actually addressed her in English. Was it like she was walking around with a sign that read: "Only English Spoken?" Lulu turned around to discover Niel's smiling face, complete with a smattering of irresistible stubble on his chin.

He looked even cuter wearing his school uniform. As a sophomore in the coed college, Niel wore lightweight khaki chino pants with a shoreline blue solid vintage oxford, button-down cotton short-sleeved shirt.

"Oh, I thought you worked here." Lulu lowered her head slightly, finding his intense gaze distracting.

"I do…during summer vacations and help out when I can. This is my auntie's shop," Niel said, nodding to a gray-haired woman who eyed Lulu suspiciously. "My Auntie Mei practically helped raise me and my siblings."

"Your parents are separated?"

Niel shook his head. "No. *Tatay* works as an engineer in Saudi Arabia. He visits about twice a year."

Lulu's eyebrows knitted in confusion.

He shrugged. "You'll find there are some kids here whose parents work abroad. That's common here since everyone knows you can make more money abroad and you don't have to be an engineer or a nurse. I have cousins who, after graduating from college here, work as live-in caregivers for elderly people in Italy, Germany, Canada and the States and they get paid really well." Niel cocked his head to the area where Lulu scanned for ingredients. "What are you shopping for?"

Lulu told him about her participation in the contest and her dilemma about which ingredients to use. She skipped her temptation to mention she thought the whole contest was silly until she knew where Niel stood on the issue. She didn't have long to wait.

"This school pageant is ridiculous, if you ask me," he said, leaning against one of the shelves.

"I didn't want to participate but my class voted me in," she said, picking up some bars of dark chocolate.

Niel stood up straight suddenly. "Why don't you use ground cacao for your chocolate mousse? It's all natural and freshly ground."

"I'm not sure how well that kind of chocolate will blend with the other ingredients," she said, tossing a few bars in a basket. "Is there any other kind of milk besides the powdered or sweetened condensed kinds? I need something in place of whipping cream."

Niel suggested using sweetened condensed milk only if the chocolate bars were unsweetened and Lulu thought she should give it a try. She didn't have to do an audience tasting—she decided the demonstration was enough and chocolate mousse was something people weren't accustomed to so it promised to be quite a novelty dessert.

While she was paying for her items, Lulu noticed several college girls stopping to chat with Niel, in Tagalog of course, and she tried to make out what they were saying. It sounded like they were discussing a class project but the girls giggled and squealed like the discussion was about more than business. She attempted to do something bold. After all, what did these college girls have that she didn't?

"Thank you so much for suggestions for my recipe, Niel. See you around." Lulu smiled at him sweetly, ignoring the college girls, with their raised eyebrows, dressed in their navy blue pencil skirts and button-down white short-sleeved cotton shirts and black leather two-and-a-half-inch pumps.

Sashaying away gracefully, her pleated and plaid uniform skirt swaying behind her, Lulu tried to imagine Niel's expression. What was she doing flirting with an older guy? Niel was eighteen, so that wasn't really old. An eighteen-year-old was a high school senior back home and she reminded herself that in two years, she would be in college anyway. Plus Niel, she justified, was just too attractive to resist. She didn't care if they did things the old fashioned way here and that it was normally the guy who did the courting. Lulu had set her sights on making him hers.

***

Five twenty-five. The face displaying the time on Lulu's watch glared at her. She couldn't believe it was that late. Had she really taken too much time wandering around the market and chatting with Niel?

Frustrated, Lulu ran to just about every jeepney that pulled up at the jeepney stop only to be beaten by other students and older, more experienced, passengers, the weight of her backpack plus her groceries slowing her down.

Just as she began walking away from the crowd waiting for jeepneys or to hail a tricycle, another mode of transportation, a jeepney slowed by her. She glanced up at the window with a large sign that read "Out of Service" and continued walking.

"Lulu!"

She turned toward the jeepney. How could she have missed the jeepney's bold sign the first time? The second she saw the name "Lucky Star" her heart started racing. And to her delight, Niel sat at the driver's seat smiling at her.

"Would you like a ride home?"

Without waiting for an answer, Niel parked the jeepney, got down and took her backpack and grocery bags from a stunned Lulu. She climbed onto the passenger seat, careful not to catch her skirt on the vicious, unfamiliar hooks around the vehicle. The last thing she wanted was a repeat of her unforgettable first-day-of-school incident.

"Thanks, Niel. You came at just the right time," Lulu smiled shyly at him. "What are you doing driving the jeepney anyway? Part time job of yours?"

He smiled. "Kind of. The driver's been sick and I've been helping out."

Niel was cautiously on the lookout for passing motorists and pedestrians before steering, weaving and swerving the jeepney into the busy traffic flow leading outside of town.

"You left my aunt's shop too quickly," he noted. "I wanted to ask you more about how school was going for you so far."

Lulu felt her cheeks flush. *He wanted to talk with me more.* "Well, I figured you were busy chatting with your classmates. Sorry, I could've waited."

He smiled. "No problem. They were asking all these questions. I didn't want to be rude."

They like you, can't you tell? Lulu thought. *Just like I like you.*

"College must be difficult," she offered, trying to shift the focus on him—wanting to know more about him. She appreciated him telling her about his parents. She wanted to know his dreams, his goals, and—she admitted to herself hoping he couldn't tell she was blushing—everything else about him.

Niel shrugged. "It's challenging to juggle all the reading and writing papers and presentations. But you're more independent in college. I think you'll find that your high school education here will prepare you for college."

"What's left of my high school education, that is," she said suddenly.

He quickly glanced at her, his brows knitting together. "What do you mean?"

Amid the blasting horns and crowds shuffling on the streets and tricycles whizzing by, Lulu was impressed with the way Niel expertly and calmly weaved and swerved "Lucky Star" through the town chaos and finally toward the road leading to the *bukid,* the farmland.

As soon as they left town limits, the long open road stretched out in front of them, as verdant rows of sugar cane and rice fields greeted them on both sides of the jeepney as they passed by. Lulu caught a glimpse of some children in front of their homes playing jump rope or basketball, probably taking a short break in between doing homework and having dinner. Some adults sat on their terraces chatting. From a distance, she could see a woman hanging out her laundry on a clothesline despite the threatening gray clouds looming above.

"Well, it's kind of funny and weird how I left the States as a ninth-grader and enrolled in school here as a junior—a third-year high school student," she said, relishing the fresh air that whipped her face but unfortunately tossed her hair into a solid mess.

Niel laughed. "At least you get to graduate high school about two years earlier than your classmates back in the States."

"Only if I pass Tagalog classes—and math," she said, smiling wanly.

He cast her a quick glance. "I can help you with both of those, if you want."

Lulu felt her body quake, like a squeal of delight imploding within her. "That would be so generous of you, but I'm sure you're too busy with your own classes."

Shooting her another glance, he said, "I can handle it. I would really like to help you."

And I would really really like it if you do. "Okay."

"Okay. It's settled then," he smiled.

They sat in silence for a minute—Lulu holding her breath to keep from screaming aloud in excitement. Inside, her heart was doing a pirouette. *A gorgeous guy wants to tutor me!*

Her euphoria was short lived as a realization hit her.

"I—I just remembered," she said, the disappointment sinking down to her toes, rendering her feet numb. "My friend Aprilyn offered to tutor me."

He nodded. "Well, you can have more than one tutor, you know. The more you practice, the better you'll get."

She flashed him a wide grin. How could she think she had a dilemma on her hands? "You're right. That totally makes sense because nobody here really speaks Tagalog to me anyway. Aprilyn can be my official tutor and you—my Tagalog practice buddy and math coach."

"Yup, that's me, Math Coach. I didn't major in business for nothing," he laughed as Lulu laughed along with him. "I wonder if you're up for a challenge."

Lulu raised her eyebrows at Niel. "What kind of challenge?"

He flashed her a smile she found to be wickedly irresistible. "How about trying to speak only Tagalog to me?"

Laughing, Lulu shook her head. "Then you probably wouldn't get a word out of me at all. That would be the best way to keep me quiet."

Niel quickly glanced at her. "I wouldn't want that. I just want you to do whatever feels comfortable to you."

She eyed him sheepishly. "Maybe when I'm better prepared, then I'll take you up on your challenge."

"Whenever you're ready." He flashed her what appeared to be a sympathetic smile.

The jeepney passed a few homes where women were tossing rice in their *bilaos* on their terraces while chatting with each other, when one of the women caught Lulu's eye. Though she resembled Lola Josefina, it wasn't her. Suddenly, she remembered the chilling encounter in the girls' bathroom.

After another moment of silence, Niel glanced at Lulu. "What's on your mind?"

The soothing, calm, concerned tone of his voice convinced Lulu that if there was someone she could trust with her fears, it was Niel. She couldn't quite explain it but here was this guy she was only beginning to know, but somehow, something about him told her he wouldn't mock her or think she was weird if she confided in him.

"Niel." Still she approached the subject with a bit of caution even as something inside of her was encouraging her to take the plunge. "Do you believe in ghosts?"

He was silent for a few seconds that seemed like minutes until Lulu dreaded broaching the topic. *Oh God, he's going to think I'm psycho.*

Niel slowed the jeepney down to allow a farmer with his carabao to cross the road.

"Did you see that?" he said, as both man and animal safely made their way to the other side.

Of course, she saw the man and the carabao but Lulu was too nervous to speak. *Maybe he didn't hear my question.*

"The scared expression on the man's face. I don't blame him for being afraid," Niel continued, shaking his head. "It's sad. People and animals get run over on these highways all the time."

Lulu looked at Niel whose compassion warmed her heart. "I think he appreciated that you slowed down for him."

Niel turned to her slightly and smiled. "Thanks for your assurance. Sorry, you were asking me something?"

Biting her lower lip, Lulu quickly debated whether she should talk about something else or pursue the burning question.

"About ghosts, you said?" Niel's remark had decided it for her.

Clearing her throat, Lulu glanced at him nervously. "Um, yeah. Do you believe in them?"

"In ghosts?"

Lulu groaned under her breath. This was agonizing. She blinked.

Niel shrugged. "Yeah, sure. Don't you?"

Forming her mouth in an "O," Lulu wasn't too sure how to answer the question. "I don't know. You make it seem like it's normal to believe in them."

He chuckled. "Well, it's a supernatural phenomenon and certainly debatable depending on what your experience is."

"What makes *you* believe in them?" Lulu just had to ask. Niel couldn't just believe in ghosts for the sake of believing, could he?

"If you think I've had a ghostly sighting or anything like that—the truth is, I haven't. But I still believe in them."

"Why?"

"Because I think ghosts are spirits of people who actually lived on this earth, people whose bodies expired whether it was their time or, in the minds of some ghosts, *before* their time. But, their spirits—now that's something different altogether."

Lulu now turned to Niel hanging on to his every word.

He scratched his head thoughtfully. "I think when the physical body dies, the spiritual body still lives and is maybe still figuring out where to go or whether its being is dead or alive. Maybe ghosts are in denial or maybe they want to stay with their loved ones. Or maybe they have a message they want to deliver. There could be any number of reasons."

Lulu nodded trying to figure out Lola Josefina's reasons for "sticking around."

"I think one way to understand ghosts is probably to put ourselves in their shoes, hard as it may seem," he continued. "Think about it—if you died before your time, how would you feel? What would you do? If you died tragically before you got a chance to say goodbye to your loved ones, would you do it? Haunt them, I mean."

Like a flame that just ignited in pitch darkness, so did Lulu's thoughts about Lola Josefina. She recalled her mother telling her about how Lola Josefina died in a train accident in the States—leaving behind her family, all those children.

Smiling, Lulu patted Niel lightly on the arm then drew back at the realization of her attempt to make physical contact with the object of her—attraction.

"Thanks for helping me put the ghost thing all in perspective," Lulu said, as Niel nodded. "By the way, how do you know so much about ghosts?"

"I read about them. A lot."

The jeepney finally reached Lulu's family's compound, where a group of men sitting in front of a corner *sari-sari* store watched as Niel helped Lulu descend the jeepney and carry her groceries to the house.

"I hope we're not being fodder for gossip," Lulu joked as she strode alongside Niel. "I heard that people out in the country like to talk when they see a single girl and a guy together."

Niel shrugged and smiled. "Then let them talk. We're just friends anyway."

Lulu felt her heart take a nosedive into the abyss of teenage crush disappointment. *He just thinks of me as a friend.*

To get to the Bituin house, they had to pass by her cousins' home where Nina, dressed in a duster and flip-flops and carrying a laundry basket, happened to step out of her house.

"Hi, Nina," greeted Niel as he nodded to her.

"Hi, Niel." Nina flashed Niel a smile and only glanced at Lulu then back at Niel again.

"Hey, I think that's cool you two are classmates," Niel said to the cousins who sized each other up.

Lulu nodded and managed a weak smile as Nina scurried off toward the clothesline in her backyard.

As Lulu and Niel neared Lulu's home, Niel turned to Lulu. "So you seem interested in ghosts. Is there a reason?"

Here was Lulu's chance to confide in Niel. But just when she turned to him and before she could utter a word, Chi-Chi's shrill scream pierced the early evening air.

Lulu and Niel rushed to the kitchen annex at the back of the house. Lulu's nerves rattled. Had her sister seen a ghost?

"What the heck is going on here?"

The Titas were plucking newly-sacrificed chickens to Chi-Chi's horror and disgust.

"That's it! I'm never eating meat again!" Chi-Chi cried out, burying her face in her hands. "Those poor chickens. I just saw them roaming our yard yesterday. They seemed so peaceful pecking on the ground. They had no idea what their future held—their future as our dinner. Well, I won't take part in it!"

"Chi-Chi, quit being so melodramatic," said Lulu as she and Niel put the groceries on the dining room table.

The second the words escaped her lips, Lulu's heart filled with regret. She recalled seeing her sister faithfully feed the black and white stray cat and little rooster, unlikely friends who bonded over Chi-Chi's care. The minute Chi-Chi christened the rooster "Barako," for his robust crowing, Lulu knew her sister would never consume another animal product again. As she patted Chi-Chi's shoulder, she glanced at the Titas' plucking frenzy and immediately empathized with her sister.

"We appreciate what those chickens have done for us," said Tita Claudia as she ran cold water over the newly plucked poultry. She lifted her gaze. "Oh, Niel, good to see you."

Lulu couldn't help but smile as she watched Niel greet each of her Titas respectfully and how the women fawned over him. Tita Diding even went so far as giving a knowing wink to Lulu who blushed. Lulu turned slightly away, hoping Niel wouldn't notice.

"Niel, won't you stay for dinner?" Tita Claudia asked with a smile on her face as she rinsed her hands in the sink.

Niel cast a gaze at Lulu then at the Titas. "Thank you for the invitation, but some other time maybe. I have to finish writing an essay that's due tomorrow."

Lulu accompanied Niel to the gate of the house.

"Thank you for the ride home," she said, giving him a shy smile.

"No problem," he said, opening the gate.

Somehow, Lulu felt compelled to prolong the conversation. "Good luck on your essay."

Niel smiled, his eyes searching hers. "Thanks. Looking forward to our tutoring sessions."

As she watched Niel walk away, Lulu lamented over not telling him about Lola Josefina, then consoled herself by at least knowing where he stood on the issue.

Still she couldn't help but feel she may lose her chances with Niel if she fessed up about her ghostly sightings. She was beginning to seriously like the guy.

Chapter Ten

The next couple of weeks proved to be the most hectic for Lulu ever since she moved to the Philippines. Aside from tackling school projects, Lulu was meeting Aprilyn after school for Tagalog lessons some days, and with Niel for math tutoring on others. Nights were also spent preparing for the pageant. Lulu had to learn Philippine history and local popular culture for the Q and A portion. To her relief, the contestants didn't have to wear swimsuits or evening gowns, but were required to wear a dress. Accustomed to wearing only jeans and shorts, the thought of wearing a skirt panicked Lulu. She knew that wearing shorts was considered scandalous in the *provincia,* even in hot weather. Not wanting to court the wrong kind of reputation, Lulu knew she eventually had to get used to wearing skirts on off days just like the other girls. She couldn't be expected to wear jeans that stuck to her sweaty legs forever.

After some cajoling, and after Lulu couldn't find a suitable dress to wear at the market, Auntie Claudia encouraged Lulu to peruse some of the dress designs she created. Lulu was impressed with her aunt's balance of classic lines with a flair for trend and she enthusiastically chose an empire waist with short sheer flutter sleeves dress design that would give Lulu's prepubescent chest some prominence. The dress would be made from rhubarb-colored cotton eyelet fabric with soft ruffles on the hem. Perfect, Lulu thought.

With the dress issue taken care of, Lulu then focused on perfecting her chocolate mousse recipe, using alternative ingredients and enlisting her family as taste-testers who gave it a thumbs-up.

Just when Lulu thought she was getting all the local customs down pat, she was filled with dread when continually committing a huge social *faux pas*—showing courtesy when speaking with someone older.

"When addressing the elderly, always use *po*," Aprilyn advised.

The girls were holding their tutoring sessions after school one afternoon on the terrace of the Bituin home while snacking on a *merienda* of *kalamansi* juice, banana chips, *langka* tarts and *hopia* as the ubiquitous flies buzzed around them.

"Why?"

"Because it's a sign of respect," Aprilyn said, furiously wiping her mouth with a napkin. "You just have to say it."

"So, do I have to say it to older cousins and my parents?"

"Usually, just the elderly whether you're related to them or not. And you don't have to use *po* when you're speaking in English."

"Well, I'll just speak English then." Lulu downed the last of her juice as Aprilyn sighed and rolled her eyes.

"Also, whenever you meet an elderly relative in a social gathering, you must kiss the back of her or his hand."

Lulu gaped at her friend with a blank face. "Do you mean like kissing the ring of a Cardinal?"

Aprilyn thought about that for a second. "Well, kind of. But you don't have to kneel or bow or actually kiss the hand. Just take the elderly person's right hand with your right hand and bring the back of the hand to your forehead and say, '*Mano po.*' You'll score points with people that way. They'll say, 'What a respectful young lady she is.'"

"For someone born and raised in the States, you mean," Lulu said, gathering pastry crumbs from her skirt.

"Lulu!"

With a startled countenance on her face, Lulu turned toward the source of the shrill shriek of Aling Miling, the Bituin's new housekeeper who started work just a week ago. Though she didn't live with the Bituins, Aling Miling, who was in her early forties and a single mother with two teenage sons, came four days a week to cook, do laundry and clean house. This suited Lulu just fine since she wasn't accustomed or comfortable with the idea of a practical stranger living in her house and going through her underwear drawer.

Aling Miling had an authoritative quality about her—the minute she marched in, she practically took over. She immediately attacked the piles of dirty dishes and laundry that had stacked up for days. With Romar living and working in Manila during the week and only home on weekends, and Dimples handling Dimar and catching up with visits to her various relatives and old college friends, and with Lulu and Chi-Chi swamped with homework and school projects, Aling Miling appeared to be a godsend to the Bituin family.

And, boy, was she on top of things!

"Lulu! You should change into your comfortable house clothes. You're going to spoil your uniform skirt after I took time washing and ironing that with care," Aling Miling admonished.

With that, Lulu sprang from the rattan chair and emerged minutes later, feeling cool and comfortable in a pink cotton skirt and white T-shirt.

"Did you hang your uniform skirt properly?" Aling Miling asked, bringing the girls more *kalamansi* juice.

"*O, po*," Lulu answered, as she reached for the glass Aling Miling just refilled. Lulu looked up and smiled at Aling Miling. "*Salamat, po.*"

The housekeeper drew back as if she had been slapped on the face. "*Po?* You address me as *po?*" She glared at Aprilyn then back to Lulu whose face turned crimson at her not-so-obvious-to-Lulu-but-apparently-obvious-to-Aling Miling *faux pas*. "I'm not that old!"

Muttering to herself, Aling Miling stomped away and once she was out of earshot, the girls looked at each other and laughed.

"Lesson learned," Lulu chuckled. "I think."

***

"Aren't you sad to not be celebrating Halloween this year?" Lulu asked Chi-Chi during breakfast the morning of October 31.

Chi-Chi shook her head, pouring herself some guava juice. "Now that I think about it, Halloween is nothing more than a commercial event that lures people into buying expensive tacky costumes and promotes tooth decay."

Lulu laughed as she sliced some pineapple. That was her bright and spirited sister.

"But in place of Halloween, this year, we'll be celebrating *Araw ng Mga Patay*," said Chi-Chi, using a Tagalog accent Lulu thought sounded cute. "We learned about it in class. It means Day of the Dead or All Souls' Day in the Catholic religion, but here, people do more than just go to church. They go to the cemeteries in the morning and stay with their relatives' tombstones all day."

Nearly choking on a pineapple slice, Lulu coughed and gulped some water. "Not exactly my idea of spending the day." She shuddered. "Just thinking of being close to all the remains of dead people makes me cringe."

"Well, guess what girls? That's what we'll be doing this year," announced Dimples as she entered the dining room with a thumb-sucking Dimar in tow.

Lulu groaned as she sliced open a *pan de sal* and spread some Cheez Whiz on it. "You can count me out."

Dimples scooped up some fried rice into a bowl and sat Dimar down on his high chair. Feeding a teaspoonful of rice to the toddler, Dimples shot Lulu a warning glare. "We're all going—the whole family. Even Dad. Day of the Dead is a big deal here. Show some respect to your dead relatives."

What's the use of showing respect to people already dead? Wasn't showing respect to living relatives enough? Lulu wanted to say, but didn't.

So that day during school, thoughts about the inevitable trip to the cemetery for All Souls' Day occupied her mind. She was so preoccupied that she didn't even notice it was her turn to lead the Morning Prayer which she hadn't prepared for, nor had she memorized the lines of *Panatang Makabayan* during the daily morning flag assembly.

That afternoon, Lulu rushed to the library to check out a book for a report in English literature when she ran into Nina who was browsing the fiction section. They nodded at each other briefly then scanned the shelves. Coincidently, they found themselves reaching for the same book: *Wuthering Heights*.

"What are you doing your book report on?" Nina asked, without letting go of the only copy.

"I plan to report on the reason for the hauntings in *Wuthering Heights*." Lulu said, in what she hoped was a calm voice. "What about you?"

"I will write about the strange romance between Cathy and Heathcliff," Nina said, pulling the book off the shelf. "We can't be writing about the same thing."

Lulu eyed her cousin curiously. "But we're not writing about the same topic."

"We are writing about the same book," Nina said defiantly, holding the volume to her chest as if it were a security blanket.

"What's the big deal?" Annoyance struck Lulu in a way it hadn't before.

"There's only one book and we can't share it. There's not enough time," her cousin raised her voice.

"Sssshh!"

The girls turned to see a nun carrying a stack of books—the school librarian, otherwise known as "The Book Nun."

Lulu turned back to her cousin. "If you let me read it first, I'll breeze right through it. I can give it back to you in two days."

Nina huffed and shook her head, tightening her grip even more. "Why do you insist on having it your way?"

With an incredulous expression on her face, Lulu stared at her cousin. "What are you talking about?"

Shrugging, Nina slightly turned away. Around them, a few high school students were milling around the shelves looking as though they too were frantically searching for books to write papers on. Lulu noticed a few high school guys—a rare sight the girls had luxury to only during the morning flag assembly and obligatory masses.

Once they were the only students in that particular aisle of books, Nina gave Lulu the once over.

"I don't know why you got chosen to be our representative for the pageant. We usually take a vote. Somehow it was 'unanimously' decided," Nina said in a mocking tone, flicking up her index and middle fingers from both hands as she said "unanimously."

Lulu shrugged. "Look, I didn't make that decision. I was asked to represent our class."

Nina huffed again, reminding Lulu of the Big Bad Wolf in *The Three Little Pigs*. "You don't even want to be in the pageant. They should have picked someone who really wants to be in it."

Lulu rolled her eyes. "Okay, so I admit. I wasn't too keen on the idea, at first. But now that the pageant date is nearly here, I'm really getting into it. I'm learning a lot about our history."

Nina's eyes bulged as if the sockets weren't strong enough to hold her eyeballs in place. "It's not *your* history. You weren't even born here. You got to live like a spoiled brat princess in the States while your poor cousins who were left behind had to struggle."

Not wanting to believe what she just heard, Lulu held on to a nearby chair. Feeling slightly dizzy, she gazed up at the lights dancing overhead. *How could she make accusations like that? She doesn't know anything about me?* Lulu wanted to shout back at Nina, but in her anger and shock, she couldn't lash back.

Suddenly, Nina grunted as though some unseen force took hold of her. She struggled to hold on to the book, which loosened its bondage from Nina's hands and dropped to the floor. The girls glared at each other then at the book staring up at them open faced. Lulu bent down and quickly picked it up as Nina continued to stare at the floor as if shell shocked.

Panting heavily, Lulu pinned the book to her chest. Armed with a burst of courage and finally finding her voice, she glared at Nina. "My father and mother worked very hard to give their children a good life and didn't spoil us. They may have gone to the United States to find jobs and raise a family but they continually sent money back to relatives here to help send *you* and your siblings to school. My parents never abandoned their family here and they never will."

Lulu turned away from Nina and darted as quickly as she could to the checkout desk.

"Give me back that book!" she heard Nina wailing.

The "Book Nun" raised her eyebrows at Lulu who gave her a sweet smile.

"She will have to wait until you're done," the librarian said, turning to glare at Nina who approached the counter.

Lulu rushed out of the library, *Wuthering Heights* safety tucked into her bookbag and hoped Nina wouldn't run after her. It wasn't until she boarded a jeepney minutes later that Lulu, heart still pounding, sighed with relief. She replayed the scene of how Nina struggled to maintain her hold on the book. It seemed like she was struggling with someone. Could it have been Lola Josefina? Would a ghost help her? And if so, why?

***

Thankfully, Lulu didn't run into Nina back home and, true to her word, two days and two virtually sleepless nights later, she finished the book. On the morning of All Souls' Day, Lulu strode over to Nina's house to find her cousin preparing breakfast for her family. As a peace offering, she handed the book to Nina who glared at her and, without a word, took the book.

After breakfast, the Bituins along with the Titas, some uncles and cousins, piled into a rented, air-conditioned van, with the little cousins sitting on the laps of the adults. Noisy relatives added to the aggravation Lulu experienced on the way to the cemetery situated just right outside town. Biting her fingernails and peering out the window, she didn't know what to expect.

What she didn't expect to see were balloons—every shape, color and size imaginable. And vendors, selling everything from tropical flavored-ice creams, to banana fritters to fish balls deep-fried upon order then dipped in spicy sweet sauces. Flower vendors spread themselves out all over the cemetery that resembled a lost ancient city—with crypts piled atop more crypts resembling high-rise apartment buildings.

As they plodded through the dirt road passing a variety of grisly structures, Lulu thought the scene before her resembled more like a carnival or a town fiesta rather than a solemn burial site. Even more shocking were the visitors using crypts in family mausoleums as makeshift tables where a variety of dishes were laid out and served.

The Villareal family mausoleum housed ornate tombstones resembling miniature Roman edifices complete with pillars and marble headstones of Dimples' ancestors. There was a newly-installed headstone for Dimples' father, Rogelio Villareal Del Rosario, placed alongside Dimples' mother who died a decade earlier.

Lulu scanned a montage of several old gravestones of unfamiliar names that blurred through her mind until her eyes rested on a name she had come to know all too well: Doña Josefina Del Rosario y Villareal, b. 1867, d. 1906. Lola Josefina's name was etched on to a stone surface, not on marble like the deceased of recent decades.

Separated from the rest of the family montage, Lola Josefina's sepulcher sat quietly unadorned by itself on one corner of the mausoleum.

Lulu took a strand of *sampaguitas* that Dimples bought from a vendor, tied it into a floral necklace and draped it on to the tombstone. Tuning out the boisterous relatives and visitors milling about the cemetery, Lulu kneeled in front of Lola Josefina's final resting place and stared at the engraving on her headstone, as if trying to decipher a hidden message between the letters.

"Lulu, let's eat!" Tito Enrico robustly announced.

Turning to face her relatives, Lulu noticed a smorgasbord of food spread out on a tablecloth over a tomb. Lulu stared in aghast as she saw her family gather around the spread as though they were at home sharing a regular meal or at a party—passing dishes around to each other, holding plates as they stood or sat around eating and talking animatedly as lively music played from a portable CD player.

"*Hel-lo!* There are dead people here. Have some respect!" The words came tumbling out of Lulu's mouth. She looked at Chi-Chi who rolled her eyes at her.

"Come on, grab a plate, Lulu," urged Tito Enrico, who was swatting flies away from the food like most of her family members.

Lulu shook her head. The spread included *menudo, chicken adobo, pan de sal*, and, of course, steamed rice. Under different circumstances, the garlic and vinegar scents of the adobo would make Lulu's mouth water, but today, she was on the brink of nausea. Even though the Titas had been up cooking at sunrise, the thought of eating food alongside the remains of the dead made her cringe.

"I'm not hungry." The morose scene quickly squelched Lulu's appetite.

Romar motioned to her daughter with an impatient hand. "Lulu, come over and eat with us. You have to join the family."

"I said I'm not hungry."

The Titas raised their eyebrows. Lulu couldn't tell if they were shocked, surprised, annoyed or displeased.

"Young lady, I said, get over here! This minute!"

Lulu knew her father didn't appreciate her disobedience, especially in front of the relatives. So she got up and stood in between her mother and Chi-Chi who handed her a *pan de sal*. Lulu stared at it for a moment but somehow couldn't get it into her mouth.

"Are you thinking of Lola Josefina?" Dimples asked Lulu who nodded, thankful for her mother sensing her discomfort. Dimples lowered her voice. "You don't have to eat anything. Just stay here with the family to appease your Dad. He thinks you're just being stubborn."

Nodding, Lulu held on to her bread roll, promising to herself she'll save it for later. From her vantage point, she could see Lola Josefina's tombstone and sense her eerie presence as if she was watching her. Or maybe watching over her like at the library with Nina, who wasn't at the cemetery.

"How come Nina didn't come?" Lulu asked Nina's mother, Tita Claudia, whose normally friendly face hinted some sadness.

"Oh, Nina's busy doing homework, something about reading a book for a report," she said. "She's minding her studies even on such an important family day like today."

Lulu's heart dipped. She felt bad Nina didn't get to join the family—not for Nina particularly, but for Tita Claudia who, unlike her daughter, had always been nice to her.

After a few prayers, Lulu and her family packed up the food and tidied up. Lulu lingered a bit, taking one last look at Lola Josefina's gravesite before joining the others to scale a few yards up to the Bituin mausoleum, final resting place of Romar's ancestors.

This time, no eating took place, only prayers, to Lulu's relief. On the way home, the exhausted relatives stayed quiet in the cool van with some of the Titas nodding off.

As Lulu stared out the window at the rows of sugar cane fields and palm trees, one thought actually bugged her. Lulu had just visited the family mausoleum. So why of all places did Lola Josefina not bother to make an appearance? If she appeared to Tito Enrico and other relatives, why couldn't she show herself to everyone?

The theory of Lola Josefina only choosing to appear to certain people unnerved Lulu. She still couldn't figure out what Lola Josefina wanted from her. If only she could ask Lola Josefina herself.

Chapter Eleven

Rehearsals for the pageant began Monday at the auditorium and would take place every day after school through Friday with the big event taking place Saturday evening. Rehearsals weren't something to look forward to not so much because of meeting the other girls she would be competing against but because even in November the humidity level still sucked the life out of Lulu and it did no good to be cooped up in a stuffy, old auditorium without air conditioning. In fact, the auditorium was the newest building—built in 1963—on a campus that had been around since the late 1800s and was as old as the basilica.

Since "Miss Queen of All Saints" contestants were high school students, there were only twelve girls competing—three from every grade level, one from each class.

Theoretically, the girls should be paired with their respective high school male counterparts, but Sister Ruth, the assistant principal as well as the show's organizer and master of ceremonies, thought it best to enlist college guys to escort the contestants during the evening gown portion of the pageant.

Just as Lulu figured, Niel, with his charm and good looks, was predictably among one of the twelve selected escorts whose role entailed approaching the candidate he was paired with, handing her a rose, then taking her hand in his and escorting her to the front of the stage where she would answer her individual question for the Q and A segment.

What Lulu didn't figure was the possibility she wouldn't be paired with Niel who instead was assigned to escort statuesque Tessa Martinez, the third-year, Section A representative whose pearly, luminescent skin, cat-like eyes, pink bow-tie mouth and silky, long black hair Lulu predicted was a shoe-in for the title, money contest or not. What Lulu hoped was that Tessa wouldn't be a shoe-in winner for Niel's heart.

Niel winked at Lulu when it was her turn to appear on stage to accept the outstretched hand of one of Niel's classmates, a tall, handsome *mestiso* who wasn't Lulu's type. Since the girls had no clue which questions they would be asked at the pageant, they simply paraded with their escorts before joining their fellow contestants lined up on stage like ducks in a row. And since there were only a dozen girls, no one would be eliminated from the pageant; the judges would award prizes to the runners-up and, of course, the titleholder.

Initially, Lulu wasn't intent on winning, just getting through the contest. But recently, she thought how cool it would be if she did place in the event—at least become a runner-up. That would send a message, not just to the high school class, but the entire school what a cool girl she was. Being recognized in the pageant could be her ticket to getting into Section A for her final year in high school.

Aside from Tessa Martinez, there were other pretty girls from the classes with the less popular girls but from the looks of it, it seemed the Section A girls, no matter which grade level, dominated the show. Taking Tessa's lead, the girls sashayed their way across the stage, rehearsing the casual dress strut to the beat of techno music complete with hand on hip, turning to the right, then to the left before assuming their place in the row.

Except for a wave and a brief "Hi," Lulu and Niel barely said a word to each other during rehearsals. He seemed to know Tessa very well through her brother Cristobal who was Niel's classmate. During a break from rehearsing a group dance number to a medley of Hip-Hop tunes, Lulu watched as Tessa tossed her silky hair as if she were starring in a shampoo commercial and elicited a light, delicate laugh, covering her mouth slightly with her folding fan while coyly peering up at Niel and batting her eyelashes. *Definitely a flirty move if I ever saw one*, thought Lulu with disgust. How many rivals did she have for Niel's attention?

The Friday evening before the pageant, an exhausted Lulu grabbed her bookbag and pushed open the auditorium door to welcome the fresh air outside. While it wasn't that much cooler outdoors, Lulu was relieved to be out in the open and away from her fellow contestants, a few of them polite in her presence, but in all likelihood, talked about her when she wasn't around. Some surely had the guts to talk about her in her presence. Yesterday afternoon, as Lulu sat fanning herself furiously while watching a professional Hip-Hop dance troupe strut their stuff, her ears perked up when she heard one of the girls say "stateside."

A few of the contestants huddled a few yards from her sitting on chairs.

"*Alam mo*, the reason *kung bakit napili si* 'Stateside' is because *galing siya sa* States. *Yun lang ang* reason."

"*Si* Nina *ang dapat nilang pinili kasi siya ang makaka sagot sa mga tanong.* What can she possibly say about the Philippines? *Na suerte siya na* English *ang* Q and A."

Lulu stared hard in their direction. Though she couldn't quite speak Tagalog but could understand a bit of it—the girls speaking in "Taglish" made it easier—Lulu knew the girls were talking about her and not in a very nice way. In her anger, she boldly marched up to them.

"Excuse me," Lulu said, both hands on her hips. "I would appreciate it very much if you would please stop talking about me. I can hear and understand every word."

Jaws dropping, the girls first exchanged glances, then eyed Lulu. And with that, she stomped back to the bleachers on the side of the auditorium, picked up her *anahaw* fan and started fanning herself furiously. She needed a cool down in more ways than one. While she thought that might not have been the best way to handle it and she likely had even made some enemies, Lulu reasoned it felt good to stand up for herself. She wanted to put those girls in their place—prove them wrong.

So now as the memory of those moments lingered and began to bother her somewhat as she drummed up various repercussions resulting from that incident, a grasp on her arm jolted her from her thoughts.

"Niel!"

"You looked so preoccupied," he said, grinning, his deeply embedded dimples distracting her. "But obviously you must be thinking about tomorrow."

For a second, lost in thought, Lulu blinked at him. This was all too surreal. Just months ago, she was starting the ninth grade in the States with Kellie and Sara and now she was in the Philippines about to compete in a school pageant and the cutest boy in the world, way cuter than Stellan Abernathy, was talking to her. Would it be too much to ask if he was interested in her as well?

"Hello, Lulu! The pageant? Tomorrow?" He waved his hand in her face, chuckling a bit.

Finally out of her reverie, she nodded gratefully. "Oh, yeah, of course." They ambled in silence through the huge courtyard separating the college and high school buildings and toward the main building and former monastery that once served as a makeshift cell used to hold Filipino prisoners of the revolution captive but now housed the elementary level classes.

The bells of the basilica began to toll at their usual time at six in the evening as Lulu and Niel exited the campus and on to the plaza where jeepneys continued to pour out passengers in front of the basilica for evening rosary and tricycles buzzed around the market area like bees over a honeycomb.

"I'm going to the Internet café; I guess I'll see you tomorrow," Lulu said to Niel as she pivoted toward the path where many students still milled about in their uniforms eating street food.

"Are you hungry?" Niel suddenly asked her. "Would you like a snack?"

Thinking he'd be on his way in the other direction, she certainly didn't expect him to tag along. But she was hungry, not having eaten since lunchtime and exhausted from a long day at school and pageant rehearsals. She smiled gratefully.

"You like fishballs?" he asked, taking her gently by the elbow and directing her toward a cart where a vendor was frying food in a wok. A group of college students—identified by their uniforms—gathered around the cart, laughing, conversing and holding the skewered fish snacks.

"I've never tried them," Lulu admitted, smiling sheepishly, suddenly unsure of herself.

Niel greeted the vendor, a dark brown-skinned man with a weathered face and gap-toothed grin who handed barbecue sticks to Niel and Lulu who watched as the students pierced the remaining golden brown fishballs with their sticks then dipped them in various sauces in glass jars. The man poured more oil and fishballs into the hot wok as Lulu watched them bubble and sizzle while the man whisked them with a spatula.

"The trick is to pierce them before they deflate so that they're still crunchy when you put them in your mouth. Of course, you'll want to cool them down first before eating," Niel said, taking his stick and piercing, not just one but a total of four through the stick. After cooling them for a few seconds, he then dipped the stick into a tall jar of sauce. "Yum. Have some," he said, offering her the snack.

But until she could get really good at what Niel made look so simple, Lulu decided to pierce just one fishball. Waving it in the air, she dipped it into another jar then placed the fishball in her mouth. After taking a couple of bites, she coughed and waved her hand furiously in front of her mouth.

"Hot!" she said, her mouth still full. "I mean, peppery hot!"

Niel smiled. "You just dipped yours in chili sauce. Sorry, I should've warned you."

Lulu shook her head as she chewed then swallowed her snack. "No problem."

"Wait right here," Niel said. While he was gone, Lulu, tongue still aflame, attempted to pierce three fishballs just as Niel came back a few minutes later with two beverages, handing one to her. "This will be refreshing after your chili spell."

Niel was right. The sweet red drink, with just a hint of vanilla and gelatin and tapioca pieces with ice did quell the scorching feeling in her mouth.

"It's called *palamig*," Niel explained, piercing more fishballs. "For quenching your thirst."

After Niel paid the fishball guy, Lulu debated whether she should still visit the Internet café as it was getting late.

"I can give you a ride home when you're done," Niel offered. "Besides, I'd like to also check my e-mail."

Niel took the computer directly across from Lulu who pounded feverishly away on the keyboard eager to log-on and check her e-mail. Sadly, her Inbox only indicated she had one e-mail from the States—the rest were reminders from teachers and final instructions from Sister Ruth about the pageant.

The one, lone stateside e-mail came from Rowena, who replied to Lulu's e-mail with no subject header.

"Hi Lulu, Thanks for responding to my e-mail. Looks like things are going well for you. How are Tagalog lessons coming along? If I were you, I would read comic books and watch a lot of Philippine movies and TV shows to learn how to speak conversationally. Don't worry, you'll pick up the lingo soon. Everyone should soon be getting ready for Christmas there. They celebrate for a whole month.

"I hope you're making friends there. It shouldn't be a problem for you. Do you have any suitors yet? I bet you do! Several, I'm sure! How's the rest of your family doing?

"I'm doing fine over here. I've met some friends who like to read and watch movies. I'm getting accustomed to American slang and style and I think I'm fitting in okay. Learning American history is new and challenging for me but I guess I have to know all those important people, dates and events if I ever want to be an American someday, you know, like apply for citizenship. My parents are already petitioning my grandparents to come over here.

"Nothing much has really been going on at school, but of course, I'm sure that Sara and Kellie keep you updated on things. I can't believe half of ninth grade has gone by already. And you only have a year and half more to go of high school there. I wonder what Kellie and Sara think about that?

"Well, thanks for staying in touch and letting me know how you're doing. By the way, the answer is yes—I do believe in ghosts. Have you seen one recently? Take care, Rowena."

The words on the screen injected a dose of confidence Lulu thought she had lost. Rowena was right. She could learn to speak Tagalog comfortably in no time. She could make lots of friends and be popular again. And she could court the attention of any cute guy she wanted. But Lulu knew it was going to be all up to her and her attitude. And she had forgotten she'd asked Rowena about ghosts. Maybe Rowena would be a good person to confide in—maybe she wouldn't judge her.

Mustering all the pent up emotion she's carried for the past few weeks, Lulu eagerly hit the reply button.

"Hey Rowena, Glad things seem to be going well with you. Yeah, pretty soon you'll be in the 10th grade. Now that I think about it, you're pretty lucky in a way because you get to experience high school a bit longer. At first, I thought it was cool that I'd be finishing high school sooner than you guys over there, but now, I'm not so sure I'm ready for college yet.

"Well, things are a lot different here, that's for sure. I kind of like that we get to wear uniforms everyday because everyone wears the same thing but it's too hot to wear socks with our shoes all the time and I kind of miss wearing some of the trendy clothes. I feel I'm out of the fashion loop! But I remembered what you and Virgie said about girls being so fashion forward over here and I have yet to see that. But I think it's because all the people our age are always wearing their school uniforms. I'm going to have to convince my Dad to take me and my sister shopping in Manila one of these days.

"Oh, yeah, I'm participating in this pageant at school. My classmates nominated me actually. It's really a money contest, a fundraiser for school but the contestants seem to be taking it very seriously, like it's a real beauty contest.

"I guess I did ask you about ghosts, didn't I? Well, I'm sort of glad you do believe in them because I think I've had one appear to me quite a few times. I guess this ghost may have made her presence felt just right before I left, now that I think about it. It's like she's trying to tell me something. I feel weird even telling you all of this because, even after all that I've seen and heard, I'm still not sure I believe in ghosts. I wonder if what I'm seeing is just my imagination."

Lulu wrote about the incident with the jewelry box, the stories told by Tito Enrico, the time she saw Lola Josefina after school and at the girls' bathroom at school.

"At first, I thought this was all so creepy but now I'm beginning to get annoyed by all of this because I simply don't understand what's really going on, I mean, why me? Am I going crazy? I hope you're not getting weirded out by all of this and I would appreciate it if you didn't share this with anyone, including Virgie."

Feeling as though she was being watched, Lulu turned her attention from the computer screen to catch Niel staring straight at her from across the way. Appearing as if he was embarrassed, Niel looked down, smiling shyly and Lulu thought she might have seen a slight flush in his cheeks. Or maybe it was the heat.

She checked her watch and gasped. It was later than she thought. She had to be home in time for dinner and get some beauty rest. But first, she had to wrap up her e-mail to Rowena.

"I have to go now. Tomorrow's the Big Night of the pageant. Will tell you all about it after it's all over. Wish me luck! Lulu."

By the time Lulu got up from her chair, Niel was already at her side. As they exited the Internet café, Lulu couldn't help but feel thrilled that not only did he hold the door for her but he lightly touched the small of her back as he led her through the doorway. She sensed, though she thought she could be wrong, a bit of a possessive vibe about his touch. As if through his action, as subtle as it was, he was sending a message out to the world. And if so, she wondered, what kind of message?

Her growing infatuation with Niel made Lulu nervously talkative and at times, painfully at a loss for words. During the drive home this time around, it was definitely the latter as Lulu uneasily sat in the passenger seat trying to think of interesting things to say. There was enough talk about the pageant; she thought maybe they both needed a break from all that.

"I was thinking about our conversation the other day," Niel said, with a quick glance in her direction.

Her mind racing, Lulu tried to remember the various topics she discussed with him.

"You were asking me about ghosts, remember?"

Biting her lip, Lulu sat back, her heart pounding. Would this be a good time to bring up Lola Josefina? She wondered.

She cleared her throat. "Oh yeah, I remembered you telling me that ghosts were here for a reason—that they have unfinished business if they die before their time."

"That's right." Niel nodded, observing her pale face. "Pardon my expression, but—you look like you've seen a ghost."

Lulu smiled wanly. "I think maybe I have." *There, I said it.* She sighed. *What a relief to get that off my chest!*

She told him about her sightings and the recent incident with the book in the library with Nina.

"It's just all too weird a concept for me to grasp right now. I mean, ghost stories in literature like *A Christmas Carol*, and movies, yes, that's so far removed from real life," Lulu said, twisting her handkerchief in a knot. "Or is it? Half the time I don't know what's real and what's not and when something happens, it's so surreal, like I can't believe it's happening, like the time the book Nina was holding flew out of her hands as if someone just came and snatched it from her and she had a tight grip on that book, too."

"I understand why you feel so uncertain—this kind of thing probably isn't really talked about so casually in the States even when sightings do occur," Niel surmised.

"Well, maybe the adults talk about it, but you wouldn't be caught dead admitting you believe in ghosts at the school I went to," Lulu said, defiantly.

"From what it sounds like, though, this Lola Josefina could maybe be your protector—like your guardian angel," Niel said, slowing the jeepney down to let a farmer cross the street with his dog and a cart full of fresh vegetables.

Lulu shrugged. "I wish I really knew."

When Niel dropped her off by the family compound, Lulu politely declined his offer to walk her to her house, still conscious about what the neighbors might say as she was fully aware how conservative they still were in the countryside.

But her fears were soon set in motion when Lulu could make out a figure in the growing darkness—Nina came out holding a pail, ostensibly to fetch water from a nearby pump. Lulu wondered whether her cousin had seen her descend from Niel's jeepney.

"What are you doing out so late?" Standing under a lantern suspended by heavy wire near the water pump and wearing a T-shirt and blue cotton skirt, her hair tied in a bun, Nina seemed tired and older than her fourteen, almost fifteen years.

Lulu ignored the question. "Did you finish *Wuthering Heights*? I made sure I got it to you in time."

Nina's eyes knitted together. "No, I haven't had the chance. Unlike you, I've been so busy with chores—washing and ironing everyone's clothes including my own, cooking, washing dishes, cleaning the house—I don't have a maid like you do."

Feeling her blood rising, Lulu placed her hands on her hips. "I don't have a maid. Our family has a housekeeper who comes just for a few days and the only reason we have one is because she helps out my Mom, *your* aunt."

Rolling her eyes, Nina scrambled over and placed the pail under the water pump spout and started pumping furiously.

"The only reason your mother needs a maid is because she spent so much time in the States, she's forgotten what hard work is really like," Nina said over the rush of water coming from the pump. "She became so used to washing machines and dishwashers. All she had to do was press a button."

Lulu's hands went from her hips to her bookbag, gripping it tightly. It was all she could do to keep herself from wringing her cousin's neck. "Don't you dare disrespect my Mom, your aunt, in that way! You don't know how hard my parents worked in the States—sometimes even two jobs to raise us kids, pay off the mortgage on our house, pay for two cars and still send money here to pay for *your* education, and you don't even appreciate it!"

Wiping off her sweat with her T-shirt, Nina picked up the pail, spilling some water as she shoved past Lulu. "I've got to get back to my chores."

Shaking her head, Lulu stood staring angrily at her cousin before slowly making her way to her own house. The sound of clattering plates greeted her as she stepped inside. Aling Miling had just finished setting the table and was washing dishes. Lulu wearily ascended the stairs and passed the bathroom where Dimples was singing a song to Dimar while bathing him. She paused silently by Chi-Chi's room and peeked around the door that was ajar to find her sister sitting cross-legged on the floor mending her doll's clothes.

Lulu made a beeline across to her own room only to be stopped by her father's voice.

"Lulu!" He must have arrived earlier instead of after dinner late on Friday nights from Manila.

Lulu stepped towards the master bedroom to see Romar sitting on a lounge chair, holding a newspaper, peering at her above the rim of his eyeglasses. "Are you just now coming home?"

The hands on the nightstand clock seemed to be insinuating her delinquency as it sneered ten past seven.

"I had rehearsals for the pageant tomorrow, Dad," she reasoned, clutching her bookbag for support, as if it would give her any.

"Mom said rehearsals ended at 5 p.m.," Romar said, setting down the newspaper on his lap. "Did you have a hard time getting a ride home?"

"No, Dad." Lulu lowered her eyes, suddenly afraid to meet her father's eyes for fear he might read into them. But what might he read? Guilt? Over liking a boy? Nothing wrong with that, Lulu supposed.

Aling Miling joined the Bituins for dinner as usual when she was around and Lulu was thankful for her presence as she sensed a bit of tension from her parents for her coming home so late. She wished they would cut her some slack—it's not as if this was a regular offense, but her parents sure treated it as if it were with their unusual silence. They really didn't give her that much of a hard time when she went out with Sara and Kellie late on a Friday night. What's all the big deal now?

"*Siguro excited na excited ka sa pageant bukas, 'no?*" Aling Miling said to Lulu, who nodded, understanding.

"Yes, Aling Miling, I am a little nervous about the pageant," Lulu responded, raking her tilapia and vegetable stew with her fork.

"Is that why you seem to have no appetite?" Romar asked, his eyebrows narrowing.

"I ate some fishballs after rehearsal," Lulu said, putting her fork down and reaching for her glass of *kalamansi* juice.

"What did I tell you about eating snacks so close to dinnertime?" Dimples said, shoving a spoonful of rice in Dimar's mouth.

Lulu sighed. She really didn't want to be arguing with her parents the night before the pageant when she should be in a relaxed mood. "It was just a snack. I hadn't eaten anything since lunch."

"What happened to the fruit Aling Miling packs for you every day? That should be your snack," Dimples said, wiping her own mouth with a napkin. "You're not throwing that in the garbage are you? In favor of those greasy fishballs?"

"No, of course, I don't, Mom! Why would I do that?"

"Don't answer back to your Mom!" Romar blasted, gripping his fork and spoon with his hands.

Not wanting to make matters worse, Lulu forced herself to finish her dinner in silence then retreated to her bedroom afterward. Why were her parents being so difficult? Didn't they know how nervous she was about the pageant?

Although beauty sleep was crucial, Lulu's anxiety about the pageant and her parents kept her up half the night so she slept in until nearly noon awakened by the relentless sun's rays piercing their way through the shades and the mosquitoes that managed to sneak their way into her mosquito net.

Dreading the event that lay ahead and wondering why she ever got talked into representing her class in the first place, Lulu momentarily thought it would have been best if maybe Nina had been selected the class candidate since she seemed to have wanted to represent the class so desperately. But after Nina behaved so badly last night, Lulu wanted so much to prove to her cousin, that she deserved to be in the pageant.

"Oh, well, too late to back out now," Lulu told herself as she made her way out of the tangled mess of mosquito net over her bed. One of these days, she reminded herself, she was going to have a serious talk with her dad about investing in some mosquito-proof screens for the windows and doors. Plus adding some AC would be nice, she thought, as she pulled her nightshirt off her sweaty back.

But for now, the task at hand was the pageant. She wasn't set on winning—just getting through it.

By the time Lulu made her appearance downstairs in time for lunch, her parents pounced on her as though she were a house mouse with no hole to escape to.

"You're finally up," Romar said, sitting down on the dining table across from Lulu and impatiently spooning loads of steamed rice on his plate.

She knew just about everyone living in the province was up at the crack of dawn doing chores, taking early morning baths, selling fish and vegetables, buying fresh-baked *pan de sal*—whatever they usually did to start their mornings. And because there wasn't much to do, except watch TV or share stories with relatives after dinner, people usually went to bed early. So getting up late was a huge no-no no matter how late you went to bed. Lulu knew Romar frowned on the concept of sleeping in. She remembered how her Dad would constantly talk about how, when he was a teenager, he would rise at the crack of dawn to the tune of the rooster crowing every morning to do chores before going to school then do more chores *and* his homework after school.

"Where were you really at last night?" Romar grilled Lulu as she listlessly helped herself to some leftover vegetable stew.

"After rehearsals, I went to check e-mail at the Internet café," she said, hoping her Dad would get off her case already.

"That's not what I heard," Romar huffed, glaring at his daughter while furiously wiping his mouth with a napkin as if he couldn't wait to unload all the words that would ultimately come tumbling out.

"What did you hear?" Lulu fixed her eyes at her Dad, then at her Mom and back to Romar again. She wasn't so sure she wanted to hear what they supposedly heard from some unknown whom.

As if he couldn't hold his frustration any longer, Romar's face twisted like a dried santol fruit. "We heard you were out on a date—alone with a boy."

Lulu didn't know whether to laugh or get mad. Since when did she go out on a date? She wasn't even allowed to date in the States. "Uh, Dad, usually when you go out on a date, you *are* typically alone with your date."

She immediately regretted her remark as soon as Romar's face turned red. "Don't get smart with me! You were on a date and you lied to me!"

This time she had to put her fork down. "Dad, I wasn't lying to you. Who told you I was on a date?"

"Nina said she saw Niel drop you off late last night," Romar said, breathing heavily as though he might have high blood pressure any second. "He should know better. I thought I could trust that boy."

Burying her face in her hands, Lulu shook her head. She couldn't believe this conversation was even happening. How dare Nina twist things around!

"Dad, I wasn't on a date with Niel. He and I were rehearsing for the pageant and he treated me to fishballs because we were both hungry then he went to the Internet café to wait for me because he offered to take me home. It was getting late so I went home with someone I trusted instead of taking a tricycle ride late at night, something you told me never to do. And that's the whole truth and nothing but!"

Thinking she delivered her speech in the most convincing manner, Lulu sat back and turned to give Chi-Chi a look that said, "Help me get out of this mess!"

But it became obvious Romar wasn't convinced. "If Niel wants to court you, he should do the respectable thing by coming here to the house. But he'll have to wait until you finish high school." Romar scratched his head as Lulu's eyes bulged. "Wait, on second thought, I don't think I want him here in this house after he's disrespected me."

"What!" Lulu couldn't believe what she was hearing. Had her father gone ballistic? *And what century are we living in?*

"Now, Dad, you're being too hard on Lulu, she's a teenager, almost fifteen," Dimples intervened, taking a whimpering Dimar out from his high chair and placing him on her lap. "I'm sure what she told us is the truth. I think Nina had overreacted."

Lulu cast her Mom a grateful look. *Exaggerated was more like it.* She was awfully glad Dimples wasn't taking her wretched niece's side. "Mom's right. Nina hates me. She'll do anything to cause trouble. She said some awful things about you last night—about how you had life so easy in the States and I told her she better back off because she had no right to disrespect you two after all the money you'd been sending to her family."

Romar pushed aside his plate as if he'd had enough of both the food and the discussion. "At least she's not cavorting alone with some *kanto* boy, disrespecting her parents."

Lulu suddenly felt tears of anger welling in her eyes. She heard what a *kanto* boy meant: a vagabond, a good-for-nothing, a loser…everything Niel was not. "Dad, just how did I disrespect you?"

Romar sighed impatiently. "People talk here in the countryside, okay? I don't want a daughter of mine getting a bad reputation. We are a respectable and proud family. I worked hard to put you all through a good school and put food on the table. The least you could do is treat me with respect. You don't understand. I'm doing this for your own good."

Lulu knew her Dad was strict but never this strict. As Romar got up and threw his napkin on the table as a signal the conversation was over, Lulu knew better than to utter a word. Instead, she looked down at her plate, barely seeing her food, tears clouding her vision then tumbling on to her plate.

When she heard the gate latch open and close, Lulu knew her father went out for a walk, probably to blow off some steam even in the hot afternoon.

"Your Dad is a little hard on you," Dimples said, letting loose a squirming Dimar who anxiously broke free from her clutches to run to the living room to play with his Lego blocks. "I think he's especially being difficult because we're living here in the Philippines and things are done differently and more traditionally here in the provinces."

Lulu folded her napkin and sat back not interested in eating anymore. "But I'm not disrespecting you or Dad."

Dimples drank from her water glass. "I don't think you are either but your Dad just wants you to conduct yourself a little bit more carefully." She gave what Lulu thought was a gentle, compassionate gaze. "What I really believe is your Dad is realizing you're becoming a young lady now and that pretty soon you'll be in college. Think about it—just a few months ago, you were in the ninth grade and now you're in your third year of high school. That's quite a leap." She sighed. "It's been an adjustment for all of us."

"Well, hasn't he considered how I feel? It's a huge leap for me, too!" Lulu wailed. "I'm still a bit mad at Dad for moving us all here and totally changing my whole life. I was happy back home. Now, I can't wait to finish high school so I can go back to the States for college."

Dimples got up to give Lulu a hug. "Don't be mad at your Dad. He's just doing what's best for the whole family and he thought it would be a great opportunity for his children to learn about their heritage by living and going to school here. And it won't be forever. Just be patient with your Dad. And be patient with yourself." Dimples gave Lulu and Chi-Chi a smile. "Give yourselves some credit for learning new customs, a new language—it's not easy."

Lulu spent some time after lunch composing herself before retreating to the terrace, since it was too hot in her bedroom to review Philippine trivia for the pageant Q and A. Chi-Chi sat down on a rattan chair across from her with books on her lap.

"You're not here to give me a hard time, too, are you?" Lulu said, annoyed her solitude was disrupted.

"No. I want to help you prepare for the Q and A," Chi-Chi said, sorting books on the patio table. "I have all kinds of books here you might find useful."

The assortment of books included *Presidents of the Philippines, Flowers of the Philippines, Birds of the Philippines*, and *Islands of the Philippines*, and Lulu's favorite so far—*Tropical Fruit of the Philippines*—books containing basic cultural information the typical Philippine high school student, except for Lulu, already knew.

The sisters spent the next two hours quizzing on topics such as: who's the Philippine national hero—Jose Rizal; national flower—*Sampaguita*; famous natural wonders—Chocolate Hills of Bohol and the rice terraces of Baguio. Gradually, Lulu felt her confidence coming back.

After bathing, Lulu changed into her cotton eyelet retro dress and Dimples applied makeup—a pink duo eyeshadow combination: a hint of blush, and pink chocolate lip gloss, giving Lulu's face a more natural, as opposed to a "painted on" look.

Minutes before leaving for the pageant, while she closely assessed herself in the mirror, she couldn't help but think that whatever the outcome of the event, this experience could change her life forever.

Chapter Twelve

Even though she managed to block out her earlier rift with her father, Lulu still couldn't shake the ever-present jitters that plagued her nearly all week. Her popularity and acceptance by her peers depended on how well she performed in the pageant.

"Maybe if you relax a bit, you might enjoy it," Aprilyn told her one day after a Tagalog tutoring session.

The school auditorium was packed by the time Lulu arrived there in an air-conditioned van that Romar rented especially for this day. She appreciated not having to ride a jeepney, which would surely spell disaster, as far as hair and makeup were concerned. All twelve contestants were already backstage engaging in last minute preening sessions with their respective *bakla* stylists dressed in neon outfits with just a hint of spandex who were constantly flailing and wailing about the heat while fanning their charges and fanning themselves and blotting oil from the contestants' faces. Lulu stood there alone—sans *bakla*—trying hard not to stare.

One of the more flamboyant *baklas*, dressed in head-to-toe pink capri pants and spaghetti-strap tank top with gold hair and tons of mascara and burgundy lipstick complete with a prominent, but fake mole near the lip, sized Lulu up and down.

"Ano ba, di?" the bakla said, in a baritone voice then

pursed lips. "You don't have your own *bakla?*"

The *bakla* and her charge, a Section A fourth-year high school student named Crickette, burst into laughter. Lulu didn't know if they were laughing at her or the fact that she didn't have her own stylist. Glancing at herself in the mirror, Lulu thought she looked fine—quite simple and natural. She hoped her natural look would stand out in the bevy of glamour pusses whose makeup, accessories and dressy outfits transformed her competitors into appearing too grown up for her taste.

After the girls performed a Hip-Hop dance number, they went into formation across the stage—six on each side and stood there as each girl took turns introducing herself. The order of introduction began from the lowest section of the first-year high school students to Section A first-year and so on for each level. Top section class representatives, people Lulu began to refer to as the "A-Listers," garnered the most rousing applause, whistles and catcalls. Lulu's own introduction elicited a decent show of support. After she said her name, she waved and smiled when she recognized her parents, Chi-Chi, the Titas, Uncle Enrico, Aprilyn, Jolie and some of her cousins, standing and cheering.

Clearly, the crowd favorites were Tessa and Crickette. It seemed the two girls were in a heated competition for the most boisterous applause and cheers as they sashayed on the stage. Tessa, with her lithe frame and shampoo commercial-like hair tossing on her shoulders, glided on stage wearing a pink polka dot cotton poplin dress and navy peep-toe pumps. Lulu thought Crickette, with her Spanish *mestisa* looks—reddish-brown hair and aquiline nose—wearing a smoke-grey silk sateen sheath strung with topstitched roses, confidently catwalked her way on stage with feet adorned in metallic pumps. It seemed to Lulu that Crickette was no stranger to modeling. Maybe Tessa and Crickette lead secret lives as models—one seen on TV commercials and the other on the runway.

Just as Aprilyn and Jolie predicted, mostly all of the contestants either sang or danced their way through the talent competition. The songs were all ballads and pop tunes, the dances ranging from Hip-Hop to jazz ballet. A perky second-year high school "A-Lister" performed a rousing baton twirling number, which got the audience clapping and cheering.

To her relief, soothing jazz music played softly in the background as Lulu demonstrated how to make chocolate mousse. For this portion of the competition, she changed into jeans and a white and sky blue cotton gingham blouse which was fortunately covered with an apron as it came in handy when her jittery fingers accidentally squirted some chocolate syrup over her bosom area. Lulu eyed the judges seated in the center of the front row but found it hard to read their expressions as they were busily scribbling notes on their legal pads.

Her talent seemed to get a polite response from the audience and, of course, more cheers from Lulu's own camp. Backstage, the girls who had completed their talent performances were already changing into their evening dresses, touching up their makeup and some gathering their tresses in updos, assisted of course by their respective *baklas.*

As stealthily as she could, Lulu sought refuge behind a stash of boxes where she stepped into her gold chiffon evening dress which she was barely able to zip all the way up by herself, sweat beads racing down her back and chest by the time the dress was on. Even though she couldn't see herself in the mirror, Lulu remembered being satisfied with the way she looked at a recent fitting with Tita Claudia who expertly made the gown for her within a week. Along with that fitting was the memory of Nina lurking in the next room of her house as her mother chatted away while she pinned and preened her gown.

After gathering her personal belongings and clothes and stuffing them in a suitcase, Lulu held on to one of the boxes for support as she slipped into three-inch heeled cream satin shoes that belonged to Dimples, and immediately she regretted not making time to practice walking in those shoes before the pageant. Platforms and wedges, she was used to, but stilettos were a different story. She straightened her body to steady herself, and just as she had read about in books about posture, she imagined a string connected to the top of her head pulling her frame upward.

As she tried to figure out whether to walk on the stilettos—heel to toe or toe to heel, using the balls of her feet for transitioning—all around her the rest of the contestants were in evening gown frenzy—*baklas* tousling hair, cans of hairspray whizzing, perfume misting around the room amid makeup touch-ups, and girls twirling around confidently, preening themselves one-by-one in front of the lone full-length mirror as various electric fans hummed around and contestants vigorously fanned themselves.

Suddenly, it occurred to Lulu that she failed to enlist help from someone to act as her stylist, and as she stood staring at the mad rush backstage, her hands went to her hair which was still in a ponytail from her talent competition look—an easy style that kept her long hair away from her face and the mousse she was concocting. But for an evening look, she wanted something more polished, sophisticated. Taking a cue from a *bakla* styling Tessa's long, lush tresses, Lulu watched as the hair was teased with a comb front to back with a light wave of hairspray for a finishing touch.

Lulu rushed back toward her suitcase to grab her comb when she heard the strum of romantic, Spanish guitar music, signaling the beginning of the evening gown competition. There was simply no time for hair styling. As the girls started to line up to promenade on stage, Lulu hurriedly and ungracefully lumbered over on her heels to a makeshift styling station one girl had just vacated. Bending over, she ran her fingers through her hair then tossed her head back up. To the surprise of one of the *baklas*, Lulu grabbed a can of hairspray and, holding it a few inches away from her head, started spritzing away.

"*Salamat!*" she smiled at the stunned *bakla*, as she set the hairspray can back on a table.

Making the trek in her heels to take her place in line wasn't as difficult a feat as she thought. *Just take a deep breath and it will all be over in a few minutes*, she coached herself, as the contestants ascended up a small flight of stairs toward the stage.

Once on stage, as rehearsed, the girls would descend down another small staircase toward their waiting escort. When her turn came, she looked down in horror. Suddenly, she felt as though she were about to go downhill on a ski slope with little or no training. Amid the clapping after her name was announced, her eyes floated across the stage—at the contestants who already safely landed from the flight of stairs toward their waiting escorts. She met Niel's eyes from where he was standing and he smiled brightly at her. Lulu hoped that smile meant he was pleased by what he saw as it's not often he gets to see her all dressed up. He looked pretty sharp himself, Lulu thought, wearing a black tux, appearing cool despite the heat, his hair newly cut and slightly spiked up with styling mousse.

Feeling self-conscious, Lulu unlocked herself from Niel's gaze and tried to focus on her own smiling escort whose hand was outstretched, the other hand holding a long-stemmed red rose. It was as though he was beckoning her to come down from the mountain she had climbed; his expression seemed to encourage her that all would be okay. *Just take the first step*, she coached herself.

And so she did. Lightly, slowly at first as she didn't know how much her heel had to go to reach the next descending step. Once her right foot was firmly planted, her left foot followed onto the next step. While mentally cursing herself again for not wearing her heels to rehearsals, Lulu tried not to look down as she took each step and tried to hide her consciousness behind a smile, while scanning the audience for familial support. Countering her uneasiness, Lulu tried to envision herself winning the contest, becoming popular, more popular than at her old school, being an "A-Lister" at her new school, and becoming friends with Tessa and her clique. Just thinking about these potential rewards made Lulu smile as brightly as she could. She could picture her post-pageant self—Lulu Bituin, "Miss Queen of All Saints," the school's new It-Girl from the States and a shoo-in for Section A. The school wouldn't even wait until her senior year before promoting her to the A-List class, where she rightfully belonged. She was just a few mere steps away from earning her place among the privileged again.

Then she saw her—that one familiar face—standing on the far right aisle next to an exit. The image was so unexpected that a stunned Lulu lost her footing and skipped the two remaining steps she needed to make a safe landing. It happened so quickly; she didn't have a chance to grasp her escort's hand and in a flash Lulu laid in a crumpled heap of gold chiffon. The audience was stunned to silence.

The next few minutes were all a blur. An assortment of faces were swimming above her—her escort's face, Sister Ruth's, some contestants' faces—and Niel's face. Someone gripped her hand and in a few seconds she was up, feeling woozy but upright nonetheless. Lulu turned to where she saw Lola Josefina standing but no one was there. Then she saw her family. Dimples smiled at her daughter with eyes that seem to say "We're still so proud of you, honey." Chi-Chi regarded her with wide, hopeful eyes.

Just when Lulu scanned her surroundings unsure of herself and flushing a deep red, suddenly, a burst of applause erupted from the audience. Smiling, her escort took her hand and handed her a rose. She shyly returned his smile as he placed her hand in the crook of his arm and escorted her over to the center of the stage where she took a bow. To her relief, she was able to make it to her place in the formation.

Once she had a moment to realize what just happened, a surge of hot blood seemed to rise to her temples. She was livid at Lola Josefina. The nerve of that woman, that ghost, or whatever the heck she was, to show up at the pageant, of all places and catch her off guard. Was this some kind of cruel joke she was playing? Lulu wondered, suddenly feeling silly for being mad at a ghost. Lulu thought about what Niel said—that every ghost has a purpose. What was Lola Josefina's purpose? Did she not want Lulu to succeed in her new school?

Lulu tried to smile through gritted, angry teeth. If Lola Josefina was an obstacle to Lulu's popularity, something had to be done. Maybe she could find someone who exterminated ghosts.

The audience cheered even louder and just when Lulu thought the cheers were for her, she turned to see an ethereal goddess in an aqua silk satin hand-painted dress. Behold Tessa with her beautiful tresses flowing past her shoulders and Niel alongside her with an enormous grin on his face as his eyes drunk in the sight of her. Lulu strained to maintain a genuine smile and as she watched, she couldn't help but think how cute they looked together.

Then Niel did something no other escort had—he kissed Tessa on the cheek, a move that seemed to surprise even Tessa. There was a gasp from the line of contestants as a few of them squealed in delight. Lulu glanced at Sister Ruth whose lips were pursed as she held the microphone.

After representatives from sections C and B of the graduating senior class made their evening dress promenade, cheers and applause rivaling those garnered by Tessa's walk erupted as Crickette made her entrance wearing a canary yellow silk chiffon asymmetric dress with black silk sash detail. Lulu had heard backstage that none other than famous Filipino designer Joey Samson had designed Crickette's dress. *It pays to have connections in high places*, Lulu thought. She couldn't figure out why Crickette, a member of one of the province's wealthiest families, was attending school in the countryside. Was it because if she were to go to school in Manila she wouldn't be as popular? Would she just be another girl from the *provincia*?

Sister Ruth, miscast in her role as emcee because her lisp was so pronounced by her use, or rather misuse of the microphone, wasted no time in getting to the Q and A portion, which wasn't exactly what Lulu expected. Instead of it being in quiz show format on Philippine trivia that Sister Ruth had said it would be, the girls were asked to comment on what they could do to promote Philippine culture to the world. But while the questions were along that same theme, to keep contestants on their toes, each was asked a different question: "If you had to design a dress using a natural fiber native to the Philippines, which would you choose and why?" "If you were to write a history book about the Philippines, which era would you choose and why?" "In your opinion, which person made the most impact on the Philippine economy and why?" "How would you explain to the world the Philippine custom of Flores de Mayo?"

Lulu placed her hands with her fingers crossed behind her back when her turn came. Satisfying the judges with a great answer could be a way to redeem herself.

"If a foreigner asked, 'What do you think is the single most prominent trait that describes the typical Filipino?' what would you say and why?"

It seemed like the audience was holding their breaths along with Lulu, waiting for her answer. How do you answer a question like that? Her mind racing, she rifled through her mental file cabinet for a folder that was labeled "Typical Filipino Character Traits." *Let's see, what I have noticed so far about Filipinos since I've lived here?*

Her anxiety barometer reached an all-time high again. Unable to breathe, Lulu exhaled hoping a smile and some words would come out along with that exhalation.

"Well, it seems like Filipinos like to emulate whatever is in style in America. Take the jeepney for example. A lot of jeepneys are named after American celebrities and the music that's played in jeepneys are all American soft rock songs. And kids here seem to enjoy dancing to Hip-Hop or singing hits from American Top 40." The words just kept tumbling, a mad rush out of Lulu's mouth, even creating a stampede before she had a chance to figure out whether what she said made sense.

Sister Ruth's eyebrow arches remained suspended as she peered at Lulu with an expression that seemed to wonder what planet she came from.

"Ah, yes, thank you for that comment, Lulu," Sister Ruth said, already turning her attention to the next contestant.

When Lulu returned to her place, she heaved a sigh of relief. The pageant was nearly over. No matter how she fared, she had done her part.

While the judges took a few minutes to decide the winner, the contestants went backstage as a dance troupe delivered another Hip-Hop number.

Most of the contestants gathered and chatted among themselves but Lulu preferred to stand behind a curtain on the side watching the dance number. She didn't want to overhear what the girls might say about her fall and response to the Q and A.

Finally, the wait was over. To the rhythmic beat of salsa music, the contestants took one last walk across the stage in a line and this time Lulu and her high heels prevailed. She just wanted to get this whole thing over with.

During rehearsal, Lulu remembered Sister Ruth insisting that although the pageant was a fundraiser in which all the contestants had to raise funds to participate, "Miss Queen of All Saints" wouldn't necessarily be chosen on the basis of whoever raises the most money nor was this a popularity contest.

"It's all about who is the all-around best representative of the high school—the winner will have beauty, brains and good character," Sister Ruth said, this time addressing the audience and reminding the contestants of the pageant's mission.

Except for a drum roll by a male member of the high school marching band, the audience remained silent. While Lulu didn't normally resort to prayer, she closed her eyes and silently wished she could at least be a runner up.

"The third runner up is Maria Liezl Mendoza, Second Year, Section A," announced Sister Ruth.

Cheers, mostly from Liezl's family, reverberated through the auditorium as student volunteers did their obligatory awarding of sash and bouquet. Clapping politely, Lulu eyed her relatives in the audience. The Titas were smiling hopefully at Lulu and clapping as if to tell her "You still have a chance."

"The second runner up is Miranda Deanna Ocampo, First Year, Section A."

More cheers and applause. Lulu and the remaining contestants shifted uneasily in their seats. There were only two remaining spots left in what Sister Ruth dubbed as "The Queen's Court." Lulu thought she may actually have a chance at winning this thing. Perhaps she showed grace and dignity when she rose after the fall—just as a strong person would do in real life. Rising after falling.

"The first runner up is Cristina Katrina Claire Marasigan, Fourth Year, Section A."

A thunder of mixed emotions erupted when Crickette's name was announced. There were cheers from people who probably didn't want Crickette to win—or maybe cheers from those who were relieved she had actually placed in the competition, the latter being utterly ludicrous, Lulu thought. *Crickette, of all people, not place in the Queen's Court? She could have easily won the title.*

"And now to crown our new Miss Queen of All Saints," said Sister Ruth. "She will represent our school in official engagements, participate in the San Juan fiesta, and will be the newest board member of the school's fundraising committee. Ladies and gentlemen, our new Miss Queen of All Saints is…"

Closing her eyes again, Lulu imagined what it would feel like to wear the crown on her head. She envisioned herself squealing in glee as soon as her name was announced. She could already feel the triumphant placement of the crown on her head and sash over her bosom and see herself taking her victory walk across the stage. Surely, the judges would reward her for her poise and character, dignity and ability to maintain grace under pressure after her fall.

She could almost smell the sweet scent of success in her new school—she was just one announcement away.

"Everyone please give a huge round of applause to our new Miss Queen of All Saints…Maria Theresa Anne Martinez!"

Lulu couldn't see straight as a veil of disappointment enveloped her. Did tears blind her eyes or were her contacts becoming filmy? Whatever the reason, she could barely see the sash that the former queen draped over Tessa's shoulder, the crown that now adorned Tessa's pretty head. True, Lulu didn't initially care too much about winning and just wanted to get the pageant over with. But now she thought the pageant had become her ticket to success—a public declaration that she was somebody, and not just in her old school. *I had as much of a chance as the other girls, so why didn't I win?*

Her rage toward Lola Josefina intensified. She couldn't wait for the ghost to make another appearance. Couldn't wait to tell her off. Lulu decided she would find a way to get rid of Lola Josefina. For good. First she had to find a ghost exterminator. Who would help her find one in a country where ghosts were practically revered as saints?

Chapter Thirteen

Lulu could barely sleep the next couple of nights and before she knew it, it was Monday morning again. But this time she had to face her classmates and the whole school—the aftermath of the pageant.

After the event festivities concluded Saturday night, Lulu politely received hugs from her family and from Jolie and Aprilyn. Though she didn't think there was a reason to celebrate, Romar offered to treat the whole group to dinner at a popular restaurant called Tito Bing's, which was well known for its home-style Filipino cuisine. The bustling restaurant proved to be the essence of Filipiniana—bamboo tables and chairs, palm trees, tropical drinks such as *buko* juice served in coconut shells, waiters dressed in typical provincial costume. There was even a stage for karaoke. As the smell of sautéed onions and garlic wafted through the air, a waiter with an eager-to-serve expression on his face hurried toward the family's table. While she appreciated her dad's generosity, Lulu would rather have gone home. Especially when the runners-up and their families arrived to dine at the same restaurant.

"Hey!" Lulu said to her friends after the waiter took their group's order. "Was it that bad?"

"Do you mean the fall?" Aprilyn asked, taking a sip of ice water. "Not at all. Considering how high those heels were, I'd say you did good."

"At least you didn't fall again," Jolie helpfully offered, as she swabbed some lip balm.

"Do you think falling was what made me lose the contest?" Lulu couldn't help asking.

Aprilyn, who first exchanged glances with Jolie, eyed Lulu solemnly. "I think the judges already picked who was going to win before the pageant even started."

Just when Lulu was going to ask Aprilyn what she meant, Tessa and her entourage consisting of family and friends made a grand entrance in the restaurant. Wearing a black polka dot halter top and khaki 1950s-inspired swing skirt and red patent leather heels, her pageant sash draped across her chest, Tessa was a vision of loveliness. Lulu watched as practically everyone in the room stopped what they were doing to stare at her as she and her group made their way toward a set of reserved tables.

While her family feasted on *menudo, chicken adobo, pancit palabok*, and *kare-kare*, the whiff of the foods nauseated Lulu. She couldn't bear to be in the same room with the other winners.

"I don't want to be here. Does that make me a sore loser?" Lulu asked Jolie and Aprilyn as she picked at her food.

As if she couldn't wait to talk even with her mouth full, Jolie pointed her fork toward Tessa's boisterous group seated in the center of the restaurant, occupying three long tables.

"The audacity of the judges to pick all the winners from all Section A classes," said Jolie, stabbing her fork into a chunk of pork. "Can you believe that?"

Aprilyn shook her head. "Who else did you expect they'd pick? The contest was fixed, I tell you. It was fixed!"

Lulu shrugged. "I don't care anymore. I admit, I did want to do well—heck, I wanted to win. But now, I just don't care. I wish I hadn't participated. I made a fool of myself."

"Don't regret the experience," Aprilyn said, reaching for more steamed rice. "Win or lose, I'm sure you learned something."

Lulu gave a sarcastic laugh. "Yeah, the next time I enter a pageant, which, I guarantee you there *won't* be a next time, I'll have my own *bakla*, thank you very much. It was tough trying to prepare backstage for the competitions without any help."

Aprilyn and Jolie exchanged glances. "We're so sorry. We don't have any experience with pageants ourselves," Jolie said, refilling her glass with mango juice.

"I guess we could've gone backstage to help you out," Aprilyn said, tentatively, looking down at her plate, as if in shame.

"Whatever. It's over now," Lulu said, shoving her plate aside and observing her relatives who seemed to be having a great time despite her loss.

Dimples was trying to eat while holding Dimar who was bending a plastic straw, his makeshift toy of the moment. The Titas were laughing at some funny joke Tito Enrico was telling them. Chi-Chi sat listening to them as if trying to decipher what the adults were talking about. To her surprise, Lulu caught her Dad eyeing her. They hadn't actually spoken much before the pageant, but tonight, Romar seemed to have a more relaxed expression on his face, to Lulu's relief. She thought maybe she had disappointed him but her fears were squelched when he nodded in her direction as if to say "Sorry you didn't win, but nice try anyway," and that was enough for Lulu. For now. She still had to clear her name and her reputation regarding the "Niel incident."

Just as she wondered where Niel had gone after the pageant, the boy of her dreams sauntered into the restaurant. He stopped for a second to scan the diners till their eyes met and he nodded to her. Was he searching for her? Would he want to join her at their table?

Lulu quickly looked at Romar. It seemed like her dad didn't see Niel and if he did, she thought, so what? Neither she nor Niel did anything wrong. Unfortunately, Niel made a beeline toward Tessa's table where he shook hands with her father, patted her brother, Cristobal, on the shoulder and took an empty seat beside Tessa, whose eyes gleamed in his direction. *Now would be a good time to vomit*, Lulu thought.

Apparently, Jolie and Aprilyn also witnessed the same scene.

"Tessa deserved to win," Lulu admitted, her shoulders deflated as she wiped breadcrumbs from the cantaloupe cotton sundress she changed into. "I mean, look at her. She's beautiful. It was either Tessa or Crickette, hands down."

Her friends shrugged. "She is gorgeous—and rich," Jolie said. "But she's still what you call an A-Lister. For once, I just wanted to see someone else, besides an A-Lister, be crowned the winner. An underdog." Jolie eyed Lulu. "Like you."

"Okay, so she won the contest. But, did she have to win Niel, too?" Aprilyn said, wiping her mouth with her napkin.

"She didn't win Niel," Jolie admonished her friend by playfully swatting her with a napkin. "Did you see the way he looked at Lulu? I don't think he's interested in Tessa."

"Everyone's interested in Tessa," Lulu said, leaning back on her chair, repulsed by the food the waiter kept placing on the table. "How can he not like her? He's a guy."

"Precisely," answered Jolie, reaching for skewered barbecue chicken. "Tessa's unattainable. She's beautiful to look at, not to date. Guys like Niel are looking for real girls to be with. Not fashion models."

Aprilyn shook her head. "I have to disagree. Don't you know how many famous supermodels date ugly rock stars? Beauty prevails!"

"Well, Niel isn't an ugly rock star and Lulu's pretty," Jolie said. "And the only reason rock stars get the gorgeous girls is because they're rock stars. And they're rich!"

"Okay, guys, I've heard enough!" Lulu said, covering her ears with her hands. "Niel and I are just friends."

Jolie shot her a teasing, eyebrows-rising-and-falling look. "You're not interested in Niel? I've seen the two of you together after school—that one time by the fishballs cart when you didn't know I was watching."

Embarrassed by being caught "cavorting" alone with Niel, Lulu stared down at her plate.

"See, she's blushing!" said Jolie excitedly, as the Titas and Chi-Chi looked over.

Lulu prayed her father didn't overhear the conversation. With so much chattering going on and contemporary pop music blaring from the jukebox, she hoped he hadn't heard what Jolie said. Romar and Tito Enrico were absorbed in conversation, probably about politics, or home improvement.

Unlike the pageant, dinner passed without incident. On their way out of the restaurant, Lulu didn't even bother to face in Niel's direction. She was still embarrassed he had seen her fall on stage. Following her family to the van her father had just rented for use only on weekends and family outings when he was home, Lulu was disappointed Niel hadn't gotten up to say "Hi!" then thought the better of it. She certainly didn't deserve any congratulations. He was seated at the winner's table.

The Monday after the pageant, Lulu felt first-day jitters all over again. She didn't feel like going to school, doubting her classmates had forgotten about her fall.

When she entered the classroom, her stomach growling, the usual chatter that occurred while waiting for first-period teacher to arrive simmered down. Amid whispering, she made her way toward her desk, lifting her head only to nod at Aprilyn and Jolie seated two rows over.

"*Sinabi ko na sa inyo*," she heard a familiar voice say in a tone of authority. "We should have picked a representative who takes pride in our culture. Hospitality. *Hospitality* is the single most prominent trait that typically describes Filipinos."

Without glancing behind her, Lulu knew the source of that sardonic lip. Lulu didn't remember seeing Nina sitting in the audience with her family, but judging by the sound of it, apparently she was there. Or at least got the pageant scoop from others.

"We could've beaten Section A girls this year, but noooooo," Lulu heard Nina say loudly. "Not only did our candidate *not* know a thing about Philippine culture, she couldn't even walk in high heels."

As Lulu pretended to be going over her notes for class, the students erupted in laughter—a familiar, chilling scene for Lulu whenever a teacher from her old schools couldn't pronounce her name. But it couldn't be happening again. Not here in the Philippines where she thought she'd be an instant star in a land that revered all things American.

"And you think *you* could've done a better job, eh?" Lulu heard another voice. Aprilyn.

"As a matter of fact, yes, now that you mentioned it," Nina said.

"If we thought you were the best candidate, we would've picked you," Aprilyn answered back. "But we didn't, did we?"

"The class should've voted, plain and simple," Nina countered. "You're all just suck-ups—so enamored of anything Stateside. It's pathetic."

"Why don't you just shut up!" Jolie lashed out, to Lulu's surprise.

The minute she said that, the class broke into arguments, challenging each other now in Tagalog, with Lulu catching tidbits of the debate she could understand. Soon, she began to tune them all out. She wanted to go home. She wanted to be invisible.

At lunch, Lulu sat silently reading over Math class notes she couldn't decipher. Going over her Tagalog notes seemed easier compared to Math, but she needed a distraction while Aprilyn and Jolie ate lunch. And she needed to ignore the staring she got from various high school and college students as they walked by her on campus on the way to the cafeteria.

"Why did you let your cousin walk all over you like that?" Aprilyn said, twisting her noodles around her fork.

"Because she's right," Lulu said in a deflated tone. "I don't belong here. I don't know what I'm even doing here in this school." *Maybe I could study with a private tutor or get home-schooled.*

"That's your defeatist attitude taking over," Jolie admonished stirring gelatin in her gulaman drink. "Don't let it get the better of you."

"I'm serious. How am I going to be popular if I can't even walk in high heels without falling or if I can't answer basic questions about Philippine culture?"

Aprilyn and Jolie gawped at their friend as if seeing a stranger. "We thought you didn't care about being popular. We thought you just wanted to adjust to living and going to school here. Isn't that what matters?" Aprilyn said.

Lulu blinked, absorbing her comment. Aprilyn struck a sensitive chord, but Lulu believed she still had something more to prove.

"And high heels don't matter. It's not like we walk around in them all day."

Angry again with her father for moving the family here and angry with Lola Josefina for being Lola Josefina, Lulu took a good look at Aprilyn and Jolie. They were nice enough girls and she was thankful for them going out of their way to be nice to her, but seriously: *If I were back home in the States, would I even be caught dead having lunch with these two?*

"You can't possibly know what I want or what I've experienced," Lulu said, gathering her books and shoving them in her bookbag. "You don't know what it feels like to be me."

Aprilyn and Jolie glanced at each other as if uncertain as to what they should say. They sat in silence for one full minute that seemed to last forever. Lulu regretted what she said and the tone of voice she used. After all, the girls had been nothing but nice to her. Still, she somehow couldn't consider them as her good friends just yet.

"You're right. We don't know how it feels to be you," Jolie said, softly, peering down at her lunch as if ants had invaded it.

"We forget you said you were popular back in the States," Aprilyn added, packing up her own books.

Lulu stood up. "I'm just super anxious right now."

Aprilyn nodded. "We understand, don't we, Jolie?" Jolie bit her lip then nodded as though she didn't have a choice. "Just be patient. In time, people will forget about the whole pageant thing."

"Oh, yeah? When?" Lulu said, as she draped the bookbag strap over her shoulder. With all the books in it, she was sure she was trudging lopsided and might even be a likely candidate for back injury before she finished high school.

As Lulu, Jolie and Aprilyn headed back to class, the overcast sky that loomed ahead all morning finally unleashed relentless raindrops that pelted on their uncovered heads. Lulu could relate to the sky right now—she couldn't guarantee her happiness at her new school. High school was tough enough already—but high school in a new country was something else all together.

***

Getting through the rest of the school week depended on Lulu's ability to rationalize that while she did fall, she got back up again and that showed the entire school she had character. *And if that wasn't a recipe for success, then I don't know what is*, Lulu thought.

Tito Enrico dropped by after dinner Friday night to chat with Romar who was relaxing in the *sala*. Lulu passed them on the way upstairs eager to retreat to her room after a long school week.

"Lulu!" Romar called out, beckoning her with a wave. "Your Uncle Enrico wants to take us to visit your Lolo's hacienda tomorrow before the new owners take over."

At first, Lulu didn't think the outing would be exciting—preferring instead to have her Dad take her and Chi-Chi shopping in Manila like he promised. Yet, she was curious about the old place.

Tito Enrico nodded enthusiastically as if he read her thoughts. "I think you'll find it interesting. Lola Josefina lived there."

While she was still angry at the ghost for distracting her at the pageant, her curiosity piqued even more.

"That sounds cool," Lulu said, realizing she meant it.

Sleep didn't come easily for her that night as she tossed and turned anxious about the visit to the old house. It wasn't that she was scared. Seeing where Lola Josefina actually lived intrigued Lulu. Plus, this could be a chance to very subtly ask Tito Enrico how to get rid of the ghost.

So getting up at 5:30 to bathe and join her family for the usual breakfast of fresh-baked *pan de sal* and Cheez Whiz—Dimar's favorite—wasn't much of a feat. They set out in the van just as the sun was rising and a slight, cool breeze coming from a nearby beach passed through.

To Lulu's surprise, it took all of only twenty minutes to get there. They bypassed going into town and continued along the highway past several more *bahay-na-bato* houses until they reached a vast landscape of sugar cane fields.

Tito Enrico steered the van off the main highway onto a dirt road that seemed to be leading to nowhere. Since they were on the opposite side of the beach, Lulu knew a beach wouldn't just emerge from behind stalks of sugar cane.

Then suddenly, as she peered through the window, she saw it. Lola Josefina's old house. Surrounded by a grove of trees bearing the luscious fruity scents of mangoes, guavas and *santol*, Lulu found the structure, which had fallen into disrepair, striking in a grotesque sort of way. As she drew closer to the Spanish ancestral house, she continued to stare at the edifice, which, she surmised, had once been grand in its heyday, its architecture a combination of a Castilian and Tuscan-style façade, comprising three stories including the octagonal tower room, the most prominent feature of the house, that provided a panoramic view of the vast landscape: the sugar cane and rice fields, the verdant farmlands. Lulu and her family followed Tito Enrico on foot as he guided them to view the rounded balcony adjacent to the master bedroom which was located at the rear portion of the house. During World War II, the mansion was seized by the Japanese and used as a headquarters and watchtower, Tito Enrico informed them as they admired the balcony and the tower from the outside.

The house was certainly creepy, Lulu thought, as she noticed the detailing on the brass door knocker shaped like a hand and the long ornate, antique skeleton key Tito Enrico used to unlock the door. As the wooden floor creaked from their footsteps, she followed her family deeper into the house darkened by the closed windows and the dark, narra wood of the walls and moldings that matched the furniture. Tito Enrico pointed out that, built in the 1850s, the house boasted of classical Doric motifs, French windows, and imported etched-glass panes protected by fancy-grilled ventanillas. There were *santos*, ivory figures of Catholic saints, on virtually every dust-ridden antique table, alongside portraits of family members spanning five to six generations. With their beady, dark eyes, they seemed to be staring at Lulu and her family. Tito Enrico even kept his voice low as if not wanting to disturb the *santos*, or if they existed here, the spirits. Lulu watched as Dimar stood clutching Dimples' skirt and, with wide eyes, peered at the large *santos*, perhaps afraid they might come to life.

The floor creaked in various spots where Lulu and her family stepped. As Tito Enrico related the story behind the people who lived in the house, Lulu ambled slowly through the *sala* eyeing the various portraits. There were old, yellowing photos of a man and a woman who resembled Lola Josefina but wasn't her, though she had the same eyes. Lulu focused on a photo of the man and woman with four children—three boys and one girl. There were individual photos of the children—the little girl especially had several photos wearing fancy dresses. Chi-Chi ran her hand along the top of a grand piano, gathering dust on her fingers.

"Lola Josefina, fondly nicknamed 'Josette' when she was a little girl, was the apple of her father's eye. Little Josette was born in this house in 1867 a few years after the family moved into their new home. This was the site for grand parties—oh, Don Miguel Villareal loved to throw parties and every sugar landowner and their heirs were invited, including Tomas, the son of Don Vicente Del Rosario. It didn't matter if the Del Rosarios were wealthy. Don Miguel decided no one was good enough for his Josette. She was poised to be debutante of the year when she turned eighteen and it was said her father had planned a trip to Paris as a birthday gift. But that was not to be." Tito Enrico sighed as he leaned against the banister of the grand staircase. "Josette fell out of grace with her father when she eloped with Tomas, just four months shy of her eighteenth birthday."

Lulu caught her parents exchange a look between them. It appeared as if they were sending telepathic messages to each other. Lulu wondered, *Wasn't it typical of girls to marry young in those days*? But on second thought, after realizing Lola Josefina was just a mere three years older than Lulu's own age, marrying young gave her the creeps.

"Don Vicente Del Rosario had other plans for Tomas who was twenty-two. He wanted to send his son to live in Spain where he would marry a full-blooded Spanish girl. So, needless to say, Don Vicente disinherited Tomas, and his younger son, Julio, became the heir."

Lulu and her family pondered on Tito Enrico's story as they admired the décor, the ceilings, the moldings and the walls that had so much history. Dimples fanned herself as Dimar yawned and his eyelids began to droop. Lulu closed her eyes for a moment as she, too, held the banister and imagined what it was like living in the hacienda as a teenager and attending parties with fancy dresses. She imagined what it was like when Josefina and Tomas first set eyes on one another. She imagined what life was like then in Josefina's time—to be seventeen and in love.

"So Tomas and Josefina lived very simply in a smaller, more modest house a few miles from town but were very happy their whole married lives until the revolution began in 1896," Tito Enrico continued, wiping sweat from his forehead with a handkerchief. "Josefina's brothers—against her father's wishes—all fought in the war. Not one of them survived. Tomas, who had been missing, was eventually found wounded and barely alive. He lived long enough to father one more child with Josefina before he died shortly after."

No one spoke for a minute, as everyone stood lost in thought.

"I think, once I knew her story and what she stood for, Lola Josefina, for me, embodied a person who advocated for equality," Tito Enrico said, at last, removing his hand from the banister and leaning against a nearby doorframe. "Although she grew up well-to-do and wore fancy clothes, she chose to live among her people, the masses. It was said she never once complained as she had her eight children and cooked their meals and did their laundry. She never wanted to return to this house again. She had found happiness and a home with Tomas and their children. That was all that mattered."

Chi-Chi, ever the romantic, clapped her hands in delight. "That's such a cool love story," she said hopping lightly, her eyes bright.

Count on her sister to gush over even the sappiest of stories, Lulu thought, even though she did admit that was quite noble of Lola Josefina to leave her luxurious lifestyle behind for love. Clearly, status didn't seem to matter to Lola Josefina. If she were in teenaged Josefina's shoes, Lulu wondered if she could do what her ancestor did.

"Shall we go upstairs?" Tito Enrico said, extending his hand toward the staircase.

As she slowly went up the stairs, an eerily familiar feeling suddenly seized Lulu. It was as if she had been here before. Then, it dawned on her. She *had* been here—in a dream. Though she could vaguely remember every detail, she remembered walking down the dark hallways and walking down this very same staircase she was now ascending. She shook her head. This was all so weird. It was like *déjà vu*.

When she reached the top of the stairs, she noticed Dimples still standing below, holding on to the handrail. Romar was already upstairs with Dimar, Chi-Chi and Tito Enrico. Though she couldn't read the expression on her mother's face, it seemed Dimples was momentarily transported back in time.

"Mom? Are you coming?"

Dimples snapped back to the present. "I'll—I'll be right up. Just a second."

This house seems to have an effect on people, Lulu observed. Although, just exactly what type of effect, she had yet to discover.

Using Tito Enrico's voice as her guide, Lulu wandered down the hallway into a small room—maybe, in her estimation, the smallest room in the house, so far. In one corner of the room sat a wooden antique rocking cradle.

"This was baby Josette's room until, of course, she grew too old for it," said Tito Enrico thoughtfully.

Lulu observed the pensive expression on her uncle's face as he eyed the cradle. She guessed he missed his children and his wife back in the States who didn't want to move back with him to the Philippines when he left the Navy. She wanted to ask him about them, ask whether he was still sad, but she didn't. He probably didn't want to talk about it anyway.

Noticing her mother still hadn't joined them, Lulu wandered off to the hallway, taking quick peeks in the rooms along the way, pausing momentarily to eye the stairs leading to the ominous tower. *Shall I dare go up alone?* But concern for her mother outweighed her morbid curiosity for now. She finally found Dimples sitting on the side of a four-poster bed with marvelous carvings on the posts. Lulu noticed the bedspread's exquisite embroidery and, at closer inspection, she saw vines, leaves and flowers were intricately sewn in the fabric.

"This is awesome, Mom," Lulu could barely utter a whisper. She was so taken with the room and everything about it. "I think I want to get into sewing and crafts now for real."

But Dimples didn't seem to hear her. For a split second, Lulu thought her mother didn't even know she was in the room. She sat so quietly still.

Lulu turned her attention to a huge, wooden dresser with a mirror and admired its carvings. The armoire was equally exquisite.

"Whatever happened to that girl? Where has she gone? Will she ever come back?"

She turned to find Dimples staring down at one corner as if in a trance. Who was her mother talking about? Lola Josefina?

"Mom! Are you okay?" Lulu started to panic as she shook her mother who stared at her as if just realizing where she was.

Dimples waved her daughter away. "I'm fine, I'm fine. I'm just exhausted. I didn't get much sleep last night."

That makes two of us, Lulu thought to herself. *At least, I'm wide awake. This trip is turning out to be quite intriguing. But Mom seems preoccupied, or worried. Or maybe just tired like she said.*

"Oh, by the way, that's called an *aparador*," Dimples said motioning ahead of her with her pursed lips, acting like nothing weird had just happened.

"What?"

"What you were looking at… It's an *aparador*, a wardrobe cabinet. It's made of a special *kamagong* wood."

Lulu ran her fingers along the intricate carvings. "It's so beautiful. And so is this." She moved toward an elaborate ladies' dresser with a carved wood-framed mirror. "Everything here is beautiful."

"It certainly is," Dimples said, a pensive countenance shadowing her face again as she smoothed her fingers on the delicate bedspread.

"Whoever stayed in this room was probably pampered," said Lulu, taking a seat on a rustic armchair.

Dimples nodded. "She was." Her mother got up suddenly. "I'm going to join the others. Are you coming?"

Lulu sat up inspecting the ceiling. "In a minute."

Once her mother left, Lulu felt an intense rush—a warm sensation she'd get whenever she was alone. And these days, with all the relatives in and out of the Bituin house, solitude was a luxury. Even Romar frowned when Lulu retreated to her bedroom with the door closed.

"What's the deal with closing your door? You live in this house with your family," he said, gruffly. "You're not in solitary confinement."

Sometimes I wish I were, she thought.

But today, she got her wish, if only for a little while, in this grand house, in this grand room. She gravitated toward the window, her eyes drinking in the sight of seemingly endless miles of green landscape beyond on this overcast day. Turning, she headed towards an ornate chest of drawers and peered at small, framed photographs she hadn't noticed before.

The familiar eyes in one photo was that of Lola Josefina, back when she was still Josette—young, vibrant, beautiful. There were other photos of her with her brothers and her parents. Then a familiar, more contemporary photo sat anachronistically out of place along with the other photos. It was a portrait of a very young woman dressed in cap and gown, the kind of photo you'd see in a yearbook. Lulu peered even closer. There was no mistaking those eyes. Her mother.

But what was this photo doing here? She did remember her Mom telling her about having had Lola Josefina sightings of her own in the past. She wondered, aside from being related by blood, what was their connection?

All of a sudden, Lulu felt the presence of someone else in the room. Thinking her Mom had returned, she turned around to face the doorway, but no one stood there. Instead, Lulu felt irresistibly drawn to the dresser mirror and moved toward it. She stood back in shock. Instead of seeing her own reflection, Lola Josefina was staring right at her.

By now, Lulu thought she was used to seeing the ghost. But Lola Josefina had always managed to catch her off guard, and this time, she appeared in the form of her younger self—the way she looked in the photo—the way she looked when she was just seventeen. Instead of appearing in a dowdy, long-sleeved dress, her hair tightly wound in a bun, the ghost now possessed an ethereal, angelic glow. Long thick wavy black hair cascaded down her shoulders, framing a face of youthful innocence—imbuing the face of a girl—Josette in love, Lulu surmised. In previous visits, Lola Josefina would simply stand stoically, a blank expression on her face. This time, with her eyes fixed on Lulu's, Lola Josefina—in the form of Josette—slowly raised her right hand and pointed with her index finger.

Her throat dry, she could hardly speak for a moment as the ghost continued to point. Lulu briefly turned to glance back at the dresser.

"What is it? What are you trying to tell me?" Lulu finally found her voice. She tried hard not to panic lest her family rush over to the room and scare Josefina away.

Hearing Dimar's whimpering echo through the hallway, Lulu took a second to peer through the doorway. By the time she looked back at the mirror, the ghost was gone.

"Are you ready to go? Dimar is starting to act all crazy. I think he finds this place creepy and so do I," Chi-Chi said, entering into the room then suddenly giving it an appreciative once-over. "Wow. Cool room."

"It's more than just cool. It's incredible," Lulu said, a bit annoyed her close encounter with the ghost was cut short and they had to leave. As good-natured as Chi-Chi was, Lulu knew she couldn't confide in her about Lola Josefina. Her sister's show of fear on the night of Tito Enrico's ghost storytelling confirmed that.

"Do we have to leave now?" Lulu turned back at the mirror hoping to spot a trace of the ghost.

"Dad's getting antsy. He's in a foul mood, like he's hungry or something. I guess this is just not his thing. Mom's starting to feel uncomfortable, too."

"Great." Lulu couldn't hide her sarcasm and her disappointment any longer.

"I thought you weren't interested in Filipino culture and history—that you were gaining knowledge just for the pageant," Chi-Chi said.

She could be unapologetically blatant sometimes, Lulu thought about her sister. She merely shrugged off the comment and followed Chi-Chi out of the room. As they proceeded toward the front door, Lulu tried to absorb the interior of the house to store in her mental file cabinet. She decided somehow, someway, she'd be back. It seemed Lola Josefina had a message for her and Lulu was determined to find out what it was.

Back home as Tito Enrico got ready to leave, Lulu hurried toward him. Now was her chance to talk to him privately about Lola Josefina.

"Tito, when do the new owners move in?"

"Move in?" He laughed. "No one's going to move in. Some contractors will work on some major restorations, but definitely, no moving in."

Lulu was confused. She thought her Mom sold the hacienda to a new landowner. "What's going to happen to the place?"

"The new owner decided he wanted to buy the sugar cane fields but didn't want to move into the home because it would cost him more money to renovate it and besides, he was already living in a nice house on the outskirts of town," Tito Enrico explained. "So your Mom decided to donate the house to the Town Historic Preservation Society. She has volunteered as a board member and will help raise funds to preserve and renovate the house. I am a board member, too. We hope to turn it into a museum which will help offset the cost of repairs. Do you want to visit it again? I can take you but you will have to wait a few months, maybe in the summer once phase one of restorations are done."

Lulu pondered on this new information thoughtfully. How nice of Mom to donate the home in the name of historic preservation. Tito Enrico's being a board member also explains his interest in the house, since he wasn't a descendant of Lola Josefina but a cousin from Dimples' mother's side.

Going back to the house was a must. Lola Josefina was trying to show her something and she wasn't going to wait months to find out what. Then, a more exciting idea entered her mind. She could hardly contain herself; she was practically bursting with anticipation.

"Um, Tito," Lulu began, wishing his eventual answer to her question was what she hoped it would be. "Who has the key to the hacienda?"

She also hoped Tito Enrico wouldn't read much into her question and instead interpret it as mere curiosity.

He smiled. "I'm so glad you're interested in the history of the house. We need more young people like you interested in preserving local history. No matter what happens, the house will always be a part of your family's history."

Lulu held her breath as he scratched his head. "Your mother has the key."

Chapter Fourteen

Lulu spent the rest of Saturday figuring out how she could get the key. She couldn't just outright ask her Mom for it, could she? Not with the first phase of renovations set to begin soon and Tito Enrico not willing to take her back there until summer. She had to figure out a way to get the key and get back to the house. There had to be a way.

School on Monday was less painful than the previous Monday mostly because it appeared everyone had moved on from the pageant experience. With only four months to go until the end of the school year in March, Lulu's teachers were gradually shifting to more challenging levels of instruction to get the students ready for college. For her final paper, Lulu decided to write about "The Reasons for Hauntings in Literature" where she planned to explore some hauntings in fictional work from the 19th century. She thought work on the paper would give her the chance to learn more about life during Lola Josefina's time. Maybe even find out a thing or two about her own hauntings, though she doubted she would include that in her paper.

She ran into Niel after school at the Internet café while she was researching for her paper. When he inquired about her research, she shared some initial ideas with him.

"I can help you out with your paper, if you want," he said, sitting a bit close to her, his eyes focusing on the Web site on ghosts she was going over.

"That would be awesome, thanks," Lulu said, facing the computer screen, conscious of his closeness and afraid of what might happen if she so much as turned his way.

After taking a deep breath, she expressed her concern about being seen in public with him and what Nina and her Dad said. Niel shrugged and shook his head.

"They're making a big deal out of nothing. That's such a small town attitude, and I mean no offense, I respect your Dad and everything, but he of all people should know not to listen to an unreliable source."

Lulu nodded. "I agree.'

"I wouldn't worry about it."

And she decided she wouldn't. As Niel gave her tips on which Web sites to browse, she thought about his willingness to help her. Then she thought about the time she told him about her own supernatural occurrences. If anyone would understand, she decided, Niel would.

"Niel."

"Hmm?" With his hand on the mouse, his eyes were fixed on the screen.

"Remember that time we talked about ghosts and my own experiences?"

"Yes, I remember."

"Well." She hesitated. He turned to face her, a curious expression on his face which was mere inches from hers. Momentarily forgetting what she wanted to say, and conscious about meeting his eyes, Lulu focused on his lower facial area where stubbles were beginning to show. His lips were pink and looked moist, she wondered what it would be like if those lips met hers.

"Well, I—I think, I think," she bumbled, "that after all this time, she may be trying to tell me something and not just trying to spook me like I thought."

His eyes widened and she hoped it was with interest and not disbelief. "Hey! That's so cool, Lulu!"

His exuberance actually caused a few heads to turn.

"You think so?" Lulu was no longer afraid of confiding in Niel, afraid of what he might think of her, afraid he'd get turned off by her. Nothing could be worse than falling on stage in front of God and everybody, she thought. At least, she managed to survive that. *And he's still talking to me. It's a good sign.*

"I'm intrigued. Tell me all about it."

So she told him about her family's visit to the hacienda, about Lola Josefina's eloping with her lover and about the ghost appearing to her in the mirror and pointing toward something.

"Wow!" Niel said, as Lulu couldn't help but notice how long his eyelashes were. While she enjoyed their physical closeness, Lulu leaned back in her chair a bit to give them some space, more for her own benefit, than his. She could have easily kissed him and boy, wouldn't that send tongues a-wagging.

"I know, kind of creepy, huh?"

"But in a good way. You're right. The ghost is probably trying to tell you something," said Niel, his eyes dancing with excitement. "So, when do we go?"

Lulu's heart leapt, not just at the prospect of returning to the hacienda, but also at the sound of Niel's "we." "Well, it's like this." She then proceeded to explain that Tito Enrico wanted to wait until after the first phase of renovations but helpfully supplied the information about who had the key in the meantime.

Niel's eyes widened. "You mean your Mom has the key? Why can't you just ask her for it?"

"Because Tito Enrico said no one is to go until summer."

"But that's months away."

"I know." Lulu grumbled, leaning farther back in her chair. "But even if they let me go back, either my Mom or Tito Enrico would be there. I want to go by myself."

Niel peered cautiously at Lulu. She couldn't tell if it was an expression of disappointment. She didn't intentionally mean to leave him out.

"I mean, without my Mom and uncle. And now that I've told you about all this, you're more than welcome to come along since you're so cool about ghosts," she said, happy when Niel's smile returned.

The Internet café started bustling with even more students coming in to use the computers. Niel suggested they log off and go some place where they could talk more.

"I am getting a little hungry, aren't you?" Niel said as they exited the café.

Glancing at her watch, Lulu thought she could probably spare a few minutes. If Niel offered to take her home, she would simply ask him to drop her off some distance from her house and she'd walk the rest of the way in case anyone would see her.

They braved the early evening riotous onslaught of people grocery shopping for dinner, weaving through vendors and shoppers and the maze of the public market. Niel chose a nondescript *panciteria* similar to the one he took her and Chi-Chi to when they first arrived, which, in Lulu's mind, seemed like ages ago. Lulu liked how, despite the boisterous meat vendors across one way and rice and dry goods vendors on the other side, the eatery was tucked away quite inconspicuously. Even the other patrons at the eatery were families with small children or elderly people. Hopefully, no chance of running into someone their age, thought Lulu.

Once their orders were taken, Niel set his hands on the table and eyed her determinedly. "Okay, so we have to come up with a plan to go to the house."

Smiling, Lulu was pleased with his enthusiasm. "First, I have to figure out a way to get the key."

"Where would your Mom keep it?"

"I don't know. Maybe I could ask her casually and hope she doesn't get suspicious. Or I could search her drawers or something. I hope she didn't put it in the safe."

"Do you know what it looks like?"

Lulu tried to recollect the key that Tito Enrico pushed through the keyhole. It was antiquated at best, probably made of brass or copper. She nodded.

"I would recognize it when I see it," she said.

They agreed that once she found the key they would head to the house the very next day before contractors arrived to start work on the house.

"And if they do start work on the house before we get there, let's hope they don't change the lock on us," she pleaded solemnly. It was almost a prayer. She realized just how important it was for her to go back. Lulu was on a mission unlike anything she'd ever encountered.

When the waitress set the plates before them, Lulu closed her eyes and took a whiff of the garlic and soy sauce that wafted from her plate of *pancit*, and thought, she had never been this "Zen" about something as simple as eating before.

"Are you feeling alright?"

Her eyes shot open to read concern on Niel's face.

"I'm fine. I just love how this *pancit* smells and looks," she said, admiring the colorful array of sliced carrots and cut green beans and the golden color of the rice noodles.

"Well, it tastes just as good as it looks and smells. Let's eat!"

They spent the rest of the meal talking about school and for the first time, Niel mentioned about planning to go to the States to continue college. Despite her delicious meal, Lulu momentarily lost her appetite. As she watched Niel talk animatedly about the prospect of joining his relatives in San Francisco, she felt like she was just putting on a smile just for show—to pretend she was happy. Little did he know she would miss him if he left, even if she would most likely go back to the States herself after high school. Life had no guarantees. A lot could change in a year or two. *But why am I so concerned? It's not like he's my boyfriend or anything.*

Trying hard to push aside the thought of Niel's moving to the States, as they exited the eatery, she focused instead on a funny story he was telling about the time when he was in the sixth grade and someone whom he thought was the teacher confidently strode into his co-ed class.

"It turned out, she was a new student," he laughed, as Lulu smiled wanly and strode alongside him. "I mean, she looked so mature, so tall and she had on so much makeup and wasn't wearing a school uniform."

At that point, Lulu decided she wasn't going to worry about the future. She was enjoying her time this moment—now, with Niel and no one was going to take that away from her. She was so absorbed with being in his presence; she bumped into the person in front of her.

Startled, she found Nina's eyes piercing right at her.

"Oh. Hi, Nina," said Niel, uneasily.

Holding a bag of groceries with her backpack over her shoulder, Nina's eyes darted to Lulu then at Niel and back to Lulu again, before scurrying off toward the fruit vendors.

"Oh, God, she's going to tell my Dad she saw us," Lulu said, burying her face in her hands.

"Not if we get to your house first," he said, taking her hand in a move that surprised her. "Let's go!"

Together, they rushed out of the market. Once they emerged from the maze, Lulu wriggled her hand out of his ever so casually. They didn't say a word to each other as she followed him toward a Jeep Wrangler.

"What, no jeepney today?" Lulu said as he helped her to her seat.

"My father decided to give the jeepney to the driver he hired, this way Mang Kelso gets to run his own business," Niel explained, climbing into the driver's seat. "My father said he's making good money abroad anyway and I can continue to drive his Jeep Wrangler which suits me fine."

Just as she requested, Niel dropped her off a few yards from her family compound. Striding towards her house, she prayed Nina didn't tell anyone she saw her with Niel. So she dropped by her cousins' house and found out Nina hadn't yet come home. Upon her arrival home, Lulu also found that her father had returned to Manila.

With concern about being seen with Niel temporarily abated, she focused on the hacienda house key, wishing there was a way she could find its hiding place. That night, while she spent time writing notes for her research paper and reading books she checked out from the library, thoughts about the key kept distracting her.

In fact, the rest of the week passed without incident until Romar came home on a Thursday evening instead of Friday and announced he wanted to fulfill his promise to take Chi-Chi and Lulu shopping in Manila on Saturday. Normally, a trip to the mall would incite every nerve in Lulu's body to dance the jig, but going shopping in the city didn't interest her. She would, however, show her Dad how much she appreciated the kind offering and thought a break from the rustic life in the countryside would do her a little good.

In fact, psyching herself up for quality family time in the city helped her get through another grueling Friday of trigonometry and Tagalog lessons. That night, Lulu lay awake, partly excited about her trip, but entirely excited about going back to the house. She couldn't believe how obsessed she was about the prospect of returning.

Just when she nearly succumbed to sleep, a piercing sound that seemed to be coming from a distance slightly roused her. Despite her heavy, droopy eyelids, Lulu tried to figure out the sound then slowly drifted to sleep. But the sound got louder, this time gradually as if it was next to her ear. This time she could make out the familiar waltz of the ballerina jewelry box. Immediately, she sat up and scanned the room from inside her mosquito net. As the waltz played louder, she scrambled to get out of the net and fumbled with the light switch. No one was in her room, at least, not by sight.

"Lola Josefina?" Lulu said, softly, scanning for traces of the ghost's presence. She even peered at the mirror. No ghostly sighting. She tried a different tactic. "Josette? Are you there, Josette? *Nasaan ka*, Josette?"

Suddenly, the music stopped. Lulu fixed her eyes at her dresser. The jewelry box had disappeared! She was almost certain she had seen it there the last time she stored the chandelier earrings she wore to the pageant. Where was the jewelry box?

Chapter Fifteen

Two hours later, Lulu woke up thanks to the roosters crowing, performing their usual call and response, crack of dawn ritual. Splashing cold water on her face to depuff the eyebags that had formed, Lulu eyed her sleep-deprived visage in the mirror. She couldn't believe a ghost, a being she previously doubted existed, had practically taken over her life. And for what purpose, she was dying to know.

Lulu slept in the rented air-conditioned van throughout the entire hour and a half trip, awakened only by the sound of honking. Suddenly, she left the peaceful, countryside for the chaos that was Manila. She hadn't been to the city since she arrived months ago. She'd forgotten the way drivers whizzed past with utter disregard to traffic lights, signals, oncoming vehicles, road signs and marked lanes. There were buses, jeepneys, tricycles and cars and taxicabs that didn't resemble the cabs back in the States. These cabs were actually regular sedans people would normally drive in except they would have a taxi sign on top.

Romar expertly maneuvered the van, dizzily weaving through several vehicles until they reached a long stretch of highway known as EDSA, site of the historic "People Power" march in the 1980s, an unprecedented movement to oust the dictatorial Marcos administration. Romar related how, as a young high school student, he and several of his classmates formed a "human barricade" in front of soldiers in tanks. Romar told his daughters it was a time of unity and solidarity among Filipinos.

"Daddy, did the soldiers have guns? Weren't you scared?" asked a wide-awake, ever-vigilant Chi-Chi, who was seated in the front seat.

"The soldiers were armed and yes, of course, I was scared," admitted Romar, changing lanes and weaving through traffic. From the backseat, Lulu was impressed at how seasoned a Manila driver her Dad was.

Romar shrugged smiling. "But, you know, we were young and vigilant. It was a peaceful revolution. The nuns and priests came out to join us, armed with rosaries. There was a show of patriotism I hadn't seen in this country in years. I had never been more proud of my people."

They were silent for a while as Lulu presumed her Dad was reliving the times he was a student about her age. Before the time he met her Mom. She closed her eyes and tried to imagine what her parents were like when they were in their teens. Instead, the image of a teenaged Josette popped up in her mind. Josette wearing an elegant dress made of the finest embroidered *piña* fabric. And she was smiling as she reached out to accept a rose that someone was offering her.

A sudden jolt interrupted her thoughts. Had she fallen asleep again? Romar had entered a huge parking garage for an even larger building that seemed to take up three city blocks.

"We're here at the mall, at last," said Romar, happily, as if pleased with playing chauffeur to his daughters for a day.

"Dad, great job on the driving," Lulu said, thinking her Dad would appreciate a compliment for all his efforts. "When I get my license, I would never drive here."

"If you ever attend school in Manila, I wouldn't let you drive. It's too dangerous," he said, as they were getting out of the van. "I'd rather hire a driver for you girls."

There goes my overprotective Dad again, Lulu thought, not wanting to argue and ruin a family day. *Well, I don't intend to stay here past high school anyway*, she assured herself.

It turned out just as Dimples had promised. The mall was indeed impressive, Lulu thought, scanning the entire interior, amazed at how many floors—five in all—there were and how expansive. The center of the mall had a mini amusement park for kids, complete with kiddie rides and looking up at the ceiling, Lulu admired the glass dome that towered over the entire center area. Even the shops were impressive. In addition to the usual American brands, the mall also boasted its share of European name brands as well as Philippine labels. Chi-Chi and Lulu entered one of the local clothing boutiques. Lulu's experienced hands rummaged through racks and racks of clothing—a pretty, eyelet yellow cotton sundress here, a pink, ruffled cotton tank top there.

"These clothes are just as cute as the American name brands, even cuter, I think," observed Chi-Chi, holding up a kelly green mini skirt.

"And way cheaper," Lulu sang out, as she snatched up a mandarin shift dress in her size that another girl put back on the rack.

After liquidating a couple of Philippine clothing shops, the girls decided an early lunch was in order.

"What are you craving?" Romar asked as he and his daughters headed toward the food court.

"Pizza!" the sisters said in unison, looked at each other, and then laughed.

Minutes later, Lulu and Chi-Chi were in pizza heaven.

"Oh, how I missed this," said Chi-Chi, using her index finger to wind up a chewy, long piece of cheese that hung from the end of her pizza.

"It's a nice big slice of home," Lulu said, sighing, momentarily wistful.

Romar blanketed his daughters with assuring eyes. "Well, the Philippines is your new home now, girls. This is your chance to make new memories and cherish them."

It depends on the kind of memories, Lulu thought. Having your skirt ride up and showing your panties on the first day in a new school and falling down in front of an audience during a beauty pageant weren't exactly memories worth cherishing. But, she knew, she had to let these embarrassments go. *Maybe one day I'll look back at them and have a good laugh*, she thought.

"Dad, how about if we stop at a few men's stores?" Chi-Chi offered, wiping her mouth with a napkin.

Dear Chi-Chi, bless her heart, thought Lulu. She should be the first saint canonized while still alive.

Romar smiled and patted her daughter softly on the arm. "Thanks, *anak*, but today is your day—yours and Lulu's. Besides, I'm here in Manila most of the week, you know."

After a few more jaunts to clothing shops and a nice, long, leisurely browse at a mega bookstore, the girls had just about had it with shopping, at least for now. While she enjoyed trying on clothes, shopping at the mall didn't give her the same thrill as it once had. Maybe it was because she and Chi-Chi wore school uniforms most of the time.

She had to admit, though, the shopping kind of took her mind off the mysterious disappearance of her jewelry box. She didn't have time to find it that morning as they practically rushed out of the house after bathing and eating breakfast—Romar not wanting to get caught in the usual weekend city traffic.

On the way home, Lulu stayed awake, looking out the window as they left the chaos that was Manila behind and welcomed back the serenity of the provincial landscape where the air was cooler, fresher. Halfway into their trip back, they made a pit stop at Tagaytay, a hilltop city, several degrees cooler, one that boasted a breathtaking view of the Taal Volcano—located on an island within a lake within an island–the centerpiece of Lake Taal, with the beautiful blue expanse of sea surrounding the vista below.

Wind whipped Lulu's face as she stood admiring the astonishing view down below of the small volcano and the serene lake, and felt at peace for the first time in months.

There was something about the view that moved her in a way she hadn't felt in a while.

Once at home, Chi-Chi and Lulu kissed their Dad on the cheek. He must think he's done the right thing by taking his family to the Philippines, Lulu thought. Still, there's nothing to keep me here, except family, her immediate family, that is. Sure, the Titas and Tito Enrico were all nice enough but, she didn't have a future here. Niel wasn't even going to stay here. But then again, she reminded herself, Niel wasn't her boyfriend. And he probably didn't have feelings for her anyway. And Nina. Nina, she definitely could do without.

Remembering the missing jewelry box, Lulu ran upstairs to her bedroom, tossed her shopping bags on her bed then inspected underneath her bed, inside her closet and drawers for the jewelry box. She ran back downstairs.

"Mom! Mom! Where are you, Mom?"

She whipped from one corner of the house to the other.

"I'm here," Dimples called from the downstairs bathroom where she was bathing Dimar. "What in the world are you frantic about?"

Lulu panted heavily by the door of the bathroom. "Mom, where's my jewelry box?"

Eyes fixed on her daughter, Dimples wiped sweat from her forehead with her arm, as she kneeled by the bathtub. Dimar was happily splashing around his toy trucks in a pail of water.

"You mean the jewelry box you keep cursing at? The one you don't seem to like?" her mother said, eyebrows knitting. "Don't think I don't hear you at night yelling at that jewelry box."

Eyeing her mother incredulously, Lulu said, "Mom! That jewelry box creeps me out. It just pops open for no reason and plays that music and keeps me up at night."

"Oh, maybe it's haunted," Dimples said with a hint of sarcasm in her voice as she shrugged.

"Mom, you're the one who believes in ghosts remember? So, explain to me why the lid keeps popping up?"

Dimples got up to close the lid on the toilet and sat on it. "Sweetie, I don't know. Maybe it's broken. It's old, you know. Remember, your Lolo gave it to me."

"And, might I remind you, *you* gave it to me. Now, where is it?"

Dimples brows furrowed. "Don't talk to me in that demanding tone, young lady. Look, you haven't really shown interest in that jewelry box until now. So, what gives?"

Lulu stood back a bit as she thought of what to say next. "Well, I just wondered where it was, that's all."

With that, Dimar let out a piercing squeal of delight as he splashed water on his already drenched mother. Sighing, Dimples poured water over Dimar with a *tabo* then reached over to grab a towel.

"It's on my dresser table," she said. "You're not really using it that much anyway."

"It's not that I don't appreciate the gift, Mom, but you're probably right, the jewelry box needs a different location. Maybe like some kind of feng shui thing."

Dimples raised her eyebrow as she began to dry Dimar, who threw his toy truck back into the tub.

She didn't really care whether her Mom took the jewelry box back or not, she was just relieved she knew where it was.

So she wasted no time running upstairs to check. Sure enough, there it was, prominently displayed in the center of Dimples' dresser. Lulu magnetically drew toward it, and without really knowing why, her heartbeat increased. Taking a deep breath, she opened the lid. The waltz music played and the ballerina twirled as usual but something else caught her eye. There among the earrings and rings and necklaces. The antique key.

Jumping up and down, Lulu couldn't restrain her joy. She reached out and took it from the box, letting it rest on her palm, inspecting it closely like it was a rare specimen. Then she closed the lid and, with key in hand, left the room. Midway to her own room, she stopped, suddenly faced with a dilemma. Should she take the key now or wait until she told Niel first? Since she didn't know how soon she would get to the house or get in touch with Niel, she thought maybe she should leave the key in the jewelry box, in case her Mom would go hunting for it. But, it wasn't like Dimples needed it anytime soon. Or did she? What were the contractors going to use? A spare key? Lulu shook her head. No. It's an antique house. There were probably no spare keys during the time the house was built, she thought.

She headed back to return the key to the jewelry box, vowing to contact Niel immediately. She'd have to borrow one of the Titas' cell phones without rousing suspicion.

She practically sprinted back to her room in time just as Dimples headed upstairs carrying a towel-wrapped Dimar. But, at least she knew where the key was. She'd return to the old house sooner than she hoped.

That night, Lulu slept a somewhat peaceful sleep. Except the music came to her in a dream she had of Josette in the arms of her young lover, Tomas. They were dancing a waltz, the very same waltz from her jewelry box. They were smiling and looking into each other's eyes. Then, suddenly, Josette was crying, as though she had been slapped. She held her right cheek with her hand. Then Lulu saw her running, in a long white nightgown, Tomas trailing her. They clasped hands. And then…there was darkness.

The next morning, Lulu awoke with her head throbbing. She heard voices coming from downstairs. Her parents' voices, and judging by the tone, they seem to be arguing. Over what? She wondered, getting up slowly. While her parents didn't fight too often, when they did, the tension made Lulu uncomfortable.

Too anxious to bathe, she crept slowly downstairs in time to hear the disagreement. She stood on the other side of a wall that divided the living room from the dining room.

"I don't want her around that boy!" Romar huffed.

She could hear plates being cleared from the table. "You're blowing this all out of proportion, Honey. *Dalaga na ang anak mo.* You'll have to face the fact that your children are growing up."

"Yes, but under my rules as long as they live in my house," he demanded. "That means no dating until she's finished with high school—or college—for that matter. Besides, kids don't date in the provinces and boys are a distraction anyway."

Dimples sighed. "They're not dating, they're just friends. Besides, if ever Niel or any boy wants to court our daughter, he can do so."

"Anyone else except Niel," Romar grumbled.

"He is the sweetest boy!" Dimples said. "Lulu tells me how much he helps with her Tagalog and with Math."

"I bet he does!"

"Romar! You're being ridiculous. *Tama na*! Enough! Don't believe the things Nina tells you. She's being vindictive."

"Who else am I going to believe? My own daughter won't even talk to me."

Lulu heard footsteps then dishes piled into the sink. "You won't listen to her. That's your problem. *Diyos ko*, Romar. She's a teenager, let her have some fun. You do trust her, don't you?"

Romar muttered something inaudible.

"She's not going to end up like Gemma, so don't worry," Dimples said, softly.

Leaning back against the wall—her makeshift refuge—Lulu wondered who Gemma was.

"I don't know about kids these days." A chair pushed back, then footsteps out the door.

When she deemed it was safe to come out from hiding, Lulu slowly made her way to the dining room just as Dimples was gathering up the rest of the dishes, studying her daughter with uncertain eyes.

"I heard, Mom," she said, sitting down. "Looks like Nina told on me again."

"Is it true? Were you really with Niel the other day after school?"

Lulu sighed, grabbing a piece of *pan de sal* and tearing it piece by piece mercilessly. "It's like you said, Mom. We're just friends. Why is it such a big deal? Can't girls and guys hang out? It's so, so backward here."

"Your Dad is just looking out for you, that's all."

"What? Like Niel's some kind of serial killer?"

Dimples shook her head and stepped to a nearby counter to set the dishes down. "No, of course not. But your father has his reasons for being concerned."

"Yeah, just what are those reasons? He likes living in the 19th century?" Lulu laughed sarcastically as her mother seemed to regard her with annoyance. "And Dad acts older for his age. Why is he too strict? It's like we never lived in the States. And, has he forgotten? He was young once too."

"You two need to understand each other. Your Dad is afraid that you'll get pregnant at a very young age like his youngest sister."

Lulu shot her mother an incredulous glare. "Get pregnant? Me? I can't even go out on a date!"

Dimples sighed. "Be serious, Lulu. People don't really date here in the province, at least not until college but even then, boys are expected to call on the girl at home."

"We seem to be living in the Dark Ages," Lulu sighed, and leaned back on her chair, chewing her bread but not really enjoying it. "What should I do, then? Not associate with Niel at all?"

Her mother shrugged. "Maybe when there are other people present."

Lulu slammed her palm down on the table but didn't intend to do it as hard as she did. Dimples glared at her. "I don't need a chaperone, Mom."

Dimples collected the rest of the plates, shuffling her feet to the kitchen sink. "You'll have to talk with your Dad about this."

Nostrils flaring, Lulu felt the blood rise to her temples. "I don't have to. After I finish this school year, I'm going back home."

Dimples turned back slowly. "What was that?"

Lulu gulped nervously but stayed firm. "Once school's over, I'm going home—back home to California. I've had enough. I'm not happy here. And you and Dad—you do want me to be happy, right?"

There was silence for a moment. Lulu twisted the strands of her uncombed hair with her fingers. "You should give this another chance, Lu. You're not being fair."

"*I'm* not being fair—to whom? To you and Dad? What about to myself? I think it was selfish of Dad to just bring us all here in the first place. I've experienced nothing but misery here. I want out!" Even as she said this, Lulu knew that wasn't entirely true.

It was Dimples turn to slam her hand down, this time on the kitchen counter. "You're the one who's not being fair to yourself. You have the opportunity of a lifetime to live and study here, learn more about your culture and make new friends. Not many teens your age have the chance to live abroad."

Lulu rolled her eyes and stood up. "If you want me to have some culture, then send me to Spain or France to live out my teenage years. Don't our ancestral roots go back to Spain anyway?"

As soon as she turned away from her mother, she regretted the words and the tone of voice she used. She hated having her mother bear the brunt of her frustration—the frustration she should be expressing to her Dad, but somehow couldn't, at least not in a way that didn't incite an explosive argument.

She decided she would apologize to her Mom later when she herself cooled down a bit. In the meantime, there was still the plan to try to contact Niel and head out to the mansion. Even though she planned to leave once summer vacation starts, she still had unfinished business to settle with Lola Josefina once and for all.

She didn't want the ghost following her back to the States.

Chapter Sixteen

No more was mentioned about Niel or of Lulu's defiant plan to return to California because Romar had left again for Manila and Lulu had given her mother an apologetic hug and all was well. For now.

To further make good with her mother, Lulu agreed to accompany Dimples to *Misa De Gallo*, literally "Rooster's Mass," otherwise known as the Mass at Dawn in the Philippines, a holiday tradition dating back to Spanish times that takes place early morning before sunrise for sixteen days leading to Christmas. So, on the first morning Lulu had to wake up at 4 a.m., take a tricycle with her Mom to 5 a.m. mass which she barely sat through without nodding off; she regretted making this pact with her mother. But to appease Dimples who thought this was a great way for mother and daughter to bond, she had to give in. The mass was an ordinary service, except that the choir sung Philippine Christmas songs.

And the massive smorgasbord of food spread out on long tables at the parish hall after mass made waking up early worth it. On the tables were *arroz caldo, puto bumbong, bibingka, pan de sal, salabat*—ginger tea to soothe the singers' throats, keeping their voices clear and merry—*siopao, queso de bola*, *Kapeng Barako*, strong coffee from the Batangas province and cacao hot beverages. Lulu wondered whether this breakfast feast was only offered during the holidays. Her mouth started to water.

Just then a tall figure caught her peripheral vision and she turned to her right and met Niel's eyes. He gave her a slight wave as he sauntered toward her then suddenly exited through the back entrance of the parish hall. Lulu observed her mother who was deep in conversation with a few teachers and nuns she knew when Dimples attended Queen of All Saints High School years ago.

After a few minutes, she casually slipped out of the same back exit. Niel was waiting for her under an *santol* fruit tree next to a grotto of the Virgin Mary.

"Hey, I have to make this quick," she greeted him with a smile. "But I'm so glad you're here. I have good news."

She noticed that like her, he was already wearing his school uniform. She intended to do some studying in the library after mass while waiting for school to start. No sense going back home only to commute back to town again.

"Nice to know you can make it up this early," he said, scratching his head and yawning. "I don't know if I can make it all sixteen days. Do you think you will?"

Lulu shrugged, maintaining a firm grip on her bookbag handle. She needed something to hold on to—she was feeling a bit nervous holding this clandestine meeting with Niel. But she was also excited being so close to him under the fruit tree with only the statue of the Virgin Mary as witness. Could that be a good thing?

"My mom has the key in her, I mean, my jewelry box," she said, smiling. "All we have to do now is figure out when to go to the house."

"Well, I have finals this week and a bit more next week but I do want to go soon. How does Thursday after school sound?"

After consulting her mental calendar, Lulu nodded. "Where should we meet?"

"The library and Internet café are too public," Niel said, rubbing his stubbled chin with his thumb and index finger. "How about 4:30 at the coffin shop on Antorcha Street across from the gasoline station? There's a side street there. No one can see us."

At first, Lulu thought she heard him say "coffee shop," but didn't recall seeing one across from the gas station during her regular commute. But she did notice that in the town's main street area leading to the plaza, there were a lot of shops selling coffins of all sizes and styles prominently displayed near the sidewalk. She wondered if the proprietors of those shops did good business. Did "death" sell well in these parts? She shivered.

"Okay. See you there?"

She started to walk away when Niel called her again. "I noticed Nina's not around."

"She's sick today but may attend dawn mass at some point. Anyway, I'm glad she's not here or else this meeting would not be taking place."

Lulu hurried back to rejoin Dimples, who thankfully was still engrossed in conversation with the group of women friends and didn't seem to notice her absence.

"Oh, there you are, *anak*. I want you to meet my former classmates from high school," Dimples said, showcasing her trademark dimples as she probably had when she was Lulu's age.

Later, when Dimples hailed a ride back home, Lulu headed over to the school library, which, to her dismay, wasn't opened yet. She checked her watch. It was only 6:40. So she decided to go to the Internet café, which she knew opened at 6 a.m. for students who wanted to do homework. It's so lame not having your own computer at home, she thought as she entered the café.

After logging on, as expected, the only Stateside e-mail waiting for her was one from Rowena.

"Hi there, Lulu, how did the pageant go? I'm sure you did well. Remember, it's not all about winning. I'm certain you're as popular over there as you were over here, what with your good looks and, of course, the mystique that comes with being raised in the States.

"Don't worry. Your secret about the ghost is safe with me. I won't tell a soul. (Get it! HaHaHa!) Seriously, it really does sound like she could be just a friendly ghost who's out to guide you or something. I wouldn't worry. It's not like you've had any accidents or had anything horrible happen to you, right?"

Lulu paused and thought about the time she fell on stage—all because of Lola Josefina. She decided, at least for now, she wouldn't tell Rowena about that and continued reading the e-mail.

"Did you ever convince your Dad to take you shopping in Manila? What did I tell you about those malls? Aren't they incredible? Better than here in the States, that's for sure. I actually did get to go to the mall here with a few of my new friends—of course, they're not popular but they're talented and smart and busy with extra-curricular activities which I hope to get into. I don't care about popularity as long as I have good friends and good grades. I think I might join the school newspaper next year and maybe the environmental club. Everybody here's into recycling. I'm still historically-challenged, so, like you, I may have to get a tutor! I still have two more years before I can get a driver's license and a job. I can't wait!

"Speaking of which, do you think you'll be staying on there for college? Or will you be coming back here after you graduate high school as you originally planned? Well, thanks for keeping in touch. I've got to study for a big exam tomorrow. Till next time, Rowena."

Lulu couldn't help but think how confident Rowena seemed to be getting and how well adjusted she appeared to be in her new life abroad. Could it be true? Was it easier to adapt to life in America than moving out of the States and living abroad? It sure seemed that way.

Instead of boring, not to mention shocking Rowena with the details of the pageant, Lulu quickly fired back her response only mentioning that, while she hadn't won, she was grateful for the experience. She also mentioned a bit about Lola Josefina but didn't elaborate on the "haunted house" since she had yet to go back there and what if her return trip to the ancestral home didn't yield any results?

Glancing at her watch, Lulu realized it was time to assemble for the dreaded flag ceremony right before classes. The flag ceremony *and* morning prayers. Another reason to skip town, she thought. *What was I doing pledging allegiance to a country I wasn't a citizen of and reciting morning prayers if I wasn't religious?*

The rest of the school day and the subsequent days seemed to drag. *That's usually what happens when you're anticipating something—like returning to a haunted house.* Lulu thought about her Lolo's old house for a second and realized that absolutely, the house was indeed haunted. How exciting! And who better to explore it with than Niel.

The night before their planned house visit, Lulu crept to the master bedroom to retrieve the key while her mother was bathing. As she approached the dresser she suddenly heard a loud shriek. Dimar was at the doorway making funny faces.

"What are you doing here, little guy?" she said, as she carried her brother and placed him on the mat of his little play corner in the room surrounded by his toys.

Then she hurried back to the dresser and lifted the lid of the jewelry box. The familiar waltz played, and the ballerina twirled. But as she ran her fingers through the various pieces of jewelry, her heart sank. The key was gone!

"Oh, my God! Where could it be?" she wailed, staring at herself in the mirror, nearly pleading for Lola Josefina to make an appearance so she could ask for help. She stood there bewildered for a few minutes, trying to figure out what to do, when her mother emerged, wearing a bathrobe, a towel on her head.

Dimples watched as Lulu hyperventilated then cast her eyes at the open jewelry box.

"You never seemed interested in that jewelry box before," Dimples said, shaking her head then removing her towel and whisking it through her damp hair. "I think people realize the value of something when it's no longer theirs."

"But, Mom, you said, you weren't taking it back, just giving it a different location."

"Yes, I did say that," Dimples said, combing her hair and smiling at Dimar who let out a yelp.

"I'm just looking for a necklace to wear tomorrow for school," Lulu said, partly telling the truth. "Necklaces are all the rage now. A lot of girls are wearing all kinds of long chains with neat pendants hanging from them."

"The nuns don't say anything to the girls about the latest fashion?"

Lulu rolled her eyes. "Mom, it's not like they're wearing mini skirts or showing cleavage."

Dimples smiled. "That's true. Well, since you're in search of a necklace," Dimples opened her tote bag and started rummaging through it.

Sighing, Lulu thought she'd just play along and take whatever her mother would offer her even if it wasn't really what she was looking for. Her brows knitted with anguish. How in the world was she going to find that key in less than twenty-four hours before their scheduled trip to the hacienda?

"Why don't you just wear this?"

Her mother dangled a long gold chain in front of her. Lulu's jaw dropped in shock and awe. There it was. The key! Only this time, it was a pendant and looked so grand on a chain as if it belonged there.

"Oh, Mom! It's such a beautiful key—er—pendant!"

"You know what it is, don't you?"

Lulu nodded happily, accepting the gift. She couldn't believe her luck. And just in the nick of time too! Dimples just practically handed her the key and Lulu didn't even have to strain to get it.

Things were looking up.

***

Lulu waited underneath an awning that graced the door to the coffin shop. She felt uneasy standing next to a display of mahogany and bronze and copper caskets. She glanced at her watch. Niel was ten minutes late and she started to doubt whether he would show up—whether this trip would even happen.

"Come on, Niel," she said to herself, eyeing every vehicle that drove past. "We're so close."

She held on to the key attached to the chain she wore around her neck to school that day and smiled remembering the compliments she received. It was nice to hear favorable comments from her classmates about her for a change. What's more, wearing the chain didn't clash with the scapular students were required to wear over their uniform shirt collars. Scapulars were like Girl Scout badges back home—they had to be earned and signified one's indoctrination into the school. A sign she was fully accepted by her peers. Lulu wore hers like a badge of honor.

Just then Niel approached from around the corner.

"Sorry, I'm late. That final exam I took in economics nearly made my head explode," he said, taking her hand. "Let's go. My jeep is parked in the alley."

They walked in silence for a few seconds until Lulu started pulling her hand away ever so gently. They glanced at one another for a second. It wasn't that she didn't want him to hold her hand—in fact, it felt good. But she didn't want to risk being seen holding hands with a guy, and not just any guy—with Niel, at least while she still lived under the same roof as her Dad in the Philippines. Holding a guy's hand in the States was one thing, holding a guy's hand in provincial Philippines, where it seemed everyone in town knew each other and watched your every move was another matter entirely.

She chatted excitedly about the house and about thinking the key had disappeared only to materialize in its new life as a necklace pendant.

"I saw that," Niel said, glancing over to her with a wink as he drove. "Great necklace."

"Thanks."

When Niel pulled the jeep into the tree-lined dirt road leading to the hacienda, Lulu's heart pounded in frenzy as she anticipated what lay ahead. She took off the necklace, holding the key to unlock the door, taking a deep breath. When the latch clicked, her heart leapt. It was indeed *the* key! Upon entering, she noticed someone had come and placed covers over the furniture apparently to protect them from the upcoming restorations project.

"Wow," Niel whispered as he drunk in the sight of the parlor room and the grand staircase illuminated by the glow of the setting sun. Lulu followed him as he slowly wandered through the parlor, his eyes fixed on the statues of the saints, admiring the furniture and closely inspecting the carvings on the wood. Although it was nice exploring the house again with Niel, she was anxious to head upstairs to Josette's room and inspect the dresser for clues.

"Josette."

Lulu swung around to see whose echoing voice whispered in her ear. Niel, who had uncovered the grand piano and was lightly touching its ivory keys, was the only one in the room with her. The voice sounded like that of a young man's.

"This is a really neat house," said Niel, covering up the piano again.

"Niel, why don't we take a look at the dresser upstairs?"

He raised his eyebrows. "Oh yeah, that's right. It's where the ghost was pointing at something."

Together they ascended the stairs, Lulu practically racing Niel up there. They traversed down the long hallway finally reaching Josette's room. To Lulu's relief, it remained exactly just as she had left it. No furniture was moved around or taken out.

She immediately went straight to the dresser and looked into the mirror trying to remember Lola Josefina's reflection, the movement of her hand, as if pointing towards something. Lulu closed her eyes, mentally willing the spirit to move her. Taking a deep breath, she opened the first drawer she saw and rifled through old lace scarves and handkerchiefs. Nothing that seemed worthy of an apparent message.

"Find anything?" Niel said, making eye contact with Lulu through the mirror. She stared back, half admiring his reflection and half figuring out what to do next. She opened the top drawer next to the one she had already opened and found an antique mirror, hairbrush and comb and other hair adornments. Still, nothing. With the drive of an obsessive beast, Lulu continued rifling through drawer after drawer, finding old articles of clothing and sleepwear but nothing that was sending an obvious message.

"Oh, God, Lola Josefina, what are you trying to show me?" Lulu said, after shutting the bottom drawer of the antique armoire.

She stood up as Niel scratched his head. They both sat down on the bed and surveyed the room—their eyes cataloguing the drapes, the tapestry on the walls, the carvings on the wooden bedposts—anything that would provide some clue.

"What are all those old clothes still doing in there anyway?" Niel wondered.

"Well, they're thinking of turning this house into a historical museum so they probably left the clothes there for show and tell," Lulu said, running her fingers on the bedspread lace.

Niel's eyebrows furrowed. "But wasn't this house lived in for a while by some other family—descendants of Josefina?"

Lulu thought about that. She didn't know much about who lived in the house after Josefina's father died and thought that her own Lolo Rogelio, Dimples father, had lived there for a while until his wife died.

"I'm not so clear on this house's history after Josette left," she said. "Maybe someone put the old clothes back in the drawers to give this place a more authentic feel for what it was like back then. But there's nothing in those drawers that speaks to me. It's not like I was overcome by some kind of strong vibe while holding any of those clothes."

"Well, there has to be a reason why the ghost had pointed downward," Niel said. He got up and searched under the dresser. Then he removed each drawer from the dresser and peered underneath each one then shook his head.

Lulu sighed in frustration. "What do we do now? This is like a frustrating game and one I'm getting tired of playing."

Niel moved toward Lulu and placed his hands on her shoulders. "Don't worry. We'll figure it out. We've gotten this far. Don't give up."

They looked at each other for a few seconds. Lulu saw as Niel's eyes lowered slightly, as if he was focusing his attention on her lips, which she subsequently moistened nervously with her tongue. *Was he going to kiss me?* She wondered, closing her eyes.

Suddenly, a young man's face, not Niel's, flashed before her. The face was handsome and olive-toned, his hair dark and wavy. He lowered his face gently toward her. She could feel his breath on her ear.

"Josette."

Lulu's eyes flew open. Niel was still there, his hands still on her shoulders.

"Are you okay?" he asked.

"I'm feeling a bit dizzy," she said.

"Do you want to lie down?"

Not wanting him to release her from his hold, Lulu shook her head.

"You won't fall," Niel whispered. "I got you. You won't go through this alone."

She smiled at his comforting words, the gentleness in his eyes. What would she do if he kissed her? She no longer wanted to wonder if it would ever happen—she wanted to find out now.

But he dropped his hands to his sides and she reluctantly moved away from him towards the door.

"We can still wander around the house a bit more, if you want," she said, holding the doorframe for support. The image of the young man's face still on her mind.

Niel shook his head. "I can see it another time. You're obviously not comfortable being around here."

"Well, part of me wants to stay a while to see if we can come up with something."

"My theory is, if Josefina wants to send you a message, she'll find some other way to do it which may mean not necessarily coming out here. Ghosts can appear anywhere, you know?"

Lulu nodded. "I know. And apparently they can appear in any form. Whenever she does show up now, it's usually in the form of her teenage self. That makes me wonder—why?"

"Not sure why." He got up and followed her out of the room. They made their way back down the long hallway and down the creaky stairs. "But all will reveal itself in time."

They spent the drive back talking about the details Tito Enrico pointed out the time her family took a tour of the house. Then Niel dropped Lulu off some distance from her family compound.

"I really had a nice time helping you on your ghost adventure," said Niel, as Lulu got ready to hop off the jeep. "I'm sorry we couldn't find anything this time around."

They looked at each other for a few seconds. *I wish I knew what he was really thinking*, she thought. "Thanks for your help."

"See you again, soon?" Niel's eyes appeared hopeful.

Say it, Niel, say what I hope you'll one day say: that you like me and want to spend more time with me and it doesn't matter what anyone thinks.

"I'll be around," she said, getting down and shutting the door.

When she entered the house, Dimples was padding down the stairs carrying a laundry basket.

"What happened to Aling Miling?" Lulu asked, dropping her bookbag on the sofa.

"She's out sick this week," Dimples said, wiping sweat off her forehead with her wrist. "How did you do with the necklace?"

Lulu touched the key gently. "Great! It was a hit."

Dimples smiled. "You never know. That key may bring you good luck."

"Uh, Mom. Don't you want it back?"

Her mother shrugged. "Hang on to it for a while. But don't lose it. If I feel like wearing it, I'll let you know."

Lulu watched as her mother took off, carrying the laundry, then turned toward the kitchen for a snack. Finally, her mother was treating her like a young adult and not a child. That's progress, she thought.

"Oh, Lu, don't leave your bookbag in the living room," Dimples called out from the back door. "I can't always pick up after you."

Lulu rolled her eyes as she picked up her bag. *So much for progress.*

***

Friday finally came only this was no ordinary Friday. Not only was it the last day before Christmas vacation, it was the day when the principal was expected to post a list of students and their respective class sections for next school year. With only three more months to go before the end of the school year, school staff was already gearing up for next year. They wanted to plan in advance who would be placed where and how many books to order and other administrative business.

"What's the use of those stupid lists," Jolie said, as the girls sat together for lunch. "They're just going to place the same people in the same sections anyway. I won't even check the list. I know which section I'll be in next year."

"Not necessarily," countered Aprilyn, as she wiped the soda spill from the table. Aprilyn had announced that, while she ordinarily didn't drink soda, the last day of school before Christmas vacation was a good enough celebratory reason to drink it. "Some people have been known to be transferred, even midyear."

"Yeah, unless you become rich overnight or if someone discovers you have some hidden pedigree, you don't stand a chance," said Jolie, slurping her coconut water from a straw.

Lulu decided to stay out of the conversation, preferring instead to concentrate on constructing sentences in Tagalog.

"Okay, listen. Am I saying this right? '*Maraming salamat sa tulong mo*,' she said, reading from her notebook.

"Hmm. You're saying 'Thanks for your help,'" said Aprilyn. "That sounds about right. Who are you thanking and for what?"

"She's thanking Niel for helping her with her Tagalog and Math homework," Jolie said, shoving Lulu playfully in the arm.

And for helping me with my ghost hauntings in literature research paper and, of course, with the ghost hunt, and for being so nice to me, but she wasn't going to share that with the girls. Some things were not meant for broadcasting.

"Hi there, Lulu."

Lulu tore her focus away from her notes to see Tessa Martinez and her clique parading by. One of the girls who she'd seen on campus, but who had never acknowledged Lulu's existence, actually waved to her.

"See you around." And the girls ambled by as Aprilyn and Jolie looked at each other, their jaws almost dropping to the floor.

"What on earth was that all about?" Jolie said, pushing aside her coconut water carton as if it carried the plague.

Lulu shrugged, watching Tessa and her friends gliding away. "That was weird."

Although the "A-Listers" were never friendly toward her, they weren't exactly unfriendly either, Lulu observed. She did notice that occasionally Tessa did smile at her in the halls between classes and once in the girls' bathroom as they were both checking themselves out in the mirror. Maybe they weren't as snooty as Aprilyn and Jolie pegged them out to be. Maybe Tessa and her friends were just misunderstood. Lulu tried to think how people perceived her when she was popular at her old school. Did they think she was a snob?

Lulu then thought about Rowena and how calm and neutral she seemed to be. Rowena didn't seem impressed or unimpressed with popular girls—she didn't seem intimidated by Lulu, Sara and Kellie and seemed to hold her own in their presence, from what Lulu remembered of her early encounter with Rowena.

And, who's been there for her all this time? She hadn't heard from Sara and Kellie for months. Who was she going to live with when she moved back to the States after the school year?

As Lulu, Aprilyn and Jolie walked back to their class after lunch, they encountered a crowd gathering in front of the high school girls' department bulletin board in the courtyard.

"The section lists for next year," Jolie said, dryly. "I'm going back to class."

"You're not even going to check where you'll be placed?" Lulu said, as more girls were pushing and shoving their way past them toward the bulletin boards.

Jolie shook her head and scurried away.

Eyes half-shuttered, Aprilyn studied Lulu closely before taking her hand. "Come on. I'll go check with you. Let's bulldoze our way through this crowd."

Amid squeals, groans, sighs and nods of expected resignation, Lulu thought this scene resembled the day after cheerleading tryouts back in the States. Only here, who did and who didn't make "the cut" affected everyone. Once they finally made their way to the front, Lulu was overwhelmed by all the names and the lists as girls continued to shout in glee or despair, some, like Jolie, shrugging their shoulders in apparent indifference.

Someone clutched Lulu's sleeve and she turned to see Aprilyn staring at her incredulously.

"What? Did you make it? Are you an A-Lister now?" Lulu said.

Aprilyn's mouth was agape but she didn't speak. Lulu searched for their names on the dreaded list. Finally, her eyes rested on her name. There it was, in alphabetical order. Luwalhati Bituin. Fourth-year high school. Section A.

Lulu didn't know how to react. Numbness seemed to envelop her followed by a surge of awkwardness. She didn't quite know what to say. Aprilyn shoved her way out of the crowds as Lulu followed her. She reached out and grabbed Aprilyn's arm.

"That's okay, that's okay," said Aprilyn, her eyes avoiding Lulu's concerned ones. "You're where you're supposed to be."

Then she hoofed it, leaving Lulu standing there, uncertain. *Am I in shock? Wasn't this expected? Didn't I deserve this?*

Chapter Seventeen

The rest of the afternoon, before school was officially dismissed, was an awkward one at best. It turned out Lulu was the only one "promoted" to Section A, so rather than receive congratulations from her current classmates, they simply ignored her. Everyone, that is, except Nina.

After the last teacher had left for the day and the girls were packing up their belongings signaling the official start of holiday vacation, Nina, it seemed, couldn't wait to pounce like a tiger anxious to attack its prey.

"So, someone here thinks she's better than us." Without turning, Lulu knew who was sneering from behind.

"Nina, why didn't you get into Section A?" asked one of her classmates. "Aren't you Lulu's cousin?"

"I'm a poor relation," announced Nina, her voice laced with mock self-pity. "Looks like the school administrators discovered Lulu is a Villareal *and* a Del Rosario, practically royalty in these parts," she said, referring to the prominent families Lulu was connected to. "That I am not."

Despite Nina's over exaggerated comment, this much was true, Lulu thought, as even if Nina was a cousin on her mother's side, she wasn't a Villareal because Nina was a relative on Dimples' mother's "less fortunate" side of the family, and not on Dimples' well-born father's side. Lulu admitted she didn't know much about her family's background. To her—rich or poor—they were just her grandparents. In her life back in the States, it didn't matter, but apparently, now it does. Apparently, the discovery of Lulu's Spanish lineage mattered more than her Stateside upbringing. Such was the effect of a "good name," Aprilyn once told her.

On their way out, Lulu tried to catch up with Aprilyn and Jolie.

"Hey, we still have the rest of the school year when we get back from vacation," Lulu said.

"You sure you still want to spend time with us?" Jolie said, clutching her backpack, not meeting Lulu's eyes.

"Don't even bother, there's no point," Aprilyn said, holding Jolie's arm as if preventing her from crossing over to unchartered territory. "You see, Lulu, you don't really consider us your friends. We were just filling in until you find your *real* friends." She and Jolie exchanged glances. "We always knew that and we didn't expect you'd stick around."

Lulu shook her head. "That's not fair. You don't really know me at all. I do appreciate both of you for making me feel welcome."

Aprilyn opened her mouth as if to say something, but Jolie's tug of her arm stopped her.

"And now, our job is done," Jolie said, spinning on her heels, urging Aprilyn along. "Enjoy your vacation."

Lulu stood there at the top of the second floor of the building staring after the girls. She slowly made her own way down the stairs as some girls shoved past her, no doubt in their haste to start their vacations. Or was the shoving deliberate? Lulu wondered as she held on to the rail trying to retain her balance. A magnetic pull caused her to see Nina eyeing her, with thin lips in a long, straight line.

As she strode alone outside the campus and into the basilica courtyard, Lulu decided to head to the Internet café to e-mail Rowena. She needed a sounding board, even if it was on cyberspace. Vacation time was supposed to be a happy time and she got into Section A, so why didn't she feel happy?

"Lulu!"

She turned around, expecting to see Aprilyn or Jolie. Instead, Tessa and her coterie strolled up to her.

"Congrats on making it to our class for next year," Tessa cooed, twisting her long necklace chain around her index finger.

"Thanks." For the first time, Lulu was intimidated in the presence of popular girls. She casually regarded the girls in Tessa's group: a light brown hair and fair skinned, tall and thin one with freckles who appeared to be of Chinese descent, an olive-skinned Spanish *mestisa* with long, thick black hair and long eyelashes, and a girl with a creamy complexion who had a pretty smile and striking doe-like eyes behind her rectangular, tortoise-shell "librarian" glasses.

"Oh, this is Precious, Lucky, and Musette," said Tessa, her hair shining under the afternoon sun. "We want to invite you to an after Christmas-before New Year beach party."

"A beach party? In the middle of December?" Lulu suddenly felt conscious of how silly her comment sounded.

"Of course!" laughed Tessa. "This is the Philippines, remember? We're tropical here. We go to beaches all year round. Except, of course, during typhoon season, and that's not until next year."

Tessa gave the details of the picnic which, turns out, was on a beach not far from where Lulu lived.

"Oh and there's going to be boys there," said freckle-nosed Lucky, as the girls squealed, held hands and hopped lightly in glee.

"Yes!" Tessa gushed, looking dreamy-eyed all of a sudden. Could she be thinking of Niel, Lulu wondered.

"Will you come?" The girls appraised Lulu, acknowledging her existence as they waited for her response.

As she scanned their faces for signs of authentic interest, for the first time since discovering she was placed in Section A, Lulu smiled.

"Of course," she said, trying to sound as light-hearted as Tessa.

She did deserve this. It was what she was waiting for. This was her future.

***

After attending *Misa de Gallo* with her mother and seeing Nina there, Lulu opted out of attending the next few remaining days. Niel attended a few times but they didn't chat, only nodded at each other from across the church or parish hall, careful not to make any obvious contact under Nina's hawk-eye observance.

Towards the last few days of mass at dawn, Lulu was getting exhausted from waking up early. Why should she when she didn't see Tessa or any of her friends there? It's not like attending early morning mass guaranteed her a spot in Tessa's class or in Tessa's social circle, for that matter. She was already in! Lulu leaped with delight as she reminded herself, getting up at a more acceptable hour of 9:30 rather than 4:30 in the morning, brushing her teeth and washing her face with more gusto than usual.

"What are you so happy about?" Chi-Chi said, folding her just-laundered clothes in the sala.

Lulu stopped whistling, putting down the black leather shoe she was polishing. She was getting her school uniform ready, even if they were still on Christmas break. She couldn't wait to go back to school and finish the last three months of the school year. Knowing she would be in Section A the next school year somehow made going back to school more exciting, more meaningful.

"So you got into Section A for your senior year in high school, big deal," Chi-Chi said.

"You got into Section A, too," said Lulu. Chi-Chi would be starting high school next year at the ripe young of age of 13—bypassing seventh and eighth grades. "You're not excited?"

Chi-Chi shrugged. "I guess. But you seem happy. I thought you weren't planning on sticking around here. Mom said you were putting up a stink about leaving after this school year. But where would you go? Who would you live with in the States?"

Lulu smiled, tossing her long tresses. "I've already thought that through. I'm not going back, at least, not just yet. I've decided I'll stick around through the rest of high school then go back for college."

"Does becoming an 'A-Lister' have anything to do with your decision?"

"Maybe."

"What about your friends—Aprilyn and Jolie?"

"What about them?"

"Are you still going to hang out?"

Lulu shrugged. "I don't know." She picked up her shoe and briskly started polishing it again. "You have to realize, Chi, that high school is such a transitory period in your life. It goes by so quickly. Look at me, I'm nearly done. You have to make the most of the experience."

Chi-Chi sighed, folding some cotton blouses with care. "Yeah, but you only get one chance at high school and you want to do it right."

"Exactly."

"This means you want to make sure your friends are your true friends and reflect who you really are. You love hanging around them no matter what, right?"

The sisters exchanged glances before Lulu continued her polishing.

"I think your shoes are as shiny as they can be, Lu," Chi-Chi said.

Lulu gathered her shoes, polish, brush and cloth, putting the cleaning supplies in a bag. "You're right. High school's going to be such fun. You'll see."

***

On Christmas Eve, as Lulu's family was getting ready to attend Midnight Mass, Lulu overheard her father talk to her Mom about how relieved he was that Lulu decided to forego "that going-back-to-the-States rubbish" as he called it.

Seems like Chi-Chi told Dimples before Lulu got a chance to talk to her mother about her decision. She decided that since it would be hard for her to be on her own if she was to return to the States, if things got worse at her provincial school, she could at least see about attending high school in Manila, find out what the experience was like. But that would mean living with her Dad, whose work was in Manila most of the time and Lulu didn't know if that option was ideal now that she was growing up. Section A or not, she couldn't wait until high school was over.

But being an "A-Lister" meant she was going to finish high school in style. She couldn't wait until Christmas was over and couldn't wait until the beach party.

"You're not going to wear a two-piece bathing suit and most certainly not a bikini," said Dimples, when she told her mother about the invitation. "You want to give your Dad a heart attack? Remember, you live in a very conservative part of the Philippines."

"So what do I wear then? A turtleneck and jeans?"

"Don't get smart with me, young lady," Dimples said, opening Lulu's drawers and rummaging through them. "Here, wear this nice cotton skirt and T-shirt. You'll be cool and look proper. Wear shorts underneath in case you want to dip in the water."

"You want me to swim in the ocean fully clothed?" Lulu's voice barely squeezed through her constricted vocal cords. *This was insane*, she thought.

The basilica was packed during midnight mass. Even if her family arrived a few minutes before the mass started, all the pews were already full, so they had to stand on one side of the church with other latecomers. Lulu spotted Nina sitting in a pew with Tita Claudia who waved at them with her fan. Again, Lulu had to wonder, how in the world did such a sweet woman like Tita Claudia have such a wench of a daughter as Nina?

Tessa was also there sitting with her parents and brother in the front of the church. Niel attended with Cyril and Madonna and their aunt and uncle but Lulu didn't wave or smile in Niel's direction lest she get caught by either Nina or Romar.

Then, there she was again. Lola Josefina. Or at least, someone who bore a resemblance to her. Lulu couldn't be sure as the woman in question stood further toward the front of the church staring straight at her before turning towards the front. The next second, the lights went out and a collective cry erupted from the churchgoers. Seconds later the lights came back on again. The woman was gone. Lulu spent the rest of the mass figuring out why the ghost, if that indeed was Lola Josefina, didn't appear as her younger self. Not that 39, the age Lola Josefina was when she died, was old, but it probably was considered so back in her time, Lulu surmised.

When the family went back home, they gathered with some of the relatives for *Noche Buena*, an after Midnight Mass feast, but Lulu was too preoccupied to eat. She was more excited about the beach picnic and who was going to be there. She was also worried about what lay ahead and what she might discover. Were Niel and Tessa really an item? Did Niel just want to be Lulu's friend?

She realized she was so absorbed with getting into the popular girls' class that she temporarily forgot about Lola

Josefina. Then it hit her. What if Lola Josefina's whole purpose was to help Lulu adjust to her new life in the Philippines by enabling her to become part of the in-crowd?

***

The day of the beach picnic finally arrived and since Lulu hardly slept the night before, she was up at the crack of dawn that morning. Christmas came and went and proved to be a quiet gathering instead of the usual, commercialized, pressured mad dash to the local mall to get everyone gifts. In lieu of exchanged gifts, Dimples bequeathed some family heirlooms she inherited from her ancestors.

"I thought you would appreciate getting something old with a lot of history and value rather than receiving some new trend that would eventually fade," Dimples said as she handed little sachets tied with ribbons to her daughters.

Chi-Chi received a pair of vintage drop pearl earrings that Dimples' mother wore on her wedding day. Lulu opened her sachet and out poured a long gold chain with a porcelain cameo pendant.

"My father, your Lolo, gave this to me when I turned eighteen," Dimples said, tracing the cameo with her index finger tip. "He always gave me something memorable and someday you will both inherit all that he gave me."

Chi-Chi turned to give Dimples a kiss on the cheek. "These are beautiful, Mom. We will take good care of these treasures, won't we, Lu?"

"Of course," Lulu whispered, admiring her new gift that Dimples helped her put on as Lulu held her hair up.

"Mom, did you have a nice eighteenth birthday ball here like I've heard so many girls had," Chi-Chi asked, trying on her new earrings. "Isn't that some kind of tradition?"

Dimples stood in front of Lulu to view the necklace that once adorned her neck. "Yes, I did have a ball and a grand party. It's called a debut." Dimples said the word "*day-boo*," as it's pronounced in the Philippines.

"Did you have it at the old mansion?" Chi-Chi asked.

Silence ensued a bit until Dimples smiled wanly. "As a matter of fact, I did. And it was lovely. I wore a nice dress and I danced in a cotillion."

"What's that?"

"A cotillion is when a bunch of girls wear fancy gowns and dance with guys dressed in tuxes," said Lulu, touching her new pendant.

"Yes, it's something like that," Dimples said. "It's a coming-of-age ball." She looked at her daughters. "A tradition I hope you will both get to experience here."

Lulu bit her lower lip wondering where she'd be when she turns eighteen.

"Did you grow up in that mansion, Mom?" Chi-Chi asked.

Dimples sighed. She turned from her daughters and picked up the little sachets they left on the bed and started pulling on their ribbons. "Yes, I did actually."

"I thought you and Lolo moved out when your mother died," Lulu said.

"No. Your grandfather and I stayed on until," Dimples paused, as if speaking suddenly became laborious. "Until I…Until I moved out."

"To go to college?" Chi-Chi asked.

Dimples regarded Chi-Chi as if uneasy with her daughter's curiosity then nodded. "Um…Yes, that's right. Until I moved away to college." She diverted her eyes elsewhere. "I have to check on your brother now." She left Chi-Chi and Lulu hanging still wanting to know more about their mother and her life at the old mansion and why she never talked about it all these years.

That conversation crossed Lulu's mind the morning of the beach picnic, as she was putting on her obligatory blue cotton A-line skirt and T-shirt. She imagined her Mom going to the beach, perhaps the same beach she was going to, and meeting boys, and maybe it was the same beach where she met her Dad. Maybe Dimples had other suitors besides her Dad. She made a mental note to ask her Mom how her parents really met. Courtship stories used to embarrass Lulu but now that they were here, hearing stories like that of Josette's, actually helped to bring them back to life in a way, Lulu thought.

"Are there going to be chaperones at the beach party?" Chi-Chi asked as she stood in the doorway of Lulu's room.

Lulu shrugged. "God, I hope not. It's not like it's a school party. Can you imagine the nuns on the beach?"

"Wearing their habit?" Chi-Chi laughed. "I think not." She eyed her sister's outfit. "Why aren't you wearing a bathing suit?"

"Because Mom said this is still a conservative neighborhood. The girls wouldn't be wearing bathing suits. I imagine there won't be much swimming. Just a picnic by the beach."

"What is this? The 19th century? You're going to a beach party—of course there will be swimming." Chi-Chi tilted her head to one side. "And bathing suits."

Lulu sighed as she examined her outfit in the full-length mirror nailed to her closet door. "I just don't want to get in trouble—have the 'loose' American girl image, you know."

"But not all American girls are loose. Is that what people think?" Chi-Chi said, her cheeks flushed.

"No, but I think that's what people who live in the provinces think," Lulu said, throwing up her arms and shaking her head as if surrendering to the judgment brigade. "I don't know anymore. My motto: better to be safe than sorry."

From the corner of her eye, Lulu could catch Romar eyeing her outfit as he drove her to the beach which was a few miles from their house. Even though he wasn't facing her, she assumed her outfit met his approval since he didn't protest. They passed a few *bahay kubos*, or Nipa huts made of bamboo elevated by hardwood stilts and set alongside palm trees.

Her stomach started to flutter as Romar drove off the highway into a dirt road leading toward the beach. She really didn't know what to expect and hoped she wouldn't embarrass herself in her first real outside-of-school teen social event since moving here.

"These used to be actual homes where families lived but ever since the volcano erupted, people have been building concrete homes that can withstand Mother Nature," Romar explained, coasting their van toward the seashore. "Now these homes had been moved here to this part of the beach that's become a resort area."

He stopped the van in front of one of the bamboo huts closest to a path that lead to the beach.

Lulu turned to her Dad. "You're just going to drop me off here?"

Romar raised an eyebrow. "Unless you want me to walk over there with you?"

"You're joking, Dad, right?" She kissed Romar quickly on the cheek and opened the passenger door.

"Don't do something you'll be sorry for later. Pick you up here at 5:30," Romar called out just before she shut the door.

Ahead of her, the path could lead to happiness or disappointment, though she couldn't imagine it could be the latter. She had wished her way into the popular group and that way could only lead to happiness, right?

Once she made her way through a grove of tropical trees, she gasped, struck by the sight of the ocean—how the blue sky met the seascape, how the effervescent waves caressed the white sand. The beach was practically deserted, except for a small group of people lounging on mats and blankets. From her vantage point, they seemed to be her group so she walked over. As she neared the people lounging on blankets on the sand, she didn't recognize anyone and they were mostly boys and only two girls. It wasn't that she was shy around boys—that surely wasn't the case as boys used to constantly flock to Lulu—white boys, that is. They considered her to be an exotic enigma: a slender, Asian girl with café au lait skin tone and an unusual last name. Because she didn't join any Filipino youth groups back in the States, she wasn't used to being around a coed group of young Filipinos, called a *barkada.*

"Hi! You must be Lulu. I'm Girlie," said one of the girls who looked anything but—sporting a short spiky 'do, long white T-shirt and loose, knee-length madras shorts, Lulu thought she appeared more like a boy. "Tessa will be here with her friends shortly. We're Cristobal's classmates."

The rest of the group nodded at her as Girlie introduced them but Lulu was dazed. Who was Cristobal? Oh, that's right—Tessa's brother—Tessa's college-aged brother. And these were his friends. Lulu suddenly felt intimidated. She was the only high school student there. To pass time as they sat in a circle eating sandwiches and chatting, she thought they would ask her questions about what it was like growing up in the States. Her classmates in her current section seemed fascinated with her previous life—especially Aprilyn and Jolie and surely Tessa must have told her brother's friends that Lulu was raised abroad. Surely, they must have detected her American accent even though she barely said a thing. Instead, they practically ignored her as they continued their own conversations about school and their instructors and which girls the guys liked and so on.

"*O! Nandito na si Maldito*!" one the guys called out as the other guys chimed in. "*Maldito*!"

Lulu turned to the object of their hollering only to meet a familiar pair of eyes. Niel squinted his eyes, as if he wasn't really sure it was her. He and Cristobal approached the group carrying bags of more food: an assortment of chips, macaroni salad, corn, and fried chicken, reminding Lulu of picnics past.

Wearing shorts and a T-shirt, Niel sat across from Lulu, glancing at her from time to time with an expression of uncertainty; it was hard to believe they spent some time alone together in the grand haunted house recently. Being around his rowdy friends didn't help matters much; she and Niel barely said a word to one another. Lulu was feeling more uncomfortable by the minute as she was definitely in the minority—one of only three girls and the youngest as everyone was at least eighteen or nineteen. Her eyes scanned the beach. When were Tessa and her friends going to show up? Or will they show up? Was this just a ruse to test her? Were Tessa and her friends being mean?

Lulu wished she had a cell phone to call her Dad to pick her up but no such luck. She'd have to ask for one on her fifteenth birthday which wouldn't be until May. Sitting stone-faced, she endured what seemed like another endless hour of college talk and ribbing.

Another fifteen minutes later, Tessa, with her entourage of Precious, Lucky and Musette in tow, arrived. Upon seeing the girls dressed in t-shirts and flowing skirts, Lulu felt relieved—she was appropriately dressed after all. The guys cast admiring looks at the girls, especially Tessa. Lulu even caught Girlie cast Tessa a wink.

"Sorry we're so late guys," Tessa drawled in English sweetly, batting her eyelashes in Niel's direction. "I hope you saved us some fried chicken."

"Yeah, I hope you didn't eat it all up," said Musette, sitting cross-legged next to Cristobal.

"Of course not. We knew you were coming," said Ray, one of the college boys who was practically drooling at Tessa.

"I can't believe you're actually going to eat fried chicken," said another of the college boys. "I thought you girls were watching your figures." Then he and the other guys feasted their eyes on the pretty foursome. *Apparently, the girls weren't the only ones watching their figures.*

"Beauty titleholder notwithstanding," said Precious, kneeling on one of the blankets, her eyes gazing at the spread of food. "Tessa has the right to indulge every now and then. Isn't that right, Tess?"

The new arrivals proceeded to enjoy the food and beverages as a lively banter in Taglish among the group ensued. Lulu picked up bits of the conversation. Something to do with daring each other to see who could swim the longest without getting wrinkly-prune skin. The college boys, who were drinking beer earlier, began to pass bottles of beer, fresh from the cooler, to the girls as a shocked Lulu looked on.

"Oh, Lulu, so nice of you to join us," Tessa cooed as she held a chicken leg in one hand and licked the fingers of her other.

"Did you forget you invited her? She's been here all this time," said Connie, one of the college girls who, by the sound of her impatient tone, seemed to be a tad bit annoyed with Tessa and her friends.

"Well, of course not," Tessa said, waving her chicken leg, then finally tossing it into a garbage bag. "I was just so hungry, that's all." She turned to Lulu. "You're not having a beer?" Tessa surveyed the beverage options. "Damn, who forgot to bring the Margarita mix?"

After a quick glance at Niel, whose curious gaze focused on her, Lulu smiled wanly at Tessa and her friends, grateful for finally being acknowledged but uncomfortable with being asked why she wasn't drinking. *Uh duh, I'm only fourteen. Aren't you guys the same age?* While observing Tessa and her friends, Lulu was taken aback by how indifferent they seemed. But then, she thought, taking a deep breath, all she needed was some time to get to know them better. Whatever it took to be fully accepted into the popular group. Then, a realization suddenly dawned on Lulu—a mere invitation to Tessa's beach party didn't guarantee she'd be one of them.

Finally, Tessa stood up and stretched as if she had been lounging on the beach for days. Lulu caught the guys' eyes widen when Tessa's shirt rose as she stretched to reveal her navel. It seemed Niel wasn't affected at all by this subtle exposure. In fact, Lulu couldn't read his expression at all.

"How about a swim? It's time we make good use of this beach," Tessa suggested. To Lulu's amazement, Tessa whipped off her shirt and slid out of her flowy, pink skirt. She stood in front of the group, in full disclosure—clad in a navy blue bikini with kelly green polka dots. Tessa stood for a second, tilting her face to the sun as she tossed her beautiful, long, silky hair, like the beautiful models did in shampoo commercials, like she was giving everyone a moment to admire her soft, luminous pearly skin. Then, as if on cue, Lucky, Musette and Precious followed suit, revealing their own two-piece versions in emerald green, purple and checkered black and white respectively, although the styles of the three girls' suits weren't quite as sultry and provocative as Tessa's. The boys stood up, staring at the girls as they removed their shirts and to Lulu, it seemed they were trying hard to keep their jaws from dropping on the sand.

"Would someone do the honor of rubbing sunscreen on my back?" Tessa drawled, turning to cast a flirtatious gaze at Niel.

As Girlie raised her hand, Musette pulled Tessa's arm. "C'mon, let's just go. You've already slathered your body with sunscreen." Tessa glared at her friend.

If this scene were taking place on a California beach, with a group of young people over the age of twenty-one, it wouldn't be an issue. But this was happening here in provincial Philippines. If these teenagers were tourists, then it didn't matter. But Tessa and her friends were locals—underage locals. Clearly, that fact didn't seem to matter around here, Lulu thought.

Suddenly, everyone's attention turned to Lulu, who tried her best not to show her shock.

"Aren't you going to join us?" Tessa cocked her head toward the beach.

"Uh, I didn't—I didn't bring—wear a suit," Lulu said, stuffing her hands in her skirt pockets.

"Aww, that's too bad. You're going to miss out," Tessa said, twisting a strand of her long hair around her finger.

"It's your time of the month, right?" Lucky said.

Lucky's bluntness shocked and embarrassed Lulu in front of the boys. But even if it wasn't her time of the month, Lulu nodded sheepishly, and hoped they would buy into that notion and leave her be.

Which they did quite promptly. Lulu watched as the girls ran to the beach screaming as their bodies hit the waves. She watched as the girls squealed when the boys started play-attacking them. A slight rustling to her left startled her.

"Niel, what are you still doing here?"

He reached over and grabbed some chips out of the bag and offered her some. She shook her head violently. She was still embarrassed and now angry she hadn't thought of wearing a swimsuit underneath her clothes.

"What are *you* doing here?" he casually asked. "Not that it isn't nice to see you."

"I was invited. I have the right to be here." Lulu found herself becoming defensive for some reason.

"I didn't say you didn't. But, it's just that…"

"It's just that, what?"

He scratched his head, as if he was unsure what to say, or if he should say it. "These girls aren't really your kind of company."

Lulu's brows furrowed. "What are you trying to say? I'm not popular enough?"

"I didn't say that."

"You should know that I was one of the most popular girls in my school back in the States."

"I didn't doubt that."

"And!" She was on a roll now, her eyes flashing with anger. "I just got into Section A for my senior year. So there!"

He nodded. "Good for you," he said, flatly.

"You know, Niel, you really don't know me at all," Lulu said.

He sighed and nodded. "Okay, fair enough. But I'm trying to get to know you better, if only you'll let me."

Lulu inhaled and exhaled in a huff. "Why don't *you* join your friends swimming?"

"I'm keeping you company."

Lulu flashed him an annoyed glance. "I don't need your company."

Niel put a chip in his mouth and chewed, then whisked his palms together to get rid of the crumbs. He looked at her solemnly, and as he took off his shirt and threw it on the ground revealing a sculpted golden brown chest, a soft gasp escaped Lulu's lips.

"Fine. If that's how you feel. You're a Villareal—descendant of a wealthy landowning dynasty. You don't need me around."

As he made his way toward the waves, Lulu felt a lump growing in her throat. The lump seemed to fester into a mass and she nearly choked first from anger, then from immense guilt. She was mean to Niel and didn't know why. Where did that attitude come from? While she knew that Niel's family wasn't rich, he was Cristobal's good friend and Niel's good looks, intelligence and charm and his association with Cristobal made him popular in his own right. Did he feel he belonged in this group? Even though Lulu was a descendant of a landowner, did that guarantee bragging rights? Automatic acceptance into the popular group? In the end, were Niel and Lulu just a pair of misfits?

Except for the occasional person coming out of the water to grab some snacks or a drink, Lulu spent the next hour sitting by herself watching her schoolmates laughing and frolicking; she felt even more pathetic about not wearing a swimsuit, forfeiting the idea of joining them clad only in her underwear. At this point, she didn't care what her parents thought if she was caught wearing a swimsuit and splashing around with boys. She just wanted to be a normal teenager again. But part of her wished she could ask Niel if he could drive her home. Her throat tightened as she remembered the implausibility of that coming into fruition after their spat.

Despite her first social *faux pas* as an "A-Lister," Lulu thought that she could possibly endure the rest of her high school term now that she was part of the popular group. Or maybe she wasn't?

She heaved a sigh of relief once the group made their way back to dry land and after toweling off, settled onto the towels and blankets and commenced round two of grazing and boozing. Some of the boys began to doze off as the girls chatted about their goals for the New Year. Lulu decided her New Year's resolution was to try to stay afloat in the sea of high school popularity.

While she contributed very little to the conversation, Lulu seemed more at ease as Tessa and her friends included her in the conversation, an act probably bolstered by their beer consumption. She was still stumped as to why they hadn't yet bothered to ask her about her stateside upbringing. The answer came at last—Tessa and her friends had cousins living in Europe, Canada and the United States. Tessa herself had visited the States dozens of times. To them, it wasn't a big deal.

Niel continued to ignore her—or maybe he was hurt by the way she treated him. She couldn't very well apologize, just yet, in front of Tessa and friends.

When the food ran out, the girls stood up and stretched.

"Leaving so soon?" Girlie asked, after chugging her soda.

"We're going shopping in Manila early tomorrow," Tessa said, sizing up Lulu. "Would you like to come with us?"

While Lulu sensed Tessa may consider her fashion-challenged, her heart leaped. "Yes! That'd be great!" She would, of course, have to ask permission. "I'll have to ask my Dad."

"That's fine. Text us if he says it's okay and you could meet us at the town plaza. We can all go in our van. Cristobal will drive," Tessa said, combing her wet hair. "Niel, will you be joining us?"

"I'm not the shopping type," Niel said, his eyes lowered as he sat drawing spirals in the sand with his finger. "Besides, I'll be helping out my Tita at her store."

"Ooo, you're such a boy scout," Tessa cooed.

The group trekked together toward the row of huts where the cars were parked. Tessa and her friends piled into Cristobal's van while the others climbed into Niel's jeep.

Romar was nowhere in sight.

"Are you sure you have a ride?" Girlie asked from the passenger side of Niel's jeep.

"Yes, I think my Dad should be coming soon." Lulu couldn't remember what time Romar said he'd pick her up.

"We'll take you, I'm sure Niel won't mind," Girlie said, winking at Niel who shrugged. He still hadn't made eye contact with Lulu.

"What if my Dad comes? What if he's on his way?"

"We'll flag him down," Ray suggested. "Let's go!"

Catching Tessa's eyes on her, Lulu climbed into the jeep.

"You can sit on Ray's lap, if you want," Girlie said, and the boys, except Niel, laughed as Lulu squeezed herself in the back seat with two of Niel's classmates.

"Where do you live, Lulu?" Girlie asked, leaning toward the backseat area.

"I know where she lives," Niel said, his voice gruff, before Lulu could say anything.

"Oo, been there before have you?" teased Girlie.

Niel ignored her comment as they drove off and conversation switched to planning a trip to a beach resort before school starts. Girlie conversed with Ray and their other friend as Niel and Lulu kept silent. As the wind whipped her face, Lulu caught him eyeing her through the rear view mirror but couldn't read the expression in his eyes.

He stopped the jeep a distance away from the compound just as he had in previous times and after Lulu thanked Niel and said goodbye, the jeep was off. Since she got accepted into Section A, Aprilyn and Jolie barely spoke to her and now…Niel. Did this mean she was in transition? Were Aprilyn, Jolie and Niel only transitory, temporary friends? What about Niel's affiliation with Tessa's brother? Was he just popular by association or by default? Could she still be friends with Aprilyn and Jolie? What did the future hold for her and Niel?

As Lulu approached her house, she noticed her father's van was nowhere in sight.

"Oh, my God! Lulu!" Dimples came running toward her.

Lulu's heart leaped in panic. Had something happened to her father?

"Your father went to go pick you up," Dimples said, twisting a dishtowel in her hands. "How did you get home? Why didn't you wait for him?"

"I didn't see his van so I hitched a ride with some schoolmates," Lulu said, clenching her skirt in her hands.

"Why didn't you wait for him?" Dimples said, worry lines marking her forehead. "I'm going to call his cell phone and tell him you're home."

"See, Mom, this is why I need my own cell phone!" Lulu ran upstairs to change out of her beachwear.

Half an hour later, Lulu, propped on several pillows on her bed reading, heard her father roaring in the sala.

"Lulu!"

Sighing, Lulu put down her book then headed downstairs. Romar didn't even wait until she had both feet planted on the first floor to bombard her with questions.

"Who took you home? Why didn't you wait for me?"

"I didn't know what time you were going to pick me up."

"I said 5:30. You weren't paying attention."

That was true, Lulu admitted. He must have mentioned the time right when she was getting butterflies in her stomach about the picnic and didn't hear him.

"You still haven't told me who took you home?"

"Some people from school?" It was the truth, still she trembled.

"Who drove? In whose car? Was it Niel?"

Lulu could've sworn smoke was coming out of her father's nostrils. She turned to Dimples whose eyes seemed encouraging. Lulu nodded slowly unable to look at her Dad.

"*Diyos mio!* Listen to me—you're not to see that boy ever again!"

Smoke seemed to be billowing from within her own self. "Dad, you don't have to worry about that because Niel doesn't seem to care about me anyway."

Romar glared at Lulu as though she had just slapped him. "Why do you say that? Do you care about this boy?"

Feeling as though her throat twisted into a knot, Lulu couldn't speak. Her father took her silence as her answer.

"You do! You *are* interested in him! He's a good for nothing *kanto* boy, I tell you! He'll use you, Lulu. He'll use you to get to the States. Stay away from him!"

"Now, Romar, they're just friends," Dimples said, patting Romar on the arm, but he brushed her hand away.

"I don't believe that for a second! You see? Lulu couldn't even answer me when I asked her if she liked the boy."

"Of course she likes Niel. What's not to like? He's charming, good looking and a gentleman," Dimples said, calmly. "In case you haven't noticed, Romar, your daughter is growing up to be quite the young lady. She'll be fifteen soon and will be welcoming suitors."

"Not until she's finished with college!" Romar seethed, shaking his head.

"Dad, you can't be serious!" Lulu exclaimed.

"As a matter of fact, after high school, you will go to an all-girls college in Manila where I and a group of nuns can keep a watchful eye on you."

Lulu felt like she'd been just shot in the heart. "But Dad, you promised I would go back home after high school."

"*This* is your home now," Romar sneered, his voice likely booming beyond their living room. "I can't have you gallivanting with just any guy. Who knows if you'll end up pregnant? I can't bear that!"

Tears of anger and hurt welled into Lulu's eyes. "You don't trust me! That's a very serious problem for a father not to trust his daughter. I have done nothing to make you not trust me."

"That's true, Romar," Dimples said. Romar glared at them both.

"I don't appreciate you two ganging up on me—the man of the house—the breadwinner. And as for you, young lady, I don't appreciate you talking to me in that tone of voice. Show some respect!"

The tears tumbled down her cheeks. "Dad, you should show *me* some respect. I'm not a child anymore!"

"You're *my* child! And you need to be watched over and protected for your own good."

"Dad, I won't end up like your sister."

Romar glared at Lulu as if she had struck a knife through his heart. "You!" He caved in closer, his hand lifting. Lulu took a step back, afraid her Dad was about to strike her. Instead he shook his finger in her face. "You should never mention her at all in this house! Ever again, you hear! You are grounded for the rest of the school year, Lulu!"

"Please, stop!" Dimples raised her hands up in prayer.

Lulu gaped at her father as though she didn't recognize the man in front of her. "How can I respect you? You really don't care about me! The only reason why I'm around is for you to control me—the way you couldn't control your sister!"

Romar raised his right hand again and Lulu reeled back in shock. Even though her father's hand had yet to touch her, Lulu held her cheek and felt it burning from the inevitable contact.

"Romar, *Diyos mio! Tama na!* Stop it!" Dimples said clutching Romar's arm, trying to hold him back with both her hands.

Lulu didn't waste an opportunity to flee. She ran out of the house dressed only in her house dress and slippers. Her legs seemed to have a mind of their own, as she didn't know where she was going only that her legs were taking her somewhere. They were taking her straight to Tita Claudia's house.

"*Diyos ko!* What's happened to you?" Tita Claudia said as she led a distraught Lulu to the kitchen where she sat her down.

Lulu related her story about the fight she had with Romar as Tita Claudia made some ginger tea. Next thing Lulu knew, she related to Tita Claudia the argument with her Dad about Niel and even about her Lola Josefina sightings. Suddenly, she remembered Nina maybe lurking around. Her cousin would have more than enough ammunition against her to spread around at school. But Tita Claudia patted her back and shook her head as if she read Lulu's thoughts.

"Nina is at a quilting session with her grandmother and aunts on her father's side," Tita Claudia said. "You're both the same age and you're cousins. You two should get along. But I know Nina's hard to get along with. It's all that anger from her father leaving us when she was young. But it's not an excuse to be rude to you."

"I can handle Nina, Tita Claudia," Lulu said, wiping her eyes with an embroidered handkerchief her aunt gave her. "We may not become the best of friends, but you're right. We're family. We should at least be civil to each other."

Tita Claudia nodded as if satisfied. "Well, now, what about this Lola Josefina? She doesn't scare you?"

Lulu shook her head. "No, not at all. But she's baffling me. I can't really figure out what it is she wants from me. At first, I thought she wanted me to become popular so I could tolerate going to school here, but now…I don't think that's what she wants. I wish I knew."

Tita Claudia scratched her head as she scanned the ceiling. Then her eyes brightened. "You know, Lola Josefina still has one child living—a daughter, Esmeralda, living in town. She's an elderly spinster—never wanted to have anything to do with the hacienda or with Dimples or her father, your Lolo, though he was her great nephew."

Temporarily putting aside her woes with her father, Lulu's face shone. "Oh, Tita Claudia! Do you think we could visit her? Talk to her?"

Tita Claudia sat lost in thought for a second. "Well, she's very old. Don't even know if she's lucid. Even though she was an infant when Lola Josefina left for the States, rumor has it that her older siblings taught her to hate their mother for abandoning them and so they have an intense dislike for their mother's side of the family—that includes your grandfather, your mother and…you too."

"But she doesn't even know me!" Lulu said, hands gesturing her enthusiasm and excitement at the prospect of meeting Lola Josefina's sole living child. "I need to see her!"

"Well, we don't want to upset the old woman. We really don't know what kind of shape she's in."

"Who's been taking care of her all these years?"

"When her siblings died, her relatives on her father's side have been caring for her," Tita Claudia said, pausing to sip her tea. "I do remember seeing her attending mass when she was still stronger as I was growing up. She used to teach at your high school and I heard she was strict though she was never my teacher. She retired just when I started high school and your mother was still in elementary."

"So she and my Mom never had any contact?"

Tita Claudia shook her head. "None that I'm aware of. You can ask your mother. Esmeralda's the only direct link to Lola Josefina but I'm not sure she could tell us much since she was a mere infant when her mother died."

Try as she could, Lulu couldn't shake the idea of wanting to meet Esmeralda, wanting to speak to her. But what if Tita Claudia was right? What good could come out of meeting the now elderly woman who spent her entire life hating her own mother for abandoning her?

***

Lulu and her father ignored each other the next couple of days. She was still mad at her father for saying those awful things—for not trusting her, for comparing her to his estranged younger sister. She didn't know how he was feeling and, for the moment at least, she didn't care.

On New Year's Eve, Dimples and the Titas prepared a feast at the Bituin house. Even though Nina was there helping with the chopping of vegetables, Lulu stayed clear of her, preferring to read a few magazines in the dining room where she was still within earshot and had a birdseye view of the kitchen.

"*Bakit hindi tumutulong ang princesa?*" Lulu heard Nina, as she sliced onions for the chicken adobo. Lulu knew Nina intended for her to hear and understand her comment, too.

"You don't mean Lulu?" asked Tita Claudia, washing green beans and carrots. "Don't talk about your cousin that way."

"We're fine. There's enough of us preparing food as it is," said Tita Clara, seasoning the *bangus* which she was preparing to fry.

"I'll help with the dishes!" Lulu called out.

Hours later, Tito Enrico joined the Titas and Lulu's family for dinner. Since there were too many of them to fit around the dining room table, the feast, consisting of *pancit bihon, lumpia, fried bangus, chicken adobo*, garlic fried rice, steamed rice and *gulaman* and *bibingka* for desert, was served buffet style.

After dinner, the Titas and Lulu hurriedly washed dishes. Tita Diding wiped the metal lids from the pots and pans and handed a few lids, pans and wooden spoons to Lulu and Chi-Chi who watched her with puzzled faces.

"For banging in the New Year," Tita Diding smiled.

Then together, metal lids in tow, Lulu and her relatives headed toward the front of the family compound where several people from the neighborhood were gathered around a man playing folk music on a guitar. Lulu searched her surroundings, hoping to steal a glimpse of Niel but couldn't venture too far away from Romar's watchful eyes. Niel was probably off celebrating the New Year at the town plaza or some beach resort complete with a spectacular fireworks display. A pang of jealousy struck her as she imagined Tessa and Niel possibly snuggling as they spend a romantic New Year's Eve together. She shook her head violently as if to erase that horrid image from her mind.

Amid the anticipated chatter among the crowd and the guitarist playing celebratory music, Lulu stood with her family as they waited for the countdown to New Year. Suddenly, the chatter ceased, and the only kind of music Lulu could hear was the familiar waltz from her jewelry box.

It was as though all around her, everything was occurring in slow motion to the rhythm of the waltz—people jumping up and down beating and clanging pots and pans with smiles on their faces, the guitarist strumming a folksy tune with his fingers. And in the middle of all the hoopla stood Lola Josefina—seen only by Lulu—the ghost staring at her and nodding, as though giving Lulu a sign to proceed with whatever it was she had in mind.

And what she had in mind was finding Esmeralda. But what would she say to her?

Chapter Eighteen

New Year's Eve came and went and soon the current school session would resume again then, in just a few mere months, the school year would be over by March. Lulu partly wished it was her final year at school already—she couldn't wait to begin her year as an "A-Lister." But if her unlucky streak continued—Aprilyn, Jolie and Niel not wanting anything to do with her and she and her father at odds—she wasn't sure if being part of the popular group was worth all the trouble.

On the first day back at school after the Christmas holiday, the reception of Lulu's current class was split—there were those who regarded her with renewed reverence, like she was some sort of celebrity—and those who shunned her either because they didn't think they were "in her league" or were seemingly unimpressed with her status as a Stateside girl who also happened to be a descendant of a wealthy deceased landowner.

"I don't really see what the big deal is," Lulu overheard one of Nina's friends say in between classes. "It's not like their family still owns the hacienda."

"It's the prestige," said one of the other friends. "You know, like being a Kennedy. It doesn't matter if you've done drugs or gotten in trouble with the law. Once a Kennedy, always a Kennedy. She's a descendant of the Villareal and Del Rosario families and obviously, that's what got her in. Even if the Del Rosarios cut off their only son and heir who happened to be Lulu's great-great grandfather, I guess, that still makes her kind of a blue blood in this area."

Lulu was expecting a snide remark from Nina but surprisingly none came. And it came as no shock to Lulu that the girls knew about the Kennedys; it seemed Filipinos here had always been fascinated with anything American celebrities did. She spent lunch in the library since Aprilyn and Jolie didn't invite her to join them and she surely wasn't going to invite herself for fear she'd get snubbed. Surprisingly—or maybe not surprisingly, Tessa and her entourage had opted out of showing up for school on the first day back so lunching with them wasn't an option. She'd heard through the school grapevine that Tessa and her friends were rumored to have overstayed their welcome at a popular beach resort north of Manila.

Lulu was rewarded, however, with a brief glimpse of Niel as he was walking past the library. She happened to be staring out the window as she sat ostensibly studying her Tagalog lessons but in reality daydreaming of Niel. If he weren't walking alongside Girlie, Lulu would have run out to greet him taking a risk he would probably ignore her. But somehow, deep within her, Lulu knew Niel wasn't like that at all. He was hurt. She had hurt him—making him feel like, now that she was an "A-Lister," he didn't seem to fit in her world anymore.

In theory, as an "A-Lister," she could have her pick of any "A-List" guy she wanted. But the options so far—Ray, Cristobal and friends—weren't quite impressive—and that was only the college list. She had yet to canvas the high school Section A guys. But she wasn't interested. A-Lister or not, all she wanted was Niel. And she was dying to know whether he cared for her just as much.

Suddenly, Niel turned to face the window Lulu was staring out of and she froze. She looked down at her notebook, her heart pounding wildly, as her peripheral vision caught him entering the library. She figured he didn't see her as he walked past her sitting in a chair near the window. Her heart continued to thump as though it might burst out of her chest as she flipped through pages and pages of notes. Glancing up, she didn't see any sign of Niel. He ignored her for sure, she thought bitterly, and she deserved it.

Hot tears welled in her eyes as she lowered her head again pretending to read her notes. But she couldn't ignore the tears that spilled onto the page nor could she ignore the realization she could be falling for Niel—a fact that seemed more important than being part of Tessa's group. Could that be true? She truly missed the times they spent together—whether at the Internet café, enjoying a meal at the outdoor market, or exploring the haunted house. Aside from her romantic interest in Niel, these past few months, he was the closest friend she's ever had.

She was grateful for one thing—the fact that Niel was at school meant he wasn't at some resort with Tessa. Or maybe he had been with her, but sensible Niel decided he didn't want to miss the first day back to class. Lulu sighed. Her feelings for Niel were driving her crazy. Wouldn't it be easier to just forget him and move on?

"Lulu."

She didn't want to look up at first, thinking she'd just imagined his voice saying her name. But when he sat down across from her, she knew he was for real.

Quickly, she brushed away any traces of dampness from her eyes.

"Are you okay?" Niel said. Lulu thought he looked handsome wearing a light jacket over his uniform white shirt and grey pants.

She nodded.

"Any ghost sightings recently?" He rewarded her with a slight smile.

Inwardly, her heart did a pirouette. *He's forgiven me!*

She told him about seeing Lola Josefina and hearing the waltz music during New Year's Eve and about Esmeralda and the old woman's distancing herself from Lulu's family.

"We definitely have to talk with her!" Niel said too enthusiastically, forgetting they were in the library, as heads turned in their direction.

Lulu's heart leapt. "I'm glad you agree with me." She was hopeful things between Niel and her would turn out fine.

"Why wouldn't I think it was a good idea?"

Lulu's mind raced. Was this a trick question, one she had to carefully answer? "Well, because Esmeralda may not want anything to do with us."

"Psssh," Niel said, brushing off her comment. "She's elderly. I don't mean to sound cold, but the fact is: her days are numbered. I bet if you and your Mom—her long lost family members—came to visit, she wouldn't turn you away. She'd be a fool if she did."

"I hope you're right," Lulu said, more grateful that Niel wasn't turning her away.

"So, that said, why else wouldn't I think going to talk with Esmeralda was a good idea?"

Lulu and Niel eyed each other silently—the unspoken words cutting through the thick air like a knife. Evidently, he needed to clear the air.

"Because I thought that, after the beach picnic," Lulu paused, averting her gaze for a second before meeting his eyes again, "I thought that you wouldn't want to have anything to do with me."

He examined her, as if studying a rare specimen, then smiled as if he chanced upon an elusive discovery. "Ever since our trip to the haunted house, I've been obsessing about what it was that Lola Josefina kept directing you to in the dresser. And I can't seem to get that off my mind."

"Me, too," Lulu said, remembering how fun it was to explore the mansion with him—remembering what it was like being alone with him.

"But that's not the only thing that's been on my mind."

As his head lowered, peeking at her through his long, thick lashes, immediate guilt surged into Lulu's bloodstream which threatened to burst the levee of regret if she didn't get the words out soon enough.

"I know and I'm sorry."

Niel looked up puzzled. "For what?"

"What else? For being such a jerk at the picnic."

His searching eyes glazed over her face. "Oh, that. I'm over it. Besides, I know that wasn't really you."

"It wasn't? I had told you how being popular was important to me, more than anything else and you didn't think that was shallow?"

He shrugged, then leaned forward until his face was just a short distance from where she sat. "I don't care whether you were popular back at your old school or not or who your ancestors were. I just happened to think the girl I've gotten to know these past few months, well—she's pretty cool."

Lulu smiled, in spite of herself, as she leaned back to absorb his compliment.

"Now about that other thing that's been on my mind," he said, his eyes flickering, his grin devilish. "I doubt this is really the place or the time to say this but—what the heck, there's no time like the present, right?"

"Or the past, if you take into account Lola Josefina," she teased, wanting to brush the strand of hair from his forehead. "So, what else has been on your mind?"

"You."

It was just one word—he said it quite simply, naturally still the word oozed with ambiguity. She sat there speechless. Waiting.

"You've been on my mind." Niel's words now seemed to flow, as if he had been anxious to unleash them. After glancing down shyly, he faced her. "The fact is I…I really, really like you…Glory Star." He winked.

She smiled at his literal translation of her name.

Pursing her lips and not minding what people said about how provincial girls should conduct themselves properly during courtship because this wasn't a typical courtship and they were in a library and not in her family's house accompanied by a chaperone, Lulu responded unabashedly. "I really, really like you, too."

As they smiled at each other, amid the students reading and browsing through the library shelves, Lulu heard a long and distinctive sigh, feminine, but not her own.

Could that be Lola Josefina, her "fairy godmother," or Josette, her teen angel's way of telling Lulu, she heartily approves?

***

They had to meet clandestinely and carefully, with so many eyes and ears all around them, dodging his classmates or her classmates through the maze that was *palengke*, when they wanted to eat lunch together or simply spend time together. With Lulu being grounded for the rest of the year, she wondered whether that also meant not being able to get her own cell phone. There was one person she longed to tell about Niel—her first real romance. Her mother. Sure Lulu's had innocent, steady boyfriends in middle school and high school before, but nothing really serious. Even Stellan, who once seemed to be a serious contender for Lulu's heart was now practically nonexistent. The huge crush she had on Stellan seemed like ages ago—so, too, was the friendship she shared with Kellie and Sara. Not that that world didn't exist—it still did, but she was no longer a part of it.

As Lulu was padding up the stairs at her home, she heard humming and thought at first it was Lola Josefina. But it was Dimples and the humming was coming from the master bedroom. Dimples was sitting on the floor, old photos strewn around her.

"Still working on putting those photos in order?" Lulu said, sitting cross-legged next to her mother.

"I've been putting it off long enough." Dimples sighed as she picked up a photo of her teenaged self standing next to her smiling father. Lulu turned to see tears rolling softly down Dimples' cheeks.

"Oh, Mom," she said, putting her arm around Dimples' shoulder. "I know how much you still miss Lolo."

"You don't know just how much," Dimples said, sniffling, placing the photo into a slot in the album on her lap. Blinking at Lulu, she made an effort to smile, patting her daughter on the knee. "So how are you doing? Just a couple more months of school left—I bet you're relieved."

Lulu smiled. "Actually, I think I'm finally getting the hang of it."

Dimples leaned back in mock shock. "What is this I hear? Could it be that you're beginning to like it here?"

"Well, yeah, a bit." Lulu glanced sheepishly at her mother who gave her a knowing look that seemed like she knew there was more where that was coming from. "Well…like a lot."

"What made you change your mind? After that awful argument with your Dad, I thought you'd force us to buy you a plane ticket to go back to the States."

Lulu sighed. "You know, Mom, the thought did cross my mind." She scanned the random assemblage of photos on the floor: Dimples wearing her school uniform. Dimples and her father dressed in elegant evening attire. Dimples wearing an evening gown and on her head rested a tiara. Lulu picked up that picture.

"That was me as Reina Elena during the Santacruzan." Dimples said. Lulu nodded. She remembered the Titas telling her about the festival honoring the Virgin Mary that took place every May where the town maidens dressed in finery and wore tiaras, each of them representing every Queenship of the Mother of God. Lulu thought that would be a great activity to get involved in. It was a Filipino custom that involved mostly young people.

"Who's the guy?" Lulu pointed to a young man in the photo with Dimples wearing a *Barong Tagalog*, the traditional embroidered men's shirt made of pineapple fibers or *piña*.

"Oh, my cousin," said Dimples. "My father was so strict, all my escorts were male family members. He kept a close, watchful eye on me at all times since I was his only child."

"Did you know Dad yet?"

Dimples smiled, as if remembering a fond memory. "Yes," she said softly. "Maybe one day, the town will pick you to be Reina Elena. It is quite an honor."

"I'm sure it would be."

Her mother nudged Lulu's elbow. "Maybe Niel could be your escort."

She dodged her mother's line of sight, her lips forming a straight line.

"It's not that your Dad doesn't like Niel," Dimples said, smoothing out Lulu's hair with her fingers like she used to when Lulu was a little girl. "He just doesn't like the idea of his daughter growing up, and too fast—that's really it."

As much as she tried to stop the tears from coming, they streamed down her face anyway. "But I like Niel a whole lot."

"And the feeling is mutual—I can tell," Dimples said, as Lulu's eyes widened, mouth agape. "Don't act so shocked. It's pretty obvious, at least to me, and probably to your Dad, too, which is why he's anxious. Your Dad just has to realize you're maturing and falling in love is part of that."

Dimples' soothing voice and comforting words gave Lulu a renewed sense of hope. She caught an expression on her mother's face she remembered seeing back at the mansion when Dimples sat on Josette's bed, lost in thought, maybe thinking about a time way back when.

"Mom, you sound like you're an expert on this," Lulu said, half-jokingly.

Dimples chuckled. "I am."

"You don't think I'm too young to fall in love?"

Her mother shook her head. "You are what you feel. Love is love whether you're fourteen or forty. And there's nothing like the experience of first love."

Drying her eyes with the back of her hand, Lulu sat up straight. "Was Dad your first love?"

Her mother smiled. "Yes, he actually was. We met at a school dance—at Queen of All Saints as a matter of fact, but I was attending school in Manila and showed up at the dance with a friend who went to school here. I begged my father to transfer me to Queen of All Saints and at first he thought it was a good idea and I started attending school here in town. But then your Lolo found out about your Dad. 'Who's Romar Bituin?' my father used to demand. Your Dad never quite measured up to the kind of man your Lolo envisioned me marrying."

"What happened then?"

"So then we eloped," Dimples said, scratching her head as if the memory wasn't as memorable in the joyful way in which it was meant. "I was nineteen and already in college but, to your grandfather, I would always be his little girl. Your Dad and I thought that if we got married secretly then told everyone once the deed was done, my father would have no choice but to accept it. But I was wrong."

Looking pensive, Dimples paused for a second as she scanned the array of photos spread out. "Then he disowned me—or at least, that's what he told me before he stopped speaking to me. He just stopped. By this time your Dad and I got working visas and moved to the States."

Lulu eyed her mother before cautiously asking the next question. "Did you and Lolo keep in touch?"

Dimples shook her head slowly. "Not really. Not directly. We would hear news about each other through various relatives who wrote letters or visited the States. Then your grandfather got really sick."

Dimples' voice started to break but she forged on. "You know, I never got to speak to him again before he died. But after his funeral, I read a letter he wrote apologizing to me for his stubborn pride and all those wasted years. He moved out of the hacienda after your Dad and I left for the States. In your grandfather's will, he left the hacienda, the mansion…everything to me."

Lulu patted her mother's back as Dimples wiped her eyes. "He did eventually forgive me, your Lolo did. And, I, of course, forgave him, but…" her voice cracked… "it was too late. We never got a chance to tell each other we were sorry."

Lulu thought about the dream she had months ago about her grandfather, whom she never met, and her mother when she was a little girl on a bicycle. She thought of Lola Josefina whose spirit still lurks among the living. Even though her grandfather's ghost hadn't appeared to Lulu, she knew he was probably making his presence felt in different, subtler ways. Lulu found this theory amusing—this coming from a former skeptic who once didn't believe in ghosts. But, she reminded herself, this was the same girl who once thought being popular was the key to happiness. This *was* the same girl.

"Mom, I'm sure Lolo knows how much you love him," Lulu said, hugging Dimples. "Not even death can take away love."

Dimples looked at her daughter thoughtfully as she smoothed her hair. "How did you get so wise?"

The laughter that followed, Lulu thought, was the antidote to all the pain that Dimples had carried all these years.

"You know, I didn't tell you this at first because I was superstitious," Dimples said. "But when you first told me about seeing Lola Josefina, I thought of history repeating itself."

Lulu scratched her head, brows furrowing. "What do you mean?"

"Well, your Lolo and I lived in the same house as Lola Josefina did and she was the only child, her father's beloved Josette, just as I was my Daddy's girl. We both occupied the same bedroom and we both eloped with men our fathers didn't approve of."

That explained Dimples behavior when their family visited the mansion. "Wow, that's a bizarre coincidence. But why were you worried about Lola Josefina appearing before me?"

Dimples smiled as she flipped through album pages. "It's silly now, but of course then, I was worried when you told me she appeared to you because she did the same thing to me right when I was secretly seeing your Dad."

It all started to make sense, Lulu realized. "So, you thought that maybe Lola Josefina was encouraging me to elope with Niel?"

This comment elicited a laugh from Dimples. "Not really. I didn't think that she would encourage it, but I thought it was a sign of things to come. And frankly, when your Dad started getting worried about how much time you were spending with Niel, so was I, but, of course, I didn't think punishing you was right. I feared your Dad's anger would drive you away."

Lulu had to smile. "You really don't think I'd run off with Niel, do you, Mom?"

Dimples' eyes cast a bit of doubt. "Would you?"

"Of course, not. Mom, I'm only fourteen!"

"Almost fifteen," Dimples said, sighing.

"And we haven't even gotten around to saying the big 'L' word yet," Lulu said, playfully shoving her Mom, like they were old friends.

"Will you say it?"

"After he says it first," Lulu said, picking up a photo of her grandfather looking dashing in his suit, perhaps on his wedding day to Dimples' mother. "A girl's gotta follow some rules."

They shared a laugh again.

"There's no need to rush," Dimples said, patting Lulu's hand. "Take your time and just enjoy the moment."

Nodding, Lulu's eyes blinked as she savored her mother's sage advice. "So, Mom, why do you think that Lola Josefina keeps bugging me?"

Dimples shook her head. "I have no clue."

"Do you think it may have something to do with Esmeralda?"

Her mother dropped the album she was holding, her fingers trembling. "How do you know about her?"

"Tita Claudia told me about her. Did you know her really well?"

Shaking her head, Dimples picked up the album. "Not really. Except that she made life a living hell for my father for many years and I didn't quite know why until I found out that it was all because we were living at the house where her mother, Lola Josefina hadn't lived in until she ran off with her sweetheart."

"I thought Esmeralda didn't want the house?" Lulu said.

"That was the rumor. I think people didn't want to paint an awful portrait of *Doña* Esmeralda Villareal Del Rosario, beloved Spanish teacher at Queen of All Saints. But she and her siblings, when they were alive, fought your grandfather in court for ownership of the hacienda which they wanted to sell to foreign investors. Your Lolo wanted to keep it in the family. He was, of course, one of Esmeralda's nephews and inherited it directly from his father, Mateo—Lola Josefina's only son and heir—your great grandfather. So, by virtue of that lineage, your Lolo won the house."

"Which you didn't want? Why not, Mom? It's such a cool house!"

"But very impractical for our family," Dimples said, gathering up a few photos. "One day, you'll understand. I think it's best to turn it into a historical museum. We found a whole bunch of great stuff."

"You mean besides the antique furniture?"

"Yes! All kinds of clothing from the late 19th century, antique books printed in Europe and a whole bunch of other things," Dimples gushed, standing up. "It was like a treasure hunt."

Dimples opened her closet door to retrieve a cardboard box that she flipped off the lid immediately after setting the box on the bed. She held up several embroidered and lace scarves, handkerchiefs, a sachet filled with necklaces and earrings and hair combs adorned with pearls.

"What are those?" Lulu pointed to a stack of envelopes at the bottom of the box.

"These?" Dimples said gathering the envelopes. "These are letters your Tito Enrico and I recently found stashed in a bottom dresser drawer.

Lulu's heart immediately soared from its dormant state upon hearing the words "dresser drawer."

"Who are the letters from? What did they say?" Lulu asked. As she flipped through the piles, she noticed a few remained unopened. The penmanship was impeccably written in an old-fashioned, long, broad script. The return addresses were all from California and addressed to a Miss Isabella Villareal Del Rosario.

"She was Esmeralda's oldest sister, the one who took care of her siblings when Lola Josefina left for the States," Dimples said, taking out a letter from an already opened envelope. "I can't believe some of these letters were left unread."

Lulu looked over her mother's shoulder at the same handwriting that scrawled across the yellowed pages.

"Even after all my Tagalog lessons, I still can't understand a word," Lulu moaned.

Dimples chuckled. "Don't worry, *anak*. This is such an old fashioned way of writing Tagalog, even I don't know a few words. But, let's see here."

Lulu sat down on the bed as she watched her mother's eyes dart from one side of the page to the other, her lips moving as she silently read.

"Well, what does it say?" Then it dawned on Lulu. Could these letters be the reason why Lola Josefina was pointing toward the dresser drawer?

Dimples sat down next to Lulu and sighed. "It's an apology letter really, probably not the first one Lola Josefina wrote. She said, 'Although the weather is quite lovely here, and I have seen the grandest of buildings, mountains and hills, I still miss home and certainly miss you all. I hope, my darling children, you will one day forgive your mother for leaving you and understand it was all for the best, as I would have never been able to give you the kind of support you needed.'"

Her eyebrows narrowing, Dimples turned to Lulu. "I thought she left to work for some rich, elderly woman so she could send money to her children or save money to bring her children to live with her. That's what I heard."

"From whom, Mom? Only Lola Josefina and Isabella know what really happened. Maybe there's more to Lola Josefina's story, which is why we should talk to Esmeralda. Even though she was still a baby when her mother left, I'm sure she'd heard about everything through her siblings." *Everything that was probably untrue.*

Dimples sighed as she set the letter down. "I don't know, Lulu. Let me think about it for a bit. This trip down memory lane has my mind spinning."

Lulu got up and helped her mother return the antique clothes back in the box.

"Once the restorations on the house are done, these will go back to where they came from," Dimples said, folding one of the lace shawls carefully.

"I'd sure like to know what's in those unopened letters," Lulu said.

Dimples cast curious eyes at her daughter, then gathered the unopened envelopes and held them out to her. "Here. Why don't you open them and read them?"

Lulu eyed her mother suspiciously as she took the stack. "Uh, Mom, I can't read this without a Tagalog translator."

Her mother gave her a sly smile and a wink as she secured the box with the lid. "Well, now, I guess you'll have to call Niel."

As Dimples stored the box back in the closet, Lulu grinned. *I have the coolest Mom in the world. I only wish Esmeralda could one day say the same thing.*

"Mom, I have an idea. How about we try to convince Esmeralda to read the unopened letters?"

***

A few days later, Lulu and Niel shared a "not-so-secret" rendezvous after school at a restaurant where Niel treated Lulu to a good, old-fashioned hamburger. Teens and college students, dressed in their school uniforms, swarmed the eatery where contemporary pop tunes were blasting from a jukebox.

"Wow!" Niel laughed as he watched Lulu devour her burger as he twisted his spaghetti noodles with a fork.

"What?" She said with her mouth full, then wiped her lips as she swallowed her food. "I'm ravenous for hamburger."

He pointed at her food with his fork. "So, how is it?"

She shrugged. The meat had a slightly gamey flavor that didn't quite taste like pure beef. She was grateful, but she had to be honest. "Not bad. But thanks for the treat."

He responded with a smile which was instantly squelched. Lulu watched as Niel's smile slowly turned into a frown. She glanced behind her to see Nina arrive with her friends. After the cousins made eye contact, the group took seats two tables from Lulu and Niel's booth.

"Oh, great," Lulu grumbled. "I don't have an appetite all of a sudden."

Niel glared at Nina. "Don't let her take control of your emotions. Who cares what she thinks? We have your Mom's approval, at least. What could Nina do now?"

Lulu sighed, shoulders deflated. "Tell my Dad."

Putting his fork down, Niel stared at Lulu intently as if to hypnotize her. "Don't let her have power over you. Show her the great, decent person you are."

"But, Niel, I'm supposed to be grounded, remember?"

Niel popped a meatball into his mouth and chewed. "But Nina doesn't know that, does she? Besides, we're sort of on official business—per your Mom's suggestion. I'm your Tagalog tutor, remember? And for today's lesson, we will translate some of Lola Josefina's letters to her children."

As Nina and her friends chatted, their eyes directed Lulu's way, she began to feel queasy. "Could we maybe do that somewhere else? I don't want to get you-know-who all curious about these letters."

Niel wiped his mouth. "Of course."

They finished their meal in silence. Then as Lulu and Niel got up to leave, Lulu felt a sudden force, a courageous rush, coming seemingly out of nowhere. She marched right up to Nina and her comrades.

"Hello Nina and friends," Lulu nodded to them. Training her eyes only on her cousin, she cleared her throat. "I'd like you to know that I intend to go to Sister Principal to file an appeal on your behalf—and mine actually." Pausing only for a second, she caught Nina glowering at her. Around them, students were chattering, perhaps exchanging adventurous experiences from the recent holiday. Niel stood directly behind Lulu. She could only imagine what he was thinking—the bewildered expression on his face.

"For our final year in high school, I wish to request that I be transferred back to Section B and," Lulu took the deepest of breaths, "and that you—you would take my place in Section A."

There she said it. She hadn't planned on saying it—or had she—subconsciously planned this? It seemed, for a moment, the whole restaurant heard those infamous words uttered. Lulu was stunned. *What did I just say? And was it really me talking?*

Nina and her friends seemed equally astonished. Her cousin's jaw was literally suspended, Lulu feared saliva would flow out eventually.

"I—I don't know what to say," Nina finally said. "Are you making fun of me? Are you joking? Are you for real? If this is your idea of a joke, Lulu, it's not funny."

Nina's friends all nodded and murmured in agreement.

"It's not a joke, Nina." Lulu remained as adamant as she hoped she appeared. "I'm dead serious." She turned to quickly glance at Niel, whose mouth was slightly open, his eyes blank.

"You would do that? For me," Nina choked, as if she couldn't believe it herself. She looked at her friends, maybe silently encouraging them to challenge Lulu, maybe asking them to pinch her to make sure she was really awake.

"Well, yes," Lulu said, shifting from one foot to the other. "And, like I said, for me, too. I'm not quite sure I want to be in Section A anymore."

"Why not?" asked one of Nina's friends, with a suspicious, raised eyebrow. "What's in it for you?"

"Nothing," Lulu breathed, inhaling relief like a drug she hadn't had for a long while. "I just feel comfortable where I'm at now is all. And I'll miss the friends I've already made."

Nina sat still her eyes staring straight ahead, as if processing the situation.

"Well," Lulu shrugged. "Just wanted to let you know that's what I intend to do."

And with that, she pivoted away, a still silent Niel following her outside the restaurant. Even with the overcast sky, the damp, sticky air struck their faces outside and as they ambled their way through vendors and shoppers, Niel took her arm gently.

"What was that all about?"

She shrugged and smiled. Around them, cars, trucks and jeepneys whizzed past—the daily afternoon streetscene in full effect.

"I'm not quite so sure myself how the words came out."

"Did you mean what you said?"

"Of course, I did."

"And…no regrets?" He stroked her hand gently—in front of God and everybody, yet she didn't seem to care who was looking.

She shook her head. "I'm feeling rather courageous. We need to seize this opportunity. Who knows, it may not come again."

"What do you want to do?"

"Instead of translating the letters for my sake, let's find Esmeralda soon and read the letters to her directly. She's old. I have this gut feeling Lola Josefina's been desperately trying to tell me all this time to find her daughter—before it's too late."

Niel nodded and without a word, he firmly held her hand as they strolled through the plaza together.

Chapter Nineteen

Before heading home late that afternoon, Lulu and Niel decided to ask around for the address of one Esmeralda Villareal Del Rosario. No one they asked at the market seemed to know. They asked as many jeepney and tricycle drivers as they could thinking maybe they had chauffeured the old woman to doctor's appointments but none of them knew who she was.

"It's likely she's had her own driver to take her to places all these years," Niel surmised as they both strolled along the small businesses on the main street.

Lulu nodded, unwilling to give up the search. But it was getting late so Niel drove her home in time for her to work on finishing her paper on ghost hauntings in literature. She admitted that researching on her paper and her encounters with Lola Josefina helped her understand ghosts more. So much so that she would never again doubt the power of the supernatural.

The following day, Lulu decided to muster the courage to approach her Tagalog teacher, Miss Espinosa, to ask her if she knew about Esmeralda. At seventy-four, Lucia Espinosa, was the oldest instructor at Queen of All Saints where she herself had attended.

After Tagalog class, Lulu rushed out to the hall chasing after Miss Espinosa whom she knew would only respond to her if she addressed her in Tagalog.

"*Excuse po, meron akong itatanong sa inyo*," Lulu said, nervously, not knowing whether she said it right.

Miss Espinosa paused and raised an eyebrow. "*Sige.*"

Lulu took a deep breath then made the plunge. "*Kilala po nyo, Miss, si Esmeralda Villareal Del Rosario?*"

Upon recognizing the name, Miss Espinosa's face softened, the corners of her lips turned up slightly. Lulu's shoulders relaxed a bit.

"*Aba'y, oo,*" Miss Espinosa peered curiously at Lulu. "*Bakit gusto mong malaman ang tungkol sa kanya?*"

Her eyebrows furrowing, Lulu understood that her teacher wanted to know why she asked about Esmeralda. But Lulu just couldn't put the Tagalog words together in response. Peering at Lulu through her horn-rimmed glasses, a waiting Miss Espinosa pursed her lips.

"Okay, you can tell me in English," she said.

Lulu beamed graciously. Now, she couldn't get the words out fast enough. "Oh, I'm so glad I found someone who knows her! My Mom and I—we're related—to Esmeralda Del Rosario. So since she's sort of like a long lost relative, we'd like to find out how to get a hold of her."

"Yes, I remember your mother, Dimples—she was my student." Miss Espinosa grew pensive. "Señorita Del Rosario I remember fondly. She was my Spanish teacher in high school."

"Do you still keep in touch with her?"

"Oh, yes, yes, I do, we've become very good friends through the years." Lulu's heart leapt as she heard those words. "You know, she's got to be more than one hundred years old."

"Oh, Miss Espinosa! If we could visit her soon, that would be great!"

The teacher's smile disappeared. "Well, I'll have to check with her first. She's been living with relatives on her father's side."

Just when Lulu's heart had risen higher than it ever had before, it sank again. "Miss Espinosa, I know about how she's been upset with her mother's side of the family." *My side of the family.*

Miss Espinosa seemed confused. "Yes, about matters that happened a century ago that she was too young to remember, but I don't see any reason why she would be upset with you and your mother." She shook her head. "It was those sisters of hers—they brainwashed her as she was growing up. But they're all gone now."

Hope began to spring within Lulu again. "So, will you please ask her if she'll see us?"

The teacher nodded as she began to shift away.

"*Maraming Salamat*, Miss Espinosa."

Just as Lulu turned to head back to class, the teacher called out to her.

"Your Tagalog is improving, by the way."

Those words put a smile on Lulu's face she doubted wouldn't fade anytime soon.

***

That afternoon, Lulu sat anxiously waiting outside assistant principal Sister Ruth's office. Twisting a handkerchief in her hands, she tried to rehearse what she intended to say. She knew she had to be firm.

"Sister Ruth will see you now," an office assistant said, opening the door for her.

Lulu had to adjust her eyes from the brightness of the hallway to the dark interior of Sister Ruth's office. The shades were drawn and the mahogany table and chairs flooded the room even more with darkness. To top it all off, the nun's black habit flowed like hot lava from where she sat. A view of the nun made Lulu uncomfortable. *Holy behemoth. Wasn't she smoldering wearing that? I would be.*

Sister Ruth motioned Lulu to take a seat. "What is it you wish to talk to me about?"

"About my being placed in Section A, Sister," said Lulu, clearing her throat. "You see, I would like to remain in Section B for the next school year."

The nun gaped at Lulu as if she had just requested to be transferred to Mars. Casting her eyes away, she shuffled the papers in front of her. "I'm afraid that is not possible."

"But, Sister Ruth, I prefer to stay with my friends," Lulu argued, shifting in her chair.

"That is not for you to decide," Sister Ruth's lips tightened in a straight line.

"I really think you shouldn't segregate classes according to social status," Lulu said, a force of courage rising within her again.

"Your opinion is of no importance to us here," the nun said, glaring.

"Of course it isn't—but money and status is, apparently," Lulu said, daring the nun to "demote" her to Section B or even C, or even suspend her. She didn't care at this point. She didn't think anyone had ever said anything about the unspoken "caste" system—till now. Something had to be said. Someone had to speak up against it.

"That will be enough, Lulu," Sister Ruth said, standing up and pointing toward the door.

Lulu stood up slowly trying to will Sister Ruth to face her—face the truth. She couldn't resist one last comment, even though it may put her at risk. "Even though I grew up in the States, I still experienced discrimination based on the color of my skin and the fact that my parents spoke with an accent and being shunned for being me was intolerable. But to face discrimination here, in the country of my parents' birth, among people of the same culture—is despicable."

"You're not being discriminated against," Sister Ruth asserted.

"But others are!"

"Do you wish to be suspended, young lady?"

As she glared at Sister Ruth, she thought of many others like her, and wanted to vomit. "No, I don't. I just wish that everyone be treated equally and fairly." She walked toward the door and placed her hand on the doorknob, then looked back. "But I guess that's too much to ask."

***

Lulu spent the rest of the day quietly sitting at her desk in class studying and reading and keeping to herself. She shared small talk with Aprilyn and Jolie who weren't mad at her but seemed a bit shy around Lulu—as if they weren't quite sure how to act around her anymore. As much as Lulu wanted to spend lunch with them and hang out, she wasn't sure how they'd react—whether they would reject her.

Since the wall facing the hallway on the second floor of their building was actually a wall made entirely of shutters which were now open, Lulu was in clear view of anyone who might pass by. She had to look up every so often when her peripheral vision caught a figure, thinking it may be Sister Ruth about to excuse her from class solely for the purpose of expelling her.

That afternoon, Lulu hurried to the Internet café to check her e-mail and, sure enough, an e-mail from Rowena was waiting for her.

"Hey, how's it going with you over there, Lulu? Just wanted to let you know that I took an editorial test and will be joining the school newspaper as a staff writer next year! I'm so excited! Also, I just found out from my parents that I might be vacationing in the Philippines this coming summer vacation. I'll let you know for sure. That would be awesome if we could get together while I'm there.

"I just want to know if you're okay. It's probably not my place to ask this but I feel I must. After all, I've considered you a friend, even though you're halfway around the world! But I just want to say how sorry I am to hear about Stellan and Sara, considering how much you liked him and all. But wait. I'm actually not really sorry. Because personally, I think Stellan's a jerk and Sara, well, she's not so nice either.

I'm sorry to say that because she's your friend and all that. But I think they deserve each other. You deserve better. Thanks for being so nice to me and for keeping in touch. At first, I thought you were like Sara and Kellie, but now I know that you're not. Sorry for my rambling and hope I didn't offend you. Please keep in touch. Rowena."

Lulu's eyes carefully scanned the computer screen, absorbing each word before going back to the top of the e-mail to reread it. Then she took a deep breath and hit reply.

"Hey Rowena, glad to hear from you again. First off, hearing about Sara and Stellan is news to me because it appears—we're no longer friends. And no, I'm not offended at all by what you said about Sara or Stellan because, frankly, I don't care." It was true, she never felt so relieved. "But thanks for the update. On a happier note, congratulations on joining the newspaper! That's quite an achievement.

"A lot has happened to me since my last e-mail. Where do I begin?" Lulu related her visit to the haunted house with Niel, her getting accepted into the "A-List," as well as suffering the wrath of Sister Ruth. She also told Rowena about her "special friendship" with Niel and her plan to visit Esmeralda.

"I never thought I'd say this, but, I'm actually enjoying it here now and no longer think I'm being punished and 'doing time.' Life is sweet. I only hope I can resolve things with my ghost, speaking of which, she's been kind of low key these days. You'll hear from me again soon. Lulu."

That night, Lulu lay in bed thinking about Lola Josefina and the mission she would fulfill for her. "Lola Josefina, am I on the right path? Do you want me to find Esmeralda, talk to her? Is that what you want me to do? Is that what all this is about?"

Instead, the silence in the darkness amid the trees rustling in the wind replied.

The next day during math class, Sister Ruth's assistant came into the classroom and spoke quietly and briefly to the math teacher whose eyes met Lulu's. Almost immediately, Lulu sat up at her desk, knowing and expecting all along she was being summoned. Every pair of eyes followed Lulu as she sprung from her desk then exited the classroom, trailing after the assistant who was a few steps ahead of her. *I should've grabbed my bookbag…I might never return.*

When she arrived at Sister Ruth's office, she was surprised to see her mother already there, sitting across from the nun's desk.

"Lulu, I was just enlightening your mother about what an opinionated daughter she has," Sister Ruth said, resembling a gigantic lump of coal sitting in her chair, her black robes enveloping her.

Lulu and Dimples exchanged glances. It was hard to read her mother's expression.

"Sister Ruth, I'm sure Lulu didn't mean to offend you," Dimples said, her eyes skimming Lulu who remained standing. "She will speak her mind, even to me."

"Yes, of course, she's a child raised in America where children do not respect their elders," Sister Ruth said, tapping her pen on her desk.

"That is not always the case, Sister Ruth," Dimples said. "My children are good people. My husband and I try our best to raise them to be responsible, decent human beings."

"Then why does your daughter address her superiors so disrespectfully?" Sister Ruth said, leaning back in her chair, glaring at Lulu who was about to say something until she caught an expression in Dimples' eyes that seemed to say: "Don't you dare say a word—Sister Ruth's question was aimed at me."

"Sister Ruth, I have not heard a complaint from any one of her teachers and if what you mean is the manner in which she spoke to you yesterday, then, I believe there was a perfectly logical reason for it."

"A perfectly logical reason for insulting me?" Sister Ruth said, sitting up, her lisp more pronounced, spit bullets firing out of her mouth. "There is no excuse for that."

"I believe my daughter was merely expressing her opinion which she, and everyone on this campus, has a right to do," Dimples said, flashing Lulu a look of encouragement. "I don't chastise my daughter for expressing her feelings as long as she shows some tact."

With her fingers of both hands clasped together over her rotund belly, the nun glared at Lulu. "What do you have to say for yourself, young lady?"

Lulu exchanged glances with her mother who nodded with an expression that seemed to say: "Just give the wench what she wants. You and I both know in our hearts what's true."

"I wish to apologize, Sister Ruth, for being disrespectful," Lulu began, but she wasn't about to give in wholeheartedly, even if it meant forfeiting her chance to enter the gates of heaven. Hmph! Lulu thought, as if Sister Ruth held the golden key. *That'll be the day!*

"But, with all due respect, Sister Ruth, I meant every word I said. I'm only sorry for the way I said it," Lulu said, feeling so liberated she felt she could take over the world one rotund, Catholic nun at a time.

Sister Ruth snorted, her nose twitching, as if she was trying to stifle a sneeze. "Very well. I have heard what you had to say and I don't have to agree with it. Apology accepted." She unclasped her hands and picked up her pen again. "You must know that I will not grant your request to remain in Section B. You are to report to Section A Fourth Year High School class the first day of the next school year. Is that understood?"

While she was happy she wasn't expelled or suspended, she wasn't too thrilled her request had been denied. But she decided, she'd get by, make the most of it.

"Yes, Sister Ruth," Lulu said, softly, her head down.

"Now, if you'll excuse me, I have a school to run," the nun said, waving them off with her pen.

Lulu and Dimples walked out of Sister Ruth's office in silence then waited until they were a safe distance away before turning to each other.

"Bravo in there," Dimples said, giving her daughter a hug.

"You're not mad at me, then?"

"Why would I be? It's about time someone stood up to Sister Ruth," Dimples said. "She was such a pain even when I was a student here."

They laughed.

"You'll do fine in your new class," Dimples said. "I'm not worried."

Lulu shrugged. "Oh, I'm not worried either. I just wanted to take a stand."

Dimples held her daughter by the shoulders. "Listen Lulu. You're trying to fight a system that's been in place since Spanish colonization—it may never change, at least not here in this town. You have to accept that. Doesn't mean you have to agree with it."

"I know. But it still sucks. I wish things could change."

"Even though things haven't changed since I went to school here, and maybe since this school's been in existence, doesn't mean it never will," Dimples said. "You know what I think?"

"What?"

"I know how you said being popular isn't a big deal to you anymore, but I think being in Section A class could give you the power to start changing things. Maybe you can be a role model somehow—by breaking barriers."

Lulu nodded enthusiastically. "Yeah, that sounds possible. I could maybe convince the powers that be to include Section B and C students in more extracurricular activities."

"It's worth a try," Dimples said, smoothing her daughter's hair. "Of course, don't expect drastic changes. You've heard the saying 'Rome wasn't built in a day.'"

Lulu and her mother exchanged hugs before she returned to her class. The room became silent immediately as soon as she stepped back in. Trying not to meet anyone's gazes, Lulu sat in her desk and opened her math book as if nothing happened.

After math class, the girls gathered their belongings and sauntered out to the cafeteria. As she glanced up, her eyes made contact with Nina's before her cousin exited the classroom. Just as Lulu tried to figure out what she'd do for lunch, she felt a hand on her shoulder.

"Lulu."

She faced Aprilyn and Jolie whose facial expressions seemed hopeful.

"Would you like to join us for lunch?" Jolie said, smiling.

"Yeah, we've missed you these past few weeks," Aprilyn said, clutching her lunch bag to her chest, unable to meet Lulu's eyes.

"Sorry, I guess, we've all been busy," Lulu said, grabbing her bookbag. "Sure, I'd love to join you."

Since Lulu forgot her lunch at home, Aprilyn loaned her some money to buy a ham and cheese sandwich and mango juice. They sat together and shared what they did over Christmas vacation.

"I have some news," Jolie said, pouring soy sauce over her leftover *pancit* lunch. "I could be moving to California in two years. My dad petitioned us a while back and finally we're making headway."

"That's great news, I'm sure you're excited to see your Dad again," Lulu said, taking a bite of her sandwich and wiping her lips with a napkin.

"I am. But I'm more nervous about adjusting to life in the States," Jolie said, after chugging her water.

"You'll do fine there, trust me," Lulu said, thinking about how well Rowena seemed to be adjusting.

Hearing boisterous laughter, Lulu turned to see Tessa and her entourage sitting a few tables over. They happened to be watching her and smiled. Before turning back to her friends, Lulu saw Tessa shrug her shoulders and shake her head.

Hmm. Wonder what that was about, Lulu thought.

During Tagalog class, Lulu kept daydreaming about Niel and wondered how he was doing. Except for seeing him and chatting with him briefly on campus, Niel was up-to-his-neck busy with a presentation and a term paper.

After class, Lulu rushed to the bathroom with the intention of returning quickly to chat with Miss Espinosa who, to her dismay, had already left the classroom by the time Lulu got back. But just as she reached her desk, she noticed an envelope wedged between the pages of her Tagalog language textbook. She tore the envelope open.

"Lulu, Miss Esmeralda Del Rosario wishes to see you and your mother. Go to 274 Buena Vista St. here in town. Tomorrow afternoon at around 4. Miss Espinosa."

The note distracted Lulu the rest of the school day so the news that the last period social studies teacher had called in sick rolled out like a welcome mat for Lulu and her classmates. After a quick goodbye to Aprilyn and Jolie, Lulu rushed out to the long sheltered pathway leading to the college building to see if she could catch Niel at study hall.

She scaled the corridors of the building, passing by college students huddled over the results of term paper scores.

"Lulu!"

Girlie caught up to her just as Lulu stopped walking. Dressed in a navy blue skirt and white shirt uniform, black pumps on her feet, Girlie's appearance seemed different to Lulu—more "girly" than the casual ensemble she wore on the beach.

"What brings you to our neck of da woods?" Girlie grinned. "It's not every day we have high school students wandering in our halls."

"I'm looking for Niel," Lulu said, eyeing the flyers on a bulletin board. There was a flyer for drama club, one for Spanish tutors and several for those wanting help with term papers.

Just then a door opened and Niel exited with a statuesque college girl who was giggling at some remark he made. Then the girl reached up and kissed Niel on the cheek, his face reddening as he and Lulu made eye contact.

Girlie looked over at Lulu who turned away.

"I don't think coming here was such a good idea," Lulu said, scurrying away.

"Lulu, wait!"

He caught her arm and she swung around trying to catch her breath.

"It's not what you think," Niel explained. "I was tutoring her in Spanish."

"Oh, I bet you were," Lulu began, angrily.

"She was just thanking me."

"Oh, I bet she was," Lulu said, biting her lip to prevent herself from saying anything worse. *Lulu listen to the guy*, she told herself. "So, who was she? An ex-girlfriend or something?"

Niel scratched his head, eyes cast down. "Or something."

Lulu peered at Niel as if he was a stranger. "Meaning?"

"Look, Lulu, she was a girl I was courting before—before…us," Niel said, shifting the books he was holding from one hand to the other.

Hot blood rose to her head. "Niel, there is no…*us*."

He appeared confused. "There isn't?"

She shook her head. "There's just you and then there's just…me."

"I don't get it."

"I mean, it's not like we're boyfriend and girlfriend or anything like that," she said, the words tumbling haphazardly. "It's not like we agreed on anything."

He took a deep breath. "Wait, back up. I'm confused. I thought we said, we like each other."

"We do. We did—say that," Lulu said, wondering what on earth was making her act so irrationally and so erratically. Why was she so jealous? This was her first real relationship—she didn't know how to act.

"Look, Lulu, I'm sorry you saw what you saw."

Her eyes blinked rapidly. "Well, what could you do? Tell her not to kiss you?"

"It just happened suddenly, without warning. You saw for yourself. Okay, why are we even discussing this? It's not a big deal."

"Maybe it's not to you." She said, veering away, fuming. Niel trailed behind her.

"You know that's nice of you to come visit me at my building," he called out to her.

She stopped and faced him. "I went looking for you because I wanted to share my good news. I know where Esmeralda lives. And she wants me to visit her tomorrow."

Niel's eyes brightened. "That's great news! So, what time should we meet?"

With her nose up in the air, Lulu shook her head. "This is strictly a family matter. Besides, Esmeralda specifically asked to see me and my mother."

He lowered his head in disappointment. "Oh, I understand." He nodded as if to assure himself that he really did understand.

"See you," she said and quickened her pace.

He continued to follow her. "Lulu, what's this about? I said I was sorry."

"I heard," she said, her head slightly turned. "Please stop following me."

Against her better judgment, and rather than sort things through, Lulu bolted away from the college building as fast as she could. Then when she reached the church she looked back and saw him standing at the school entrance staring after her.

Boys couldn't be trusted. Even though Stellan wasn't her boyfriend, Lulu really thought he was interested in her. She thought she didn't care about Stellan and Sara being together, but it seemed she probably cared more than she thought. Or maybe because she was plain scared. Navigating her way in a relationship was uncharted territory.

I've had crushes, puppy loves and innocent going steady boyfriends before, but this thing with Niel—this is for real, she thought. *Am I being paranoid? Or just insanely jealous?*

That evening over dinner, Dimples and Lulu were excited about their visit with Esmeralda the next day. Chi-Chi wanted to come along, but Dimples said to wait a bit since the elderly woman was only expecting the two of them.

"It's such a relief and a huge step for her to accept us into her home, Chi-Chi," Dimples said, passing a dish of vegetable stew to her. "We don't want to overwhelm the old lady."

"Okay," Chi-Chi said, pouring more of the stew's gravy on her rice. "But I hope there will be a next time."

"I hope so, too," Dimples said, appearing suddenly pensive. She turned to Lulu. "What did Niel think about the upcoming visit?"

Lulu shrugged.

"What does that mean?" Dimples said. "You two getting along?"

Sighing, Lulu put her fork and spoon down. "Mom, I think I blew it."

"What?"

"Niel and I got into a disagreement," Lulu didn't want to utter the words "fight" or "argument" mainly because she felt she was solely to blame. She told her Mom and Chi-Chi about seeing Niel being kissed by a girl he once liked.

"But does he still like her?" Chi-Chi asked, helping herself to a skewer of grilled eggplant.

"I don't know," Lulu said, pushing her plate aside. The fact that the earlier incident between her and Niel was senseless, unnecessary and all her doing, was sinking in. "I don't think so."

"So, I don't understand. What's the problem?" Chi-Chi asked.

"Well, she may like him still," Lulu said. "After all, she was the one who kissed him."

"*Anak*, let's say she does like him, okay," Dimples said, wiping Dimar's mouth with a napkin. He whimpered and pushed the napkin away and reached for a piece of chicken on his plate then put it in his mouth smearing barbecue sauce all over it again. "If he doesn't like her, then it's not a big deal. The important thing is how he feels about you."

Lulu sat quietly, unable to face her mother and sister.

"Let's face it," Dimples continued, putting Dimar down then wiping her own hands. "People are going to be attracted to other people—it's a fact of life—whether the person is with someone else or not. It's okay to be attracted to people. But it's not okay to act upon an attraction when you're committed to someone."

"That would be cheating," Chi-Chi said. "I don't think Niel is the kind who would cheat."

"We're not boyfriend and girlfriend anyway," Lulu said, tossing her napkin on the table. She'd given up on dinner once her appetite went A.W.O.L.

"You're not?" Dimples said. "Is it because of your Dad? Don't worry about him, Lulu. I'll handle him."

"Well, yes I am worried about what Dad will think but I really don't know what Niel and I are," Lulu said. "We still haven't really confirmed anything."

"I think it's understood, don't you?" Dimples said. "You two have what we called a 'Mutual Understanding' back when your Dad and I were teenagers. It's understood you like each other."

"But it doesn't mean people are really together," Lulu countered. This conversation was really exhausting. She couldn't very well just ask Niel, could she?

"What is it you want, *Ate?* A ring?" Chi-Chi asked, finishing up her meal. Lulu sized up her sister with envy and annoyance. Nothing seemed to faze her younger sister.

"No!" Lulu said. "Chi-Chi, wait till you become a teenager."

Chi-Chi smiled. "I'm almost there. I'll be thirteen in four months remember?"

And I'll be fifteen in three months, Lulu thought to herself. *I need to get a grip on this relationship thing.*

"*Anak*, why don't you just relax and have fun," Dimples said, smoothing Lulu's hair gently. "You're taking this way too seriously. Stop analyzing everything and trying to figure it all out. Just go with the flow."

Dimples words caressed her fears and lulled Lulu to sleep as she repeated them like a mantra. Just relax and have fun. Stop analyzing everything. Just go with the flow.

Chapter Twenty

The next day at school, Lulu thanked Miss Espinosa profusely.

"Don't thank me," the teacher said, the creases on her forehead pronouncing. "Thank Miss Del Rosario. She's becoming crabbier in her old age. But she's still smart as a whip."

Dimples met Lulu after school and together they strode toward the town's main street and turned on Buena Vista Street which was lined with traditional, ancestral *Bahay na bato* homes originating from the Spanish Colonial period. For Lulu, it was like stepping into the past. The houses had continuous moldings, capiz windows and stylized pillars. As they strolled, admiring the façades of the houses, Dimples explained that this particular part of the neighborhood, with its weathered awnings, archways and roofs, still boasted of a grander time and lifestyle among the aristocrats living in Batangas during the Spanish era.

A young woman dressed in a duster whom Lulu assumed was Esmeralda's caretaker graciously welcomed Dimples and Lulu. The smell of cooked fished wafted through the house which had a stone ground floor and wooden second floor with capiz shell windows. The caretaker, who introduced herself as Felita, led them upstairs to the wooded area of the house. Lulu was surprised that Esmeralda was staying at the second level and doubly curious about the elderly woman's health. She and Dimples gasped as an astonishing room adorned with furniture made of narra and molave wood under a grand archway greeted them. Just like the hacienda, there were miniature porcelain and wooden *santos*, posted at every corner and in the middle of the room, old photos in silver-plated brass frames were prominently displayed. Near the opened capiz windows sat a baby grand piano.

Sitting near one of the open windows, on a sturdy armchair made of narra and rattan caneweave, sat an elderly woman—Esmeralda. With her platinum hair tied in a bun that sat on the nape of her neck, Esmeralda was dressed in an ivory cotton housedress with lace on the short sleeves. She wore pink fleece slippers on her feet, her pale, bony ankles exposed. Her veined hands with long fingers rested on a threadbare celery green blanket on her lap. Esmeralda didn't seem to notice them as they slowly approached—her attention captured perhaps by the rare appearance these days of a blue sky and clouds.

The elderly woman turned slowly as Dimples greeted her softly, gently raising Esmeralda's hand to her forehead as a sign of respect. Lulu took her mother's lead, but her own fingers trembled as she drew the old, frail hand to her forehead. Esmeralda's eyes shone like dark, shiny, black beads, captivating Lulu who observed the lines, creases and wrinkles splayed across the woman's weathered face like roads and hills on a map of an area whose terrain was rough and ragged.

Lulu noticed Esmeralda observing Dimples intently. Without a word, the woman reached her hand out, beckoning Dimples to come toward her. Dimples knelt in front of Esmeralda who stared at her for a moment then ran her spidery fingers across Dimples face. Dimples smiled as tears welled in her eyes.

"Tita Esmeralda, it's so nice to meet you," Dimples said in Tagalog, taking the old woman's hands in hers. "My daughter, Lulu, and I are very grateful that you have agreed to meet with us."

Esmeralda turned to Lulu, who sat in a chair diagonally from her elderly relative.

"Good seeing you as well," the old woman responded in Tagalog, her voice hoarse.

"She doesn't get many visitors much anymore as she's outlived most of her relatives on her father's and mother's side and those still living just send money for her medicine and essentials," Felita said, gently removing the blanket from Esmeralda's lap.

The old woman glared at her caretaker as she gripped the blanket as if it was the only thing that provided her safety from the unknown. Taking a cue, Felita stepped away to sit in a chair nearby, picked up a basket, needle and thread and started mending a garment—a project she was probably working on before the visitors showed up. The caretaker would look up every now and then to check on her elderly charge.

In Tagalog, Dimples gave an account of her background growing up in the hacienda until she eloped with Romar and moved to the States to raise a family. Lulu absorbed the tales Dimples recounted, her fond memories of parties and events at the hacienda, her schooling in Manila as well as her life as a working mother in the States. As the old woman listened attentively—her eyes glistening at times—Dimples shared her grief over her father's death and wished she had been there at his bedside and spent the last few years making amends.

A wan smile appeared on Esmeralda's face as the woman reached out to place her hand on Dimples' knee.

"Worry no longer, my child," Esmeralda said. "You have carried the burden of guilt for far too long. It's time to let go. Time to accept."

By now, tears had tumbled down Dimples' cheeks. Lulu sat next to her mother and patted her gently on the back.

"Accept that my father never forgave me? Accept that we never had a chance to tell each other 'I love you' and 'I'm sorry?'" Dimples wailed, as she took a handkerchief out of her jeans pocket and blew her nose.

"My dear, have no fear," Esmeralda said. Lulu presumed the old woman was sharing the wisdom of the sages—a trait people get when turning a certain age. "I believe your father, God rest his soul, has already forgiven you. It is you who needs to believe that, forgive yourself and move on."

Dimples and Lulu studied Esmeralda for a few seconds. Then Lulu turned to her mother. *Is Mom thinking what I'm thinking? Could Esmeralda have forgiven her own mother? Was there anything to forgive in the first place? After all, Esmeralda was but an infant when Lola Josefina left.*

Drying her eyes, Dimples eyed Lulu as if reading her thoughts. Then Dimples reached into her tote bag for a bundle—the letters sent by Lola Josefina to her children. Esmeralda eyed the letters curiously.

Clearing her throat, Dimples untied the bundle letting the letters fall onto her lap.

"Miss Esmeralda, we have these letters written by your mother," Dimples began, tentatively eyeing the old woman who pursed her lips.

Silence ensued for a few seconds that Lulu was afraid she and her mother would be banished any second. But Esmeralda just sat there staring at the letters. Finally, the old woman nodded slowly.

"Go on," she urged. "Read them to me. My eyesight isn't what it used to be, you know."

Taking a deep breath, Dimples opened the first letter on the top of the pile, her eyes scanning the fancy penmanship before her.

"My Dearest Children, it is cold here, much colder than I could have ever imagined, but the wool coat my mistress gave me keeps my body warm. It does not, however, compare to my love for you and the anticipation we will all be together soon. This is what warms my heart and sustains me day to day. I long for the day when we will all be together. But you must be patient, my little darlings, for your mother is working very hard to make a better life for us all. How I wish you could all be here now—see what I see—the glorious architecture, the wondrous California landscape, the lush green hills that turn golden in the summer—the way the blue sky meets the gray blue water of the San Francisco Bay."

Dimples paused as she and Lulu kept an eye on Esmeralda whose face remained expressionless. Putting aside the letter, Dimples reached for the next letter in the pile. Esmeralda placed her hand on Dimples as if to stop her from doing so.

"You don't have to read every letter to me," the old woman pleaded. "Felita can do so in her spare time." Esmeralda pointed toward the letter pile with her pursed lips. "Why don't you read one of the unopened ones?"

Nodding slowly, Dimples reached for the letter on the bottom of the pile, opened it, and took a deep breath.

"My precious darlings, I have been here for a year now already and still long for you all to join me. I wish I could go back home but I am committed to my mistress' care. I am also afraid that, should I return home, I may lose my privilege to return here. I hope you can understand that my being here is for our own good—indeed, I believe that there is a better life awaiting all of us here in America. Please be patient with me, my dearest ones! I may have to ask my own father for his lawyer's help in processing papers so that I may finally be able to bring you all here. And as I mark my one-year stay here, I am reminded of the fact that, aside from updates from your aunts, whom I have entrusted your care to, I have yet to hear from you Isabella, my dearest child. I hope you are all keeping with your studies and I especially hope you are not frustrated with your mother as I do love you all so and am working very hard to ensure we are all together again. And should I be burdened by the wrath of your anger, please, please my darlings, please forgive your tired, but loving mother who wants nothing but the best for you and thinks of you always."

Suddenly, with a trembling frail hand, Esmeralda reached over to push aside the letter from Dimples' clutches. The letter slowly glided down and landed like a small, light aircraft on the hardwood floor.

"Enough," the elderly woman said, her breathing uneven. "I've heard enough for now."

Lulu and Dimples exchanged glances then suddenly Esmeralda turned slightly toward a corner of the room and gasped, the pupils of her eyes dilating, like a cat facing a predator.

"Argh!" the old woman cried, as she clutched her heart.

Felita got up from her chair, the sewing basket and garment falling from her lap, then crashing to the floor. She held Esmeralda who, despite her age, shoved the younger woman away.

"Let me be!" Esmeralda said, still staring at the corner of the room. Then with tears in her eyes, she reached out.

Lulu's gaze was magnetically drawn towards the corner.

"What is it? What's wrong?" Dimples clutched her daughter's arm with a vise-like grip.

Lola Josefina was standing in the corner, dressed in an ivory lace dress wearing a bonnet. And she was smiling and reaching out—reaching out to Esmeralda.

"It's Lola Josefina," Lulu said calmly, smiling at the ghost.

Just when she said her name, the apparition disappeared. Esmeralda cried out once again, then wept bitterly as Felita took her in her arms.

"I think you should go now. You have upset her enough," the caregiver said, calming the old woman.

Lulu opened her mouth to protest, but Dimples squeezed her arm firmly.

"Yes, I think Miss Esmeralda needs her rest. We're sorry for wearing her out," Dimples said, pulling Lulu by the arm to follow her. "Come along, *anak*."

Saying their goodbyes quickly, they left the house.

"We shouldn't have left her so soon," Lulu said, looking back up at Esmeralda's window as they walked away from the house.

"She'll be alright," Dimples said, tucking her handkerchief into her purse.

Lulu thought about Lola Josefina—how serene she appeared. It seemed she was finally at peace.

"Yeah, I think you're right," she said, squeezing her Mom's hand. "I think we did good, Mom."

Dimples turned to her daughter. "I think *you* did good, sweetie. It took some courage and a lot of faith to believe in Lola Josefina and help carry out her mission. You could've just dismissed her. But you didn't. I'm proud of you."

Lulu shrugged. Tricycles and jeepneys were whizzing past them, its occupants oblivious to the miracle that had just occurred.

Chapter Twenty One

That night after dinner, Lulu asked Dimples if she could have her jewelry box back.

Lulu was helping her Mom clear the dishes as Dimples turned thoughtful eyes at her daughter curiously then nodded.

"Okay," Dimples said, shrugging her shoulders.

Lulu eyed her Mom, sensing the uncertainty emanating within. "Look, Mom, let's just say I've developed an appreciation for the darn thing. I actually miss it. It was sort of my connection to Lola Josefina."

She raced upstairs to retrieve the jewelry box. But when she opened it, she was aghast to find the ballerina was gone and no music spewed from the inside.

"Mom!"

Lulu practically tumbled downstairs as though the fate of her music box signaled a bad omen—one she desperately aimed to fix. She couldn't get the words out so she simply opened the box to show Dimples her grim discovery.

"Oh," Dimples said, putting her hand to her mouth.

Chi-Chi stomped in with a wet washcloth to wipe the table when she noticed what her sister was holding.

"Dimar grabbed hold of the ballerina and broke her off," Chi-Chi said, wiping the table.

Her sister's nonchalance shocked her. Apparently, Chi-Chi was unaware of how valuable the jewelry box had become.

"How did he reach the box?"

"He didn't," Chi-Chi said, looking sheepish, as if the enormity of what happened began to dawn on her. "He was curious about the box. So I showed it to him. He squealed when he heard the music play as the ballerina twirled. The next thing I knew, he reached out and grabbed the poor thing."

Lulu groaned and sat down. She felt ill.

"I'm sorry, *Ate*," Chi-Chi said. "Dimar doesn't know better."

But Lulu wasn't upset with Chi-Chi or Dimar. She was upset at herself. She had the jewelry box all this time—a gift from her grandfather—yet she had taken it for granted. She felt she personally let her Lolo down.

"How could I fix this?" Lulu said.

"You could try gluing her back on," Chi-Chi suggested, inspecting the damage closely.

"I can't even find the ballerina!" Lulu wailed. "Lolo must be rolling in his grave. He must be so disappointed in me!"

Dimples dumped the dishes she was holding into the sink; the clanging sound jolted Lulu, as though all the dishes had broken.

"Lulu! Did you learn anything at all this afternoon? What about the lesson on forgiveness that Esmeralda talked about? Your grandfather isn't disappointed in you. I'm sure that he's proud of you, proud that you've accepted your heritage and that you're truly happy to be here."

Despite her doubts, Lulu managed a weak smile for Dimples' sake. "You're right, Mom. I did forget."

She didn't know her grandfather like she knew Lola Josefina. What if Lolo Rogelio wasn't the forgiving type?

Late at night, Lulu tossed and turned in her sleep, feeling at a loss for the first time in weeks. It wasn't just the ballerina or the music—it was Lola Josefina herself. That was it.

She actually missed the ghost.

To the tune of the daily rooster symphony, Lulu reluctantly got up the next morning after a restless, virtually sleepless night. Still drowsy, she folded the mosquito net haphazardly, placed it under her bed then propped up her pillows. A tiny object barely caught her sleepy eye.

The missing ballerina.

As if Lulu had sucked up a mug of strong coffee, her eyelids flew wide open as she grabbed the ballerina before it became a figment of her imagination—a mirage. But she wasn't imagining things. She gripped the small plastic figure in her hand then inspected its painted eyes and rosy lips and pink tutu. How did the ballerina get to her bed and how did it manage to wedge itself beneath her pillow. Had it been there all this time?

Thinking it was a good sign, Lulu changed her outlook immediately. Things were looking up. She couldn't wait to get to school to find out what kind of luck awaited her. She tucked the ballerina in her uniform skirt pocket.

During a break between classes later that day, Lulu studied her reflection in the girls' bathroom mirror. Had she really changed all that much? Outside, she appeared to be the same person. Yet, there was definitely something different. Well, it's not like she was cured of growing pains and adolescence angst. She knew the most challenging aspects of her teenage life were yet to come. But, for now, she felt an inner peace she hadn't felt in a long time.

She looked at the far end of the long, horizontal mirror that spanned four sinks—the end of the mirror where Lola Josefina had once appeared and was sad to not find her there.

Just as she turned to head out, Nina walked in. For a second, the cousins eyed each other awkwardly. Nina turned away as Lulu started to leave.

"Lulu, wait," Nina said, clearing her throat, eyes cast down at the floor. "I heard about what you did the other day—about requesting we switch sections."

Lulu shrugged. "Yeah, well, it turned out to be for nothing."

"You nearly got in trouble," Nina said.

"But I didn't. And I don't regret standing up to Sister Ruth. Someone had to. And she wouldn't listen to me or to anyone anyway."

Nina glanced at Lulu. She seemed a bit shy. "Well, I just wanted to…to thank you for—for your effort."

An inner wave of warmth swept through Lulu. "No problem."

Nina turned quickly to enter a bathroom stall as Lulu stood for a few seconds breathing evenly. She patted the outside of her skirt pocket.

The cousins didn't exchange another word the rest of the day. Lulu didn't expect they would ever be best friends. But they could at least co-exist as schoolmates and cousins. Family gatherings didn't have to be such a pain anymore.

Miss Espinosa approached Lulu after school in the hallway. She seemed more tired, more frail than usual and it just wasn't her age. The normally sleek and distinguished older woman appeared as though she hadn't slept for a month. She cast her bloodshot, puffy eyes at Lulu.

"Is everything alright, Miss Espinosa?"

"My child, I want you to know that Miss Esmeralda passed away last night, peacefully in her sleep, I am told," said the teacher, dabbing the corner of her eyes with an embroidered hanky. "She was a dear friend and mentor. She will be missed."

"Oh, my!" Lulu covered her mouth with her hand. She quickly shared the details of her visit—except the part about the ghost—with Miss Espinosa, her voice breathless.

"Miss Espinosa, I feel bad we upset her," Lulu said.

The teacher shook her head and held Lulu by the shoulders. "You mustn't blame yourself, Lulu. Miss Esmeralda was elderly. I'm sure she appreciated hearing her mother's words. She never really knew her mother—all she knew was what her older siblings told her and who knows what they said. But it was a noble deed you and your mother did—reading those letters. At least Esmeralda heard the truth straight from her mother's own words. She's at peace. She's finally with her mother now."

As soon as Lulu heard that, the peace that enveloped Lulu earlier returned.

When Lulu went home that Friday night, she and Dimples shared a long embrace when Lulu told her about Esmeralda. A couple hours later, Romar arrived from Manila. Lulu remained in her room trying to focus on reading *Pride and Prejudice* but was distracted by the voices of her parents in the master bedroom. No doubt, Dimples was updating him on the latest events.

Except for a request to pass the water, Lulu and Romar barely exchanged a word during dinner that night. While she was ravenous, she felt too nervous, too uncomfortable to eat. She still had unresolved issues with her Dad.

Air. That was what she needed. After excusing herself from the table, Lulu walked onto the terrace and leaned on the railing. She looked up at the stars and took a deep breath. The cool night air caressed her within and she closed her eyes. Thoughts of Niel invaded her, threatening to interrupt the calmness she was trying so hard to cultivate. But she knew facing him was unavoidable. If there was anything she learned about her encounters with Lola Josefina and meeting Esmeralda—it was that forgiveness and making amends was the key to happiness. She knew Niel had deliberately been avoiding her and rightfully so. She couldn't wait to seek him out. Tell him how sorry she was.

A slight rustle interrupted her thoughts. She turned to see a figure in the doorway.

"It's a nice cool night for a change," her father said, his hands in his pockets.

She turned back to face the darkness of the night. Some lanterns illuminated Tita Claudia's vegetable garden and another one softly lit the water pump for anyone needing to pump water for the next day's bath or laundry.

"Your Mom told me about facing Esmeralda," he said, standing on the other side of the railing. "That was a brave thing you did, insisting on meeting her. That was a nice gift for the old woman. I think she died happy."

"I hope so," Lulu said, her voice barely audible. From a distance, she could hear rustling near a row of banana plants, as a farmer carrying a lantern on one hand and the reins of his carabao on the other passed through. They were both trudging slowly, perhaps tired from a long hard day's work in the fields.

"I know about you and Niel," Romar said, his voice low and throaty, as though it had suddenly become dry.

Lulu lowered her head, prepared to receive the wrath of Romar Bituin. *First you praise her, and then you attack.* That had seemingly become her Dad's motto. Or forget the praise. Just attack. She braced herself for the inevitable.

Her Dad took a deep breath. "And I want you to know I'm okay with it."

A twitch above her right eye made Lulu jerk her head to one side. She didn't hear that last sentence correctly. *I had imagined he said that, right?*

She turned to face her Dad, afraid to face the truth. As if he read her expression, he nodded.

"As hard as it for me to know my firstborn is in love, I have no choice but to accept it," Romar said, with a sigh, raising his gaze up at the sky. "I guess, now that I'm older, I forgot what it feels like—being young and in love."

In spite of herself, Lulu couldn't help but grin. "Aw, Dad, you're not old."

"No! No, I'm not," he said quickly. "But I guess I was hard on you because I'm paranoid."

"Mom told me about your… sister," Lulu said, no longer afraid to face her Dad. "I promise I won't end up like her."

Romar shrugged, his eyes carrying a faraway look. "Funny thing was, she promised my father and me the same thing—that she won't end up a pregnant teen, but she did anyway."

Lulu turned away, feeling a bit dejected, but her father turned her to face him.

"But I trust you, Lulu," he said. "You're more strong willed than your aunt was. More sensible."

Searching her father's eyes, even in the dark, she could see a reflection—of the stars, of the nearby lights, of the past. There was hurt there.

"Dad, maybe it's time you should forgive her," Lulu said.

He sighed. "You know, I've been thinking about that for a long time now, but somehow I can't seem to bring myself to do it."

"Why not?"

"Because your aunt and I haven't spoken since she and her fiancé ran away to God knows where. I don't know whether they even got married or not or if she even went through with the pregnancy. Or how the child is."

"There must be a way to find her."

"Unless she doesn't want to be found."

"Dad, you don't know that."

He studied her thoughtfully, crossing his arms across his chest. "Tell me, how did you get so wise?"

Lulu smiled. Thoughts of Lola Josefina and Esmeralda popped in her head as she gazed heavenward at the stars. "Guardian angels."

"I feel a little funny having a mature conversation with my daughter," Romar said, chuckling. "I guess you are growing up."

She and her Dad hugged for what Lulu believed to be the first time in a long while. As he turned away, Lulu knew there would probably be bumps along the road toward adulthood where her parents were concerned. But for now, there was no word more beautiful in the world than forgiveness.

Chapter Twenty Two

Aprilyn and Jolie met Dimples and her family the next day to attend Esmeralda's wake at her home.

"I feel weird about being here at Esmeralda's house again with Esmeralda not here," Lulu said as they ascended the stairs to the *sala* where they heard a drone of voices immersed in praying the rosary.

"But she *is* here," Aprilyn said.

"Yeah, but dead in a coffin," Chi-Chi said.

"Shh!" Dimples admonished just as they reached the top of the stairs where they were greeted by a group of unfamiliar faces, their heads bowed, some pausing in mid-prayer to stare at the new arrivals. "I think most of these people are from Esmeralda's father's side of the family and not her mother's. But even if they're from Lola Josefina's side, I still don't recognize anyone."

Still, Dimples put on her sweetest smile which wasn't received warmly. People dressed in black garb, wearing frowns on their faces and huddled in small groups, stared at Lulu and her family curiously. A woman in a corner waved at them and hurried over.

"Good you could come," Felita said, holding Dimples' hand. "You are family, of course."

"Of course," Dimples said, as the caretaker led them to the center of the *sala* where there were empty seats. At least for Dimples' sake, Lulu was relieved Dimar was left in Tita Claudia's care.

After scanning the room for Niel, Lulu's heart sank. He had made no attempt to contact her and she wondered if he had heard about Esmeralda's death.

Once the rosary prayer concluded, a maid entered carrying a tray of pastries then disappeared only to reappear once more carrying a coffee pot on a tray filled with mugs. Guests helped themselves to coffee and pastries as they chatted quietly.

Minutes later, a priest arrived to bestow a blessing and sprinkle holy water on Esmeralda's coffin which was situated at the far end of the sala near a wall adorned with a portrait of her. Lulu thought she slightly resembled Lola Josefina—same dark-beaded eyes, same Mona Lisa smile.

One by one, guests approached the open coffin to view the body as Lulu sat still with panic. She'd never seen a dead body before—not even her Lolo's as she wasn't around for his funeral. When it was her family's turn to view Esmeralda, Dimples held on to Lulu firmly as they inched slowly toward the coffin.

To Lulu's surprise, the body wasn't grotesque as she envisioned. Instead, through protective glass, Esmeralda's tranquil countenance shone back at them, that Lulu found herself leaning closer to peer through the glass. Adorned in a linen and lace dress, Esmeralda imbued serenity as her spider veined hands entwined with an emerald beaded rosary, rested on her stomach. Her expression seemed to evoke eternal peace.

"It looks like she's just sleeping," Lulu whispered.

"She is," Dimples whispered back, touching her fingers lightly on the glass, then making the Sign of the Cross. "But her spirit lives on. I'm sure she's with her mother in heaven right now looking down at us."

A mist greeted Lulu and her family as they stepped outside from the stuffy house. Aprilyn, Jolie and her family walked slightly ahead as Lulu paused to raise her eyes heavenward at the hazy sky.

"I know you're up there, Esmeralda," she said. "Tell your mother I said 'Hi.'"

***

Lulu rubbed her palms against the abrasive texture of the *piña* fabric that would become the dress she would someday wear for Flores de Mayo, the Santacruzan in May. There was no way in hell that fabric was going to drape her sensitive skin and in this humidity no less. But being Reina Elena was a huge honor, said Tita Claudia. It wasn't just an honor that would give her the kind of positive exposure Lulu needed to further boost her image at school. Wearing the *Traje de Mestiza* gown that had once belonged to Josette was the ultimate tribute to the girl who left a life of luxury behind for love.

Even though the May festival was a long ways to go, Lulu couldn't imagine anyone else being her escort. It had to be Niel. She wondered how he was doing as she had not heard from him. Somehow, she had to seek him out—ask for his forgiveness.

At school that Monday, Lulu tensed up a bit when Tessa and her gang sashayed past as she sat with Aprilyn and Jolie at the cafeteria.

"Lulu, sorry to hear about your great-great-grand-aunt," Tessa cooed, as Precious, Lucky and Musette all nodded.

Lulu faced the girls with a wan smile. "Thanks."

"I'm inviting you to my birthday party next month," Tessa said, twisting a strand of her hair around her finger.

Aprilyn and Jolie exchanged glances as Tessa eyed them both.

"Yes," Tessa said. "All of you."

While Jolie and Aprilyn sat as if shot by a stun gun, Tessa sashayed away and called back, "Invitations will be sent out soon."

As her friends exchanged puzzled glances, Lulu nodded. *I'm not yet in Section A of my senior year of high school and already barriers are starting to come down.*

"What was that all about?" Jolie asked, stuffing her half-eaten sandwich into a paper bag. "Is she for real?"

Aprilyn shrugged. "I wish I can say 'That was nice of Tessa to invite us.' But I'm not sure what the motive is."

"Hey, what if there isn't a motive?" Lulu said. "What if she's just really being nice?"

Her friends gaped at Lulu as if she were speaking a foreign language. "Come on, guys. One thing I learned about being the new kid in school is to never judge people you don't know very well. I think Tessa's not too bad. She and I may never be best friends, but I think she's tolerable."

"Why do you say that?" Jolie said, watching Tessa and her friends gliding toward the library.

Lulu inhaled then exhaled deeply. "Well, I thought about the time when I was really popular back in my old school and how I earned a reputation for being stuck up. I probably was on the outside. But on the inside, I had the same fears and doubts and insecurities. I used to think being popular made me unattainable. But someone helped bring me back to earth."

She smiled as she thought of the time Rowena shamelessly and bravely went up to her in the early days and asked her why she didn't speak Tagalog and how Lulu looked down on Rowena then. Rowena, who turned out to be a trusted friend.

At the Internet café, Lulu poured forth her recent adventures regarding Esmeralda to her only Stateside friend.

"Dear Rowena, I think Lola Josefina has gone from my life for good and I never thought I'd say this but, I kind of miss her," Lulu e-mailed. "She was like a guardian angel to me once I got over my doubts. Her presence made me realize a lot of things about myself. Anyway, I think I should be able to carry the lessons I learned about love of family, forgiveness and unconditional love with me for the rest of my life."

She paused to take a deep breath. "I also learned about accepting people for who they are and it really took my moving all the way over here for me to realize that." A nearby group of teens gathered around a computer erupted in laughter. She smiled to herself. "You know, I never thought I'd ever say this, but, I'm really glad I moved here. Now, about you. How have you been doing?"

When she got up to leave the café, she turned suddenly thinking she caught a glimpse of Niel in the corner of her eye. But it was just another guy who resembled him. Sighing, Lulu left the Internet café, feeling some relief that Esmeralda and Lola Josefina were reunited and that all was forgiven. Still her own heart was heavy. All was still not forgiven.

Lulu couldn't figure out why she dreaded funerals. It wasn't as if she attended them regularly. If the wake was somber, the funeral could be just as gloomy. She didn't know what to expect. People couldn't very well be feasting on food like they had during Day of the Dead, would they? Would women be wailing in anguish and collapsing like the drama queens she'd seen in Tagalog movies?

A misty morning bathed mourners dressed in black at Esmeralda's final earthly gathering. The dark clouds overhead promised a later downpour but, for now, the only watery streams were the tears rolling down the cheeks of the various relatives, friends and former students whose lives Esmeralda touched. Even though she had been alone the last part of her life, Lulu heard she had been an influence to many. There were those she mentored like Miss Espinosa. And relatives like Dimples and Lulu whose lives the old woman had barely touched, yet still managed to make a powerful impact. Lola Josefina's spirit—and

Esmeralda in her final days—brought the Bituin family closer together.

After prayers, the priest gave the final blessing as mourners bowed their heads. There was silence except for the sound of the casket as it was being lowered to the ground. Slowly and almost in slow motion, mourners made the Sign of the Cross as a final farewell to Esmeralda before moving away from the burial site. Romar, Chi-Chi and Tito Enrico silently slid away as Dimples came up to Lulu and gave her a big hug. Lulu felt as though she wasn't only saying goodbye to Esmeralda, but to Lola Josefina, too, a girl who had just been like herself once, a girl in love. As she allowed herself the comfort of Dimples' embrace Lulu's eyes caught a familiar sight.

Lola Josefina stood next to Esmeralda. The hand-holding mother and daughter were bathed in a blinding glow. They were both at peace. Lulu opened her mouth to call out to them but they disappeared as suddenly as they appeared.

Dimples squeezed her daughter's hand.

"I'll be a few seconds," Lulu said, now staring at the hole in the ground—Esmeralda's final resting place.

"Take all the time you need," Dimples said, padding away. "We'll be in the car."

Closing her eyes, she was finally alone to collect her thoughts. Lulu breathed a "Thank You" to Lola Josefina for changing her life. Suddenly, a warm presence enveloped her. Her eyes opened slowly and gradually through the soft mist that moistened her eyelashes; her vision gradually focused to reveal Niel's eyes meeting hers from a distance.

Dressed in black pants and black cotton, long-sleeved shirt, Niel's stride through the mist was confident. Lulu squeezed her eyes shut and tightened her hands into fists to make sure she wasn't imagining things.

As her eyelids fluttered open, Niel took her hands into his, drawing her close as he stared at her intently with tender, forgiving eyes, his face hovering above, his lips just mere inches from hers.

Tightening her grip on his hands, she smiled up at him, just as light raindrops began descending. It wasn't her imagination, after all.

Author's Note

As of 2011, the Philippine Department of Education began offering a new K-12 educational system throughout the country. This novel was written from 2006-2008 and reflects that time period prior to the new educational system taking effect.

Acknowledgments

This book was my thesis in completion of my MFA in Creative Writing. While it's been said that writing is a solitary endeavor, editing and publishing a book, in my case, had been the result of a collaborative effort involving the assistance of many wonderful people.

Many thanks to my Thesis Advisers and professors in the MFA Fiction program at Mills College: authors Cristina García, Yiyun Li and YA author Kathryn Reiss who took time to read and critique the entire manuscript in its early stages. I would also like to extend my gratitude to my writing peers in the YA Fiction workshops who critiqued my work.

I am grateful to the book's "Godmother," cover designer and publisher, my dear friend and fellow author, Ana Galvan, for her meticulous work and attention to detail. Immense gratitude goes to Julie Abitbol, a true artist who listened carefully to my ideas, took time to absorb the story and then used her vivid imagination to create the artwork that graces the book's front cover.

Much appreciation goes to my editing team: Susan Medina and Judy Swager for copyediting and proofreading; and to Nemia Carpio, my longtime friend since my two-year high school stint in the Philippines, for editing the Tagalog sentences and phrases.

And of course my love and gratitude to my family and friends for their love and support and to my students for their continued commitment to the written word. Much love and thanks to my furry nephew and nieces, especially to Lilly, the Feline Editor, for continually inspiring me.

About the Author

Janice De Jesus resides in the San Francisco Bay Area. Her short story, *Island Tulip*, was included in *Field of Mirrors: An Anthology of Philippine American Writers.* She is also the author of two novels: *Not Just Another Pretty Face* and *Pretty as a Picture*, Book One and Book Two of the *Pretty Princess Trilogy*; and *Soulstice: Living and Loving On and Off the Yoga Mat*, a collection of short stories.

Her first nonfiction book *Omstruck: Healing Heartbreak through Yoga and Meditation* was published in 2011.

Visit http://JaniceDeJesusAuthor.Blogspot.com and follow her on Instagram: @literaryyogini

Proceeds from the sales of this book will go toward various animal welfare organizations. Thank you for your support.

Made in the USA
San Bernardino, CA
24 November 2018